THE FINAL CURTAIN

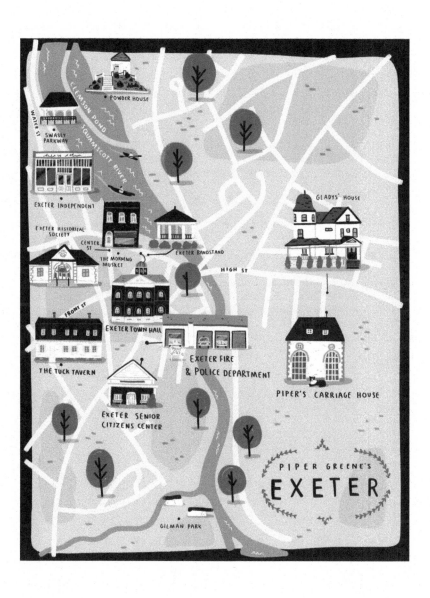

THE FINAL CURTAIN

A PIPER GREENE EXETER MYSTERY

LARA BRICKER

Exeter Independent Press
111 Water Street, Suite 5, Exeter, NH 03833

Editor: Renee Nicholls www.mywritingcoach.net
Map: Alex Foster
Cover Design/Layout: Stewart A. Williams Design
Proofreader: Cindy Black
Publisher Colophon: Lionel Hearon
Author Photo: Melissa Koren Wilson
Cover Photo: Charles Cormier Photography

Acknowledgments

The idea for this book began during a presentation about local birds given by Scott Heron at the Word Barn in Exeter. Scott's description of a local gentleman who fed birds' meat and other left-over food behind his barn immediately conjured up a murder scene in my mind. As a result, the first draft of this book was somewhat unceremoniously called "The Meat Pile Murders." But as this is a cozy mystery, the murder scene is a lot less gruesome than the one I initially imagined.

My first reader, and biggest cheerleader, Susan Nolan, who is my real-life Aunt Gladys, was with me for every step of the writing process for this book. She took my phone calls day and night, provided inspiration for Aunt Gladys's fall fashion, and not only read every draft, but gave me honest feedback that I needed to hear to make the book better.

My editor Renee Nicholls always helps me to do my best work and her contributions from the first draft to the final manuscript did just that. This book has more twists and turns than the first Piper Greene mystery, and as a fan of complicated British mysteries, Renee was the perfect person to give suggestions that made this book complete. She also knew just when I needed some encouragement along the way.

The first Piper Greene mystery made its way around the world thanks to the amazing listeners of our *Crime Writers On* podcast. So, thank you! It's hard to imagine life before my fellow New Hampshire crime writers, Kevin Flynn, Rebecca

Lavoie, and Toby Ball, decided to record that first episode of *Crime Writers On* back in 2014.

Lastly, thank you to my adopted hometown of Exeter, New Hampshire and my former colleagues at the Exeter News-Letter for inspiring me to bring Piper Greene to life.

carriage house, where I was alone except for Oscar, the formerly feral black-and-white tuxedo cat. He was perched next to a pot of dark-red chrysanthemums, and he peered at me from a safe distance, giving me a pensive once-over. Though I had spent months thinking Oscar was plotting to kill me in my sleep, he was currently giving humans a try thanks to the determined efforts of my coworker, Todd Tisden, who was renting a room in the big house, which my aunt, Gladys, owned and occupied.

"We had a cat like this when I lived on the island of Tortola," Todd had announced when he moved in. It appeared he had missed very few exotic spots before rolling into town in his camper truck, which he called the Jolly Dodger. He then had added, "A little mackerel juice and he'll be your best friend in no time."

Now Oscar scooted off when I leaned over to pat him on the head. He wandered back toward the Jolly Dodger, which hadn't moved since it had sputtered to a stop in the backyard in a cloud of smoke several months ago. Todd seemed to use it as a storage unit these days, and I'd grown accustomed to him stopping to chat with me in the late mornings when he finally emerged from Gladys's house and made his way to his camper. He operated on "Todd time," although he somehow surprisingly still managed to meet deadline. His new red scooter, Scarlett, which he used to get around town, was parked next to the camper.

I'd given myself a small window of time to stop at the Morning Musket for coffee before my rendezvous with Harry. My best friend, Jenny, who owned the bakery, got up every day around 4:00 a.m. to start the pastries, so I knew she'd be there. I walked down High Street and along Water Street to

CHAPTER 1

Getting up before dawn was for the birds. Ironically, a bird was exactly why I was awake several hours before my alarm's usual bell.

Harry Trott, the reclusive bird man of Exeter, had called me late the night before with an irresistible invitation to meet him downtown, meaning my early morning wakeup call was a given. For months Harry, a gnome-like man in his seventies, had been writing letters to the editor at the *Exeter Independent,* where I worked as a part-time reporter, about the extremely rare Ross's gull. A lone Ross's gull, normally seen only in the Arctic, had begun sharing meals with Harry's beloved common seagulls at a vacant lot on Water Street, which was now at the center of a controversial redevelopment plan. Harry's letters against that plan had been persuasive—and prolific—but the man himself was a mystery. I'd only met him a few times, and even then, I hadn't learned much. He kept to himself, content to feed his birds and return to his weathered, white colonial-style home on the edge of the prep school campus in town.

As I prepared to walk downtown, I lingered outside my

Author's Note

Exeter, New Hampshire, is a very real town and one I've been lucky to call my adopted hometown since 1998. While Piper Greene seems to find a murder a month, Exeter is a relatively murder-free zone.

The town of Exeter and its major landmarks are portrayed accurately in this book, as is the general history of the town. People and businesses are fictional and came from my own overactive imagination.

The vacant lot at the center of this book was not the site of the former Exeter Playhouse. That building was created by me and never existed. That lot was previously home to Exeter Jewelry, which burned in 1990, and it has never been redeveloped. The Opera House and the Ioka Theater both existed in real life, and like our fictional Piper Greene, many Exeter residents have fond memories of first days, movie premieres, and popcorn in the theater.

the Morning Musket, where I found the side door unlocked. I eased it open and stepped inside.

"Jenny," I called out as I entered. "I really need a cup of that crazy-strong South American coffee you have."

She popped her head out from behind a rack of cooling loaves of bread. Her red curls were tucked under a paisley headband this morning, but a few had escaped, giving her the appearance of a Viking princess.

She said, "What, you mean Prince Charming doesn't make coffee?"

I blushed at her mention of my new romance with Detective Richie Collins. "Now, Jenny," I said, in my best prim-and-proper voice, "you know I don't engage in premarital morning coffee."

She pursed her lips and gave me the look. I sighed in defeat and said, "Okay, so he didn't come over last night. But I really need to wake up." I lowered my voice, more by habit than the need to be discreet since we were clearly the only two in the building. "Harry Trott invited me to meet him this morning."

Jenny raised her eyebrows, and I knew her well enough to tell she was impressed. "That's a coup," she said. "He tends to keep to himself, as you know."

I helped myself to a cup of coffee, added two sugars, and took a long sip. "He does," I said. "But this Revolutionary-themed arcade and fun house development proposal for that vacant lot has Harry really amped up. He's determined to stop the redevelopment altogether."

She nodded. The controversial plan in our historic district was for the former site of the prestigious Exeter Playhouse, which had been vacant for nearly five decades after the building burned down. Since then, the Carmichael relatives had bickered constantly about the property, leaving most observers to speculate the only way an armistice would happen was if one of them died. But in late August, Roy Carmichael had quite surprisingly secured the majority ownership from his family and announced his plans to build the arcade. Roy owned several arcades already, including his first location in nearby Hampton Beach and another at Weirs Beach in the Lakes Region, two tourist-driven areas that, as most folks in town insisted, were not the same as our quaint and historical town. Roy's plan was now practically all locals were talking about: what could, or *should*, be built there? Debate about the empty spot, which was covered in weeds, had even overshadowed the gossip about the murder of my former editor, Charlotte Campbell, in July.

So far, it wasn't looking promising for Roy's plan. The lot's location in the town's historic district required a special level of complicated approvals. In addition to Harry's concern about the birds, people were especially horrified at the idea of an enormous likeness of one of the town's puritanical founders being lit up with red-white-and-blue neon at the entrance to the downtown like a Revolutionary War version of Bob's Big Boy. I'd half expected Tripp Bolton, the chairman of the Historic District Commission, to seize up and have a heart attack on the spot when the artist's rendering was unveiled during one of their meetings. Instead, he had just pounded his gavel so hard that it had broken in half. The proposed name, Carmichael's Arcade in Arms, added another layer of horror for those who prized Exeter's downtown charm.

"We are not a discounted tourist attraction! Have you lost what was left of your mind?" Tripp had boomed at Roy during that same contentious meeting.

I couldn't believe Roy really thought he had a chance of getting approval for the arcade, but some people weren't good at reading the room—or in this case, the town. Harry Trott and a handful of other locals had been pounding the warning drum ever since, and I could hardly wait to hear what he had to say about it when I saw him in person.

I turned my attention back to the coffee and grabbed a recyclable lid. "I hate to leave you hanging, but I've got to get there," I said.

I slipped a lemon blueberry scone into a napkin, slapped some money on the counter, and gave her a little wave before stepping back onto Water Street. The vacant lot was just a short distance up the street, sandwiched between a restaurant and a chocolate shop. Many referred to the spot as the missing tooth of the downtown, and I had to admit it was an eyesore, particularly amidst the other shops on the picturesque thoroughfare, which was characterized by historical brick buildings and charming window displays. In its heyday, the Exeter Playhouse had been a magnet for up-and-coming actors with designs on getting to Broadway. Sure, there were those who went into the further reaches of the state to perfect their craft, including the Barnstormers Theatre in Tamworth, which was once the summer home of President Grover Cleveland. However, actors who wanted to be closer to Boston, which was easily accessible by passenger train from Exeter until 1965, went to the Exeter Playhouse to hone their talent. These days, the train was actually back in operation, but the theater was long gone.

Harry Trott had been regularly feeding seagulls on the vacant lot for years. Locals called him, somewhat unceremoniously, "the bird man" because he supplied old bread and leftover shellfish from the downtown restaurants to the birds. Entire generations of seagulls had clustered on the lot every morning for Harry's feast, but over the last year another bird, this one endangered, had joined the breakfast crowd. Many of Harry's letters to the *Exeter Independent* stressed the importance of protecting the Ross's gull.

During our phone call last night, Harry had been blunt. "I don't usually talk to reporters," he had begun, "but my neighbor, Tootie Wentworth, says I can trust you."

Harry had explained the situation about the rare bird, which, honestly, I was still having a hard time swallowing. As even Roy had pointed out, there was probably a way to relocate the feeding area and keep the tiny bird content. And although the gull was native to the Arctic, it wasn't considered endangered. But that had not deterred Harry, who had kept up his avian advocating. Last night he had insisted, "I think for you to really understand the significance of the Ross's gull, you should come down with me when I feed the birds. Get a sense of what is at stake here."

Now, let's be real: the idea of standing around a pile of old clam shells and brittle bread crusts while birds ripped them apart with their beaks wasn't my idea of a great morning wakeup call. But getting an interview with the elusive bird man of Exeter was a major score, so I was trying to tamp down my queasiness. I had already slipped a container of Vicks VapoRub into my bag on the way out in case the old clam shells were too smelly, a trick I'd learned from the crime scene investigators when I worked in the city. The camphor, eucalyptus, and menthol smell could block out a lot of unpleasant odors.

I continued my trek up Water Street toward our meeting

spot, passing the Ioka Theater, another shuttered theatrical relic that many hoped would become a movie theater once again. I'd finished half of my coffee by the time I spotted the fence around the vacant lot.

A gate on the side of the fence was propped open ever so slightly. I peeked through and saw the promised flock of seagulls congregating. Behind them, mist floated up from the river, a sign the water was still warmer than the morning air, which was so cold I could see my breath. I didn't see Harry, which seemed odd given that I was a few minutes late, but I decided to go in and wait. The gate was stuck, so I used my hip to dislodge it, narrowly avoiding falling on my face. The hinges let out an ear-splitting squeak, sending the birds off like they'd heard the shotgun of a duck hunter in the marsh grass.

I peered ahead through the mist and stopped in my tracks. Two camping chairs were at the edge of the lot, facing the river, and only one was empty. From my position I could see the top of a baseball cap, but the chair's occupant was slumped forward as if he or she had dozed off. Something didn't feel right. My reporter's instinct took over and I edged closer. I slipped my phone out of my pocket and took a few photos as I approached, an almost second-nature habit for someone like me.

"Harry?" I said quietly, as I edged forward. But the person in the chair didn't move. Maybe the bird man was taking a short siesta.

"Harry!" I said, a little louder. No response. Yes, something definitely felt wrong. But as I got a better look, I noticed the hair wasn't gray like Harry's, but shiny and black like a harbor seal. I spied a bottle of Yellow Label Veuve Clicquot champagne, the kind Gladys got for New Year's Eve, resting against a chair leg. Hmm, maybe he'd dyed his hair, gone on a bender, and was sleeping it off. I inched forward, narrowly missing stepping in what I could only assume was last night's regurgitated dinner. Yuck. Emboldened now, I got in front of the chair, ready to wake the reveler.

"Son of a monkey!" I exclaimed when I saw the face.

It was Roy Carmichael. He had an empty crystal champagne flute in his lap. His face was gray, his chest was still, and his mouth was open. After a few seconds I realized that although I could still see my own breath, the air in front of his face was clear. It didn't take a medical degree to know that Roy had just had his final curtain call.

CHAPTER 2

As if on autopilot, I dialed the number to the Exeter police. I didn't look back, but I couldn't get the image of Roy Carmichael out of my mind. On one hand, he could have just drunk himself to death. But my mind always went to the other possibilities, and given his reputation in town, there were any number of people who might have wanted him dead. I could just imagine what my aunt, Gladys, always one for dignity, would say when she learned about the pricey French champagne that he'd consumed before he died: "Well, he went out with a classy final toast, didn't he?"

I moved to the edge of the lot and waited for the police to arrive. It was only moments before the first cruiser drove up and Police Chief Frank Sinclair climbed out. At about five foot ten, Chief Sinclair was barely taller than me. His kind eyes and gray hair made him look approachable, which he was. His compassionate style epitomized community policing, and he was better known for his outreach at the schools and with the elderly than for his zest for writing speeding tickets. In Exeter, where it seemed residents valued history above all else, Sinclair was considered historical by many. He was third generation in his family to serve as police chief in town, but while he was getting on in years, he had expressed no desire to leave his post just yet.

He sighed when he saw me. "Miss Greene," he said, "this is getting to be a habit, but not the type you should be proud of."

To be fair, he wasn't totally off base. I had also been present when my late editor's body crashed to the sidewalk from town hall just a couple of months earlier. Later, when I had ended up with a concussion from an encounter with the killer, the chief had given me a rather strong lecture about not getting involved in any future police business.

I looked at the growing crowd before responding to him. "Chief, this isn't what it looks like. I was meeting Harry Trott this morning …" I paused. "And I found poor Roy instead."

The chief scrutinized the crowd. "Well, that sounds plausible. I know how *you* newspaper people are. I'll just need to confirm with Harry."

He did a slower examination of the crowd, mostly early morning walkers and joggers so far. I couldn't immediately pick Harry out of the onlookers.

"Any idea where he is?" the chief asked me.

In my rush to call the police, it hadn't registered to me that Harry still wasn't there yet. Was he really running this late? *Or,* I thought, *given how he kept himself to himself, maybe he saw the mass of people outside the fence and left.*

"Hold on, I'll find out," I told the chief. I looked through my phone's record of incoming calls and dialed his number. It rang four times and went to an answering machine. I left a message, asking him to return my call.

I turned back to the chief, who was glancing around the area. He held a finger up toward me, indicating I should wait.

Then he went to talk to the uniformed officers standing by Roy's body. The officers were unrolling yellow crime scene tape around the perimeter of the lot, leaving Roy's body in the chair while they took photos and waited for the medical examiner. I took a shaky breath and moved out of the lot.

I stopped when I felt a gentle hand on my back and heard a low voice. "You okay, Scoop?"

Now this was a different kind of excitement: the thrill of a fresh, still-behind-the-scenes romance with the blue-eyed Detective Richie Collins.

"Yeah, I'm good," I said, not wanting to attract attention to our conversation, especially because I knew I was blushing, a new phenomenon anytime he was near me. We'd been seeing each other mostly at my carriage house or his apartment, and we had decided it would be best not to advertise our clandestine affair.

Chief Sinclair stepped back toward me, his expression one of relief when he saw Richie, who quickly dropped his hand.

"Good, you're here," Chief Sinclair said. "Can you get a statement from Miss Greene?"

He shot me another stern glance, the exact same way my high school principal used to behave whenever I got caught snooping in my teacher's grading book. "And remind her not to have a repeat of last time."

The chief really knew me too well. I did have a wee tendency to find myself in the middle of murders.

Richie nodded to the chief and gave me a discreet wink. Technically, it was a "big no-no" for Richie to take a statement from me when we were having a personal relationship, but given that I wasn't actually the one who had offed Roy, if indeed that was what had happened, I kept my mouth shut.

Before we could step to a quieter spot to talk, a commanding female voice cut in.

"That's my brother. Let me through."

I knew Fiona Carmichael, Roy's sister, by sight from her involvement in the local historical preservation scene. She was often vocal on the need to maintain Exeter's historical charm. Her height and vibrant auburn hair, cut in a stylish pixie, made her easy to spot in a crowd. Seriously, I could imagine her in a suit of armor marching into battle. She was edging forward to try to look through the gate toward the vacant lot.

"Is he really dead?" she demanded to know, as she found Chief Sinclair. The chief gently took her arm and led her away from the crowd. She started shaking her head, the way people do when they think something can't possibly be true, before she put both of her hands over her face. The chief guided her toward his unmarked cruiser, opened the passenger door, and helped her inside. I knew he was trying to give Fiona a safe place to sit and process the news.

Richie and I gave each other a look. Neither of us envied the chief in that moment.

Then Richie got down to business. "Okay, Scoop, you know the drill. Let's go make you an official witness ..." He paused, then added, "For the second time this year."

We stepped out of the growing crowd and walked up to the Great Bridge, the official entry to our historic downtown. The bridge had been fortified in the 1800s when the home of the noted feminist author, Tabitha Gilman Tenney, was moved to a new lot on High Street to make way for a courthouse downtown. In recent years, it had drawn people eager to watch the annual migration of the alewives up the river to spawn. The tiny fish were so important to the town that one even appeared on our town seal.

Further down the river, the crew team from the prep school was out for their morning practice, likely oblivious to the fact that a dead body had been discovered only a short distance away. Closer to me, a great blue heron stood in a shallow section of the river, poised to spear fish. Since the dam had been removed and the alewives no longer had to use a fish ladder to get upriver to spawn in the spring, their population had rebounded. Though they migrated back to saltwater after spring, it seemed other fish were returning to these waters as well, bringing more and more herons to what I dubbed Exeter's fresh fish café.

Richie flipped his narrow notebook to a clean page, took out a pen, and looked at me. "Just the basics," he said. "I'll hand this over to the state cops when they get here."

State police handled most murder investigations for smaller departments in the state. I knew Richie would like to have a bigger role in the case, but at the same time, I didn't want to put him in a position where our relationship compromised the investigation. His current job gave him access to inside information, which was always useful for me when I needed off-the-record background for my articles.

"Well, you know the ongoing sentiment about Roy's plan for the revolutionary arcade, and Harry's avid devotion to the birds," I began.

In fact, his commitment was so intense there were times I couldn't believe the force that came out of Harry's pen. "Carmichael's decision to move ahead could have permanent consequences, and one wonders how he would feel if his life was at stake," he had written in a recent op-ed.

When Richie nodded, I said, "So, Harry wanted to show me

the Ross's gull, which is apparently quite a big deal, though I have my doubts about shutting down the entire project just for that. He invited me to come down this morning."

I repeated what Harry had told me about the small pink-tinged and dove-like gull, although I was pretty sure Richie was already up to speed, given the number of birders who kept trekking through Exeter for a sighting.

"Apparently, Harry was around when they saw one back in Newburyport in 1975," I told him.

Then I went on to give him a timeline of my travels that morning, explaining how I had stopped to get a coffee, found the gate partially cracked, gone inside, and discovered Roy.

"You see anyone else around?" Richie asked.

I shook my head. "No. I don't know if Harry was running late or maybe he saw the crowd and split."

I told him I'd left a message for the bird man, and he nodded, making a note of that in his book. Everyone knew Harry's reputation around town as a loner.

Then Richie said, "Now, I'm sorry that I have to ask, but, well, I know you. Did you touch the body at all?"

If we'd been alone, I would have swatted his arm, but that felt too intimate for the audience around us. "Richie, please," I said. "I know better than that."

He laughed. "I know, but we just need to rule out any transfer DNA. You know how it works."

I did, but the fact that he even thought it was a slim possibility was unexpected.

He closed his notebook. "Well, that should do it for now." He looked around, then lowered his voice. "Come by tonight?"

Even though we'd been spending a lot of time together, it still gave me a natural buzz when we made plans. Gladys and her gentleman caller, Stanley, jokingly said I had the colly-wobbles when it came to Richie. I glanced around before I answered. "Okay."

He winked at me. "Be careful out there," he said, and I watched as he walked back to the crime scene. The state police major crime scene van had arrived and was parked in front of a children's clothing store up the street. God, what a contrast. I snapped a few more pictures on my phone. I needed to text Hap, the owner and editor of the paper, and get a story up for the website. That meant I'd need to make contact with the state police commander to get started on the right foot with the flow of information for my story. I glanced at my phone. Drat. My battery was dead. Guess I'd have to wait until I got to the office to put in that call.

I looked back at the river, trying to channel the calm of the water and the rowers as the adrenaline of the morning started to wear off. I knew what I needed to do for my story, but something was niggling at me. I couldn't shake the feeling. Where was Harry Trott? And why hadn't he appeared for our meeting?

CHAPTER 3

I wanted to find Harry, but my immediate priority was to get a short breaking news story up on the *Exeter Independent* website, so I headed for my office. I'd been working at the small, family-owned weekly newspaper, which was beholden to no one other than its role as watchdog for the community, ever since I'd moved back to Exeter earlier in the year. Initially I'd returned home to help out after my aunt, Gladys, had a fall, but then I never left. Reporting in the town I was raised in was never where I thought I'd land at this stage in my journalism career, but I couldn't imagine leaving now.

The paper was on a side street that ran parallel to the river and a short walk from the vacant lot. Roy was dead, but the streets were coming to life as families walked to Exeter's two elementary schools. An older man with an enormous gray wolfhound strode by, keeping pace with the colossal canine, while young children pressed their faces against the windows of the yellow school buses as they rumbled past me. Most shops didn't open until later in the morning, and the only places open were the Morning Musket and two other coffee shops.

I was walking so fast I almost didn't see Winnie Smart wave me over as I reached the two large granite markers at the entrance to Swasey Parkway. She held her arm up and called out, "Piper! Oh, Piper!" with more energy than I could muster most mornings. She was with the Women's Walking Club: a group of older ladies who took keeping up on town chatter as seriously as they took their exercise. It didn't hurt that the police chief's secretary, Cindy, was a regular member of the group. I headed toward Winnie.

"Is it true? Roy Carmichael is dead?" she asked.

Yes! I thought, not because I was happy about anyone's death, but because I finally had valuable information before Winnie did. As our town historian, she always knew everything about everyone—living *and* dead—in town. I glanced at the other ladies, who were doing their best to eavesdrop without looking suspicious. Chief Sinclair's secretary wasn't among them, which accounted for their late arrival to the day's news.

"Afraid so," I said. "And he went out with a pop and some fizz."

She looked confused, so I filled her in on the empty champagne bottle and flute in his lap. "And his sister, she seems like a handful," I added.

Winnie pinched her lips together like she was trying to hold back a thought before it came out. "There's a lot of history there," she said carefully. "Stop by sometime when you have a few minutes, and I'll fill you in."

I nodded and looked over at the ladies behind her. "How did you find out?"

Winnie shrugged and waited a minute before she responded. "It pays to have more than one source," she said. Then she winked and added, "You know Rhonda from the chocolate shop next door is in our group, right? She heard the police were next to the shop, so she stopped over on her way to meet us this morning."

That made sense. I could only imagine the sense of dread business owners would have upon hearing a crime scene van was next to their property. "Huh, that must have been shocking for her," I said. "I'll catch up with you later. I've got to get a move on to get a story up online. Breaking news and all."

Winnie gave a little wave, and the pack of ladies headed out behind the prep school's boat house, no doubt to see if they could catch a glimpse of the crime scene from the river side.

Given the hour, I entered the newspaper building through the back pressroom area, where a single loading dock served as the pickup spot for delivery drivers and for the one truck that supplied the area stores with physical copies of the paper. Our summer intern, Jimmy Malloy, was back at college, and aside from Todd, I was the only reporter on staff. We still heard updates from Jimmy, who was in the process of applying for a winter internship at the *Hartford Courant*. As Jimmy's uncle, Hap was particularly thrilled about this. Clara, our receptionist and obituary editor, would be in later in the morning.

As I was the only one in the newsroom, I didn't have anyone to share the sordid details of Roy's death with, so I got right to business. I fired up my computer and tapped out what was known as a quick hit, a preliminary breaking news story, which I'd update as more information became available.

PROPERTY OWNER FOUND DEAD

By Piper Greene

EXETER__*Local property owner Roy Carmichael was found dead on his vacant lot on Water Street early this morning in what police have termed an unattended death.*

His body was found by this reporter in an area commonly used to feed seabirds. He was discovered lifeless in a camping chair, an empty bottle of expensive champagne next to him. There were no visible signs of a struggle.

Police Chief Frank Sinclair said it was too early to speculate on the manner of death or if it is suspicious. He referred all further comments to the state police major crime unit, which was expected on scene momentarily.

Carmichael, an Exeter native, has been in the news lately because of his proposal to build the Carmichael's Arcade in Arms, a themed arcade and fun house, on the lot. The proposal is currently stalled before the town's Historic District Commission and Zoning Board of Adjustment.

The lot has been vacant since a suspicious fire nearly 50 years ago when the former Exeter Playhouse located there burned to the ground. The three remaining family members were at odds on what to do with the property until Roy obtained a majority ownership from his mother this year. No arrest was ever made in the arson case.

Hap Henderson walked into the newsroom just as I finished my third read through of the story. It was the second week of September and only a few maple leaves had started to turn red, but Hap was ready for the colder weather in his trademark flannel shirt. All he needed was a pumpkin spice coffee and he could be the poster boy for New England in autumn.

"I'm just finishing up. I'll send it to your queue," I told him. By this stage in our relationship, I knew what he was thinking before he asked.

He nodded his head as if still taking in the events that had unfolded before 7:00 a.m. in Exeter. Hap said, "I mean, Roy was Roy. We all know he wasn't on the Citizen of the Year list, but really, I don't know what is going on in this town lately. Exeter used to be so quiet."

He looked around the newsroom as if reminding himself that it was just us, before saying, "I want you to focus on Roy's death. I'll have Todd take over the preview story of the Beer and Chili Fest I assigned you. I'll speak with him about it when he gets in."

I wanted to say, "Don't hold your breath." Todd usually didn't roll in until the crack of noon—just in time for his lunchbreak. However, I decided to hold back.

"Thanks, that would be great," I said.

I made quick work of filling Hap in on what I knew so far. I told him I had some photos, and I found one that showed the scene without a full view of Roy. It wasn't like there was anything gruesome around the scene; other than the vomit I'd almost stepped in, I hadn't even seen any blood. However, it was widely agreed that publishing a photo of a dead body was not in good taste, especially at a community paper where local reporters had to face their readers in the grocery store or the Tuck Tavern.

Hap nodded and headed for his office at the rear of the

newsroom while I reviewed the photos again. It did look like Roy had simply fallen asleep. But I couldn't help but wonder what else was in that champagne. I couldn't wait to talk to Richie off the record and find out what he knew.

I walked over to Hap's office and poked my head inside. "So, I'm going to head out and track down Harry Trott," I said. Waiting around being patient wasn't my strength. "It was his regular bird-feeding spot, he skipped our meeting, and he didn't answer his phone. Makes me wonder."

Hap raised his eyebrows with interest, then nodded at me. "Keep me posted."

I walked the short distance up Spring Street and turned onto Court Street, a back way to Massachusetts for those who wanted to avoid the highway. Sadly, it looked like Harry's house hadn't been updated since colonial times. My foot narrowly missed going through a rotten section of wood on his front porch as I walked up to the door. I knew I was taking a chance showing up at his home, particularly given his private nature, but considering he had missed our appointment—at a vacant lot with a dead body—in the back of my mind, I had to ask if he was okay.

I rang the doorbell and waited, looking down again at the neglected porch. I leaned a little closer to the door, turning my head sideways to listen, but I didn't hear anything. Maybe the doorbell didn't work. I gave several raps on the door and waited. Two old plastic chairs and a giant bag of birdseed were the only things on the porch, a sad commentary if you asked me. God, where was he? I knocked again, then leaned forward to peek inside the window on the side of the door.

"He's not home," an older woman's voice announced.

I turned to find Tootie Wentworth, a long-retired teacher

at the prep school who lived next door—the same woman who had originally encouraged Harry to call me. She had just turned 92, a fact I knew because I'd driven Gladys to her birthday party last month.

"Oh, hey, Tootie," I said. "Any idea where he is? I really need to talk to him."

She shook her head. "Your guess is as good as mine. He left like a shot this morning in his car, just as I was headed out on my daily constitutional."

Tootie walked two miles faithfully every day, and on some days she even still played tennis at the school's courts. She'd been inspired to walk by the travels of a woman known as Granny D, a grandmother from New Hampshire who had walked across the country to raise awareness of the need for campaign finance reform. Tootie hadn't yet ruled out a longer walk for something she believed in, like green energy. Her well-loved red Prius was covered in bumper stickers for Earth Day.

"He just took off?" I asked. "Is that unusual?"

She bobbed her head enthusiastically. "Oh, yes. I dare say I've never seen him drive that fast in all the years we've been neighbors. I wanted to ask, 'Where's the fire?'"

Where's the fire indeed. More like, *Where's the dead body?* I took a minute to process this tidbit before I said my good-byes. Harry had only called me last night to invite me to meet him this morning, and he hadn't called me to cancel. So, what was so important that he left his home at dawn like a man on the run?

CHAPTER 4

My phone rang before I made it much further down Court Street. It was Todd Tisden. "What's up?" I asked as I answered.

He sounded out of breath. "First of all, it wasn't my fault," he said.

Oh boy, that was not a good sign. And his words were becoming all too familiar. Since moving in, Todd had caused a fire at Gladys's house when he tried to make beer can chicken on the stovetop, short-circuited the electrical outlet in the carriage house by plugging his beef jerky dehydrator into the wrong socket, and attracted an entire family of raccoons when he left a bag of stale marshmallows outside. Apparently, raccoons really like marshmallows. Even stale ones. Who knew?

"I'm afraid to even ask," I said.

Up ahead, a loud alarm blared from a speaker on the roof of the fire department, and an ambulance came barreling out in front of me, lights, and sirens screaming.

"Oh, God," I said. "Is it Gladys?"

Todd sighed. "Not exactly," he said. "It's Stanley. But really, don't panic. I think once they patch him up, he'll be okay."

Stanley, Glady's gentleman caller and regular visitor to her home for martinis and show tunes, was usually in good health, but he was a few years older than her. "Well," I said when he didn't elaborate, "what happened?"

Todd sounded sheepish—if that was even possible. The man seemed to lack awareness of the norms of what folks should and shouldn't do in polite society. "Well, he wanted to try out Scarlett, but he twisted the scooter's accelerator when he should have pulled the brakes." For a second he laughed, but then he started to choke. Eventually, he continued. "Went off across the driveway like Evil Knievel. Quite impressive really, like the time I was with an old girlfriend in Bermuda, and we barely made it over a drawbridge as it was going up."

Except I immediately realized that Stanley didn't "barely make it" anywhere if the ambulance was en route. Why on earth would Stanley think it was a good idea to try a scooter? Now granted, Todd's Craigslist scooter "steal" didn't go over 30 mph, but still, that was 30 mph too much for someone of Stanley's age.

Todd was still speaking. "Stanley hurtled across the driveway and hit the neighbor's new chicken coop. It could have been worse, really, if not for those feathered friends. I mean, they cushioned his fall quite a bit. If he'd hit a car instead, that really would have done a number on him."

You don't say, I thought. I almost asked if we'd be having beer can chicken for dinner that night or if the feathered friends had survived the situation. Those new neighbors were not going to be pleased. Even though our part of town was quite busy, they'd embraced a back-to-the-land, self-sustaining philosophy, which included selling their composted chicken manure at the farmer's market and fresh eggs in a cooler in front of their house.

Todd groaned on the other end of the line, and I cringed at the thought of what was transpiring in Gladys's driveway. "I'll be right there," I said, hanging up before he could babble on further. Todd, the "great adventurer" as Gladys had dubbed him for his world travels, had a story for everything. Honestly, it was hard to believe they were all true, but the few I'd been curious enough to track down had checked out. I was still amazed about his tale of escaping South America with a fly fisherman who was being chased by the police for allegedly smuggling contraband coffee beans in his fishing boxes.

But what would possess Todd to let Stanley, who was in his nineties, ride a scooter? Stanley still had a driver's license, but he never ventured beyond his senior living apartment, Glady's home, the golf club, and his dedicated seat at the Tuck Tavern.

I walked as fast as I could down Clifford Street, looking back at the swarm of police past the Great Bridge only briefly as I headed for Gladys's large purple Victorian on High Street.

The paramedics were bent over Gladys's companion when I arrived. They didn't look panicked, which I took as a good sign. I recognized the older medic with salt-and-pepper hair and a mustache. As he took Stanley's vitals he asked him, "Okay, can you tell me what happened?"

Stanley winced in pain, then responded. "Well, I guess that little buggy had a bit more spirit that I realized. And I don't bounce like I used to."

Despite the situation, I smiled at his description of Todd's scooter. Then I was quickly sidetracked by Gladys, who threw her arms around me in a huge embrace.

"Oh, Piper, dear, thank God you're here," she exclaimed. She was wearing her favorite fur stole, Suzanne, and I held back from petting her like I might stroke a cat.

Though it was only mid-September, Gladys had recently shifted to her fall wardrobe, a seemingly never-ending collection of faux fur shawls and some real ones, including Suzanne, which she had bought secondhand from a woman retiring to Florida.

"I'm saving the dear thing from the rich people, Piper. Really, it's an act of animal rescue," she had told me when she had returned home and showed me her score.

Now she frowned as she watched the paramedics tend to Stanley. "The poor dear," she went on. "I hope he didn't break his leg."

I glanced down. His left leg was bent at an unnatural angle for anyone but a contortionist or a yoga master. The remnants of a cracked eggshell and yellow yolk was visible by his knee. But I decided to keep my thoughts on the likelihood of a broken leg to myself for now; no need to cause additional alarm. I placed my fingers on her arm and gave a squeeze.

"He's in good hands," I said. "That's the paramedic who helped me this summer when I fell in the cupola. By the way, where's Todd?"

Gladys shook her head. "Oh, the poor thing, he feels just awful about this," she said. "He's calling Stanley's senior living place and his nephew to let them know what happened."

He might feel terrible, but his judgment was clearly skewed. This was another thought I might once have blurted out, but with age I knew it was better to keep this to myself.

The paramedics were immobilizing Stanley's leg with a brace. The medic who had helped me said, "Okay, Stanley. On the count of three, we're going to slide you onto the stretcher. Alright?"

Stanley nodded, and I saw him grimace in pain again as they moved him. Even so, he still looked dapper in his brown tweed blazer and emerald bow tie, which was dotted with red foxes. I also decided to refrain from the obvious statement about the fox going into the henhouse, given what had landed him on the stretcher.

I reached over and put a hand on Stanley's shoulder. "Now, Stanley, I know you've been bored lately, but did you really have to channel Hurricane Hutch?"

He smiled at the reference to Hutch, a character he and Gladys had seen in an old 1920s black-and-white movie recently. It was part of their silent-movie binge, made possible thanks to the miracle of modern technology. Hurricane Hutch had been the first man to jump a moving train on a motorcycle. Quite impressive, they'd both agreed at the time.

"Well, what a story it will make, am I right, Piper?" he said. He gave me a little wave as the crew wheeled him toward the ambulance. "Make sure you make me sound dashing in the newspaper."

The ambulance squad was efficient, and within minutes Stanley was loaded up and off toward the hospital. Thankfully, it was less than a five-minute ride down High Street.

"Oh, Piper, do you think I should go to the hospital to be with him?" Gladys asked. "The poor darling, this must be terribly scary for him."

I felt I should agree, but taking Gladys to the hospital would mess up my schedule for the whole day. Of course, I immediately chided myself for that thought. Stanley needed support, and we were his local watchdogs. I started to say, "Yes, we should go—" just as Todd, who seemed to appear out of nowhere, cut in.

"I'll take you over, Gladys," he said. "My schedule is free now anyway." He gestured toward the scooter, which had a completely flat tire and a large dent in the front. "Hap asked me to follow up on the Beer and Chili Fest preview, but it can wait until this afternoon."

He looked at me, turned back to Gladys, and said, "Piper's on a big story."

I guessed he'd heard from Hap already. Gladys looked perplexed.

"We've had another suspicious death in town," I explained. "Roy Carmichael, right on the old Exeter Playhouse lot."

Gladys's eyes brightened momentarily, which was not what I expected for someone who'd just learned of a potential murder—even someone as worldly as her. "Oh, the Playhouse," she said, as if in a dream. "Those were the days. Of course, they're gone now, just distant memories."

She looked off into the distance, no doubt seeing something only she could recall before she caught herself. She merely said, "Well, that does sound pressing. But Roy wasn't exactly making friends lately, now was he?"

She wasn't wrong. Still, I said, "Surely, though, there must be some people, like his sister Fiona, who will be mourning his passing?"

Before she could reply, Todd took Gladys's arm and helped her into Walter, the old Volvo station wagon named for her late husband, leaving me with no vehicle apart from the broken scooter and the decrepit camper. Looked like I was on foot for the rest of the day.

I glanced over at the neighbor's place, where the young wife was still corralling chickens while her husband stretched a tarp over the side of the coop that had been pushed in by the scooter. Thankfully, I didn't spot any chicken carcasses. One death in Exeter was enough for today. Before turning back toward the carriage house, I waved at them in what I hoped was a sympathetic way. Then my phone pinged with an incoming text. It was Richie this time.

He'd typed, "Everything okay? I heard the scanner call to your place."

I tapped out a fast message back and filled him in on Stanley and the scooter snafu.

"Glad it's sorted," he wrote back. "Because you might want to return to the crime scene. Medical examiner just arrived."

I quickly typed a reply. "Anything interesting?"

He texted back with a winking face emoji and wrote, "You'll just have to come down and find out."

CHAPTER 5

It turned out the new county medical examiner was a good deal chattier than the old one, who I learned had retired. He provided some initial information off the record once I swore to keep it that way, and he promised to give me the scoop once he'd conducted a complete autopsy and toxicology testing.

"Poison," he said bluntly. "It seems highly likely that's what did him in."

Now that *was* suspicious, I thought, and wondered when authorities would officially say Roy had been murdered. The medical examiner surmised that someone had slipped poison into the champagne flute, and I noted that the empty bottle was bagged up in a clear plastic evidence bag. Now that I was closer to Roy, I cringed when I saw the remnants of his partially digested dinner next to him.

The medical examiner followed my gaze and gestured toward the vomit. "That, along with the swelling on his face, lead me to believe he ingested a lethal amount of something. But I won't know for sure what until we do actual testing."

It turned out that the testing took some time, and over the next few days I found myself eager for some sort of update.

Instead, I kept rehashing what I knew. No one had heard from Harry Trott, and the police seemed more than eager to speak with him. He was an old-school kind of guy with a landline instead of a cell phone, and there was no wife at home waiting for him, so all we could do was wait.

"I'm not saying he's a suspect," Richie told me over Chinese food one night. "But it's extremely questionable that he went off the grid immediately after this happened."

He didn't have to say that again. Gladys and Tootie had been speculating daily about where he'd gone off to. I can't lie: I was half expecting another body to materialize any moment now.

With the investigation in its early days—which often meant few, if any, comments from the police on the case—I was relegated to following up on the proposal for Roy's arcade, which had been awaiting approval from the Historic District Commission. I did have the official word that the police considered Roy's death a murder, but that's all they were saying for now.

Across the office from me, Todd was spending way more time than I would have on his latest assignment: preview interviews for the town's annual Beer and Chili Fest. Given that this year's festival was going to be featured on a Food Network travel show, it did warrant some extra coverage.

"Man, one time I tried chili made with the Purple Bhut Jolokia," he said to me.

"What the heck is that?" I asked.

He paused. "A purple pepper. It's super rare, with a nice, sweet flavor and a good burn. Someone had them at the Burning Man Festival one year. Never seen them since."

I rolled my eyes. Of *course*, Todd had gone to Burning Man. What was next, a travelogue of his time following The Grateful Dead?

I decided to ignore him and got to work. I started with the current chairman of the Historic District Commission, Charles Bolton III, who went by Tripp and just happened to be married to one of my least favorite town personalities: Pansy, the head of the Rotary. I skipped past the opening sentence that first popped into my mind—"The plan is as dead as its owner"—and wrote the following lines instead.

ARCADE PLAN PAUSED AFTER MURDER

BY PIPER GREENE

EXETER__*Some locals are speculating that the murder of its owner could signal the final curtain call for a plan to redevelop the site of the former Exeter Playhouse.*

The death of Roy Carmichael remains under investigation but is considered suspicious, according to police. His body was found in a camping chair with an empty bottle of champagne on the very lot he hoped to build upon.

With Carmichael dead, the minority owner in the property, his younger sister, Fiona, says she intends to pull the plug on his plan to construct Carmichael's Arcade in Arms, a Revolutionary War–themed arcade and fun house on the parcel.

"First and foremost, I'm mourning my brother. While we disagreed on the direction his plan was going, he was my big brother and I loved him," she said.

A longtime member of the Heritage Commission, Fiona previously said she hoped to one day build another theater on the property. "Speaking on my own behalf, I was not in favor of this plan from the start," she said. "It was about as wrong for Exeter's downtown as a tattoo parlor or strip club would be."

Tripp Bolton, chairman of the Historic District Commission, a vocal opponent of the plan, declined to comment when reached by phone. "At this time, out of respect for the family, I'm going to wait to say anything," Bolton said. "You can read our meeting minutes if you want to know where I stand."

As previously reported in this paper, police were called to one of the meetings when Bolton leapt from his seat at the table and began screaming at Carmichael, "You'll regret this decision as long as you live." Audience members got between the two men, and eventually both shook hands and agreed to respect the decorum of the meeting, but later meetings were equally contentious.

The former Playhouse site has been vacant for decades since a fire ripped through the building on opening night of Bye Bye Birdie. *While the redevelopment plan drew criticism from longtime residents, it found a champion in Becky Bean, a public relations consultant in town to promote the Beer and Chili Fest this year. She'd recently started working with Roy Carmichael to handle his media inquiries.*

"I understand the hesitation from residents about his plan, but quite honestly, this is a challenge in all small towns: the need to balance growth with preservation," she said. "Roy was passionate about bringing a new energy to the downtown area, making it a place that could compete with some of our neighbors on the ocean. I'm just devastated by his death."

By the time I finished writing, it was almost dark outside. Oh, the joys of the countdown to daylight savings time. With Gladys still holding vigil over at Stanley's bedside, I knew she wouldn't be home for dinner, so I decided to get a quick bite to eat at the Tuck Tavern, where—if I was lucky—I might pick up some scuttlebutt about Roy.

The tavern was quiet when I arrived. Emily Athens, its owner, was tending bar. She'd been short-staffed ever since her last bartender, Kevin, left his post to return to the tennis circuit. She perked up when she saw me.

"My favorite newshound," she said. "What's the word?"

I knew she was referring to the murder investigation. Emily and I had gotten to know each other over the summer, and she had quickly become one of my best sources. I knew never to use her name, unless she gave the okay, and she knew she could trust me. She also really loved to trade gossip.

"Not much," I told her. I held back from what I'd learned about the poison for now, not wanting to burn my source. "I'm still waiting for the medical examiner to release cause of death, and the police aren't saying boo at this point."

She nodded. "Sounds about right. What can I get you?"

I thought on that for a minute. It was fall, after all, and Jenny had been schooling me on red wines, a passion of hers after her time living in France. "How about a merlot," I said.

She poured me a glass, filling it a little fuller than normal, and turned to take an order from Grayson Adams, who was slouching in his regular seat on the opposite side of the bar. Grayson acknowledged me but didn't jump up to say hello. He was still standoffish after his false arrest for the murder of my former editor, Charlotte, a few months ago.

I took a sip of the wine. Black cherry, raspberry, with notes of vanilla. Not bad. Jenny would be proud that I was finally starting to appreciate wine. I glanced around the bar, as was my habit, to keep tabs on the comings and goings of the regulars.

My brother, Chester, and his business partner at the law

firm, Teddy, were cloistered in the corner in a dark wooden booth. Chester was an impressive man by most people's standards. Tall, with a full head of thick black hair, he looked much like our Puritan ancestors, who were on display in the paintings in his library. His button-down shirt likely cost more than my entire wardrobe. Teddy waved me over.

"Care to join us?"

What could I say? My brother was a total pain, but Teddy was a good guy. And on a positive, with their salaries as lawyers, they'd pick up the tab.

"So, you decided not to do the book, huh?" Teddy said immediately.

My literary agent, Jack Harper, a classmate of Teddy's at the prep school in town, had been gaga over the idea of me writing a first-person account of Charlotte's murder. But after I'd recovered from my concussion over the summer, I had decided to put it on hold before I even wrote the first chapter.

"Nope, not now. Honestly, I wasn't in the frame of mind to write a book," I told him. More accurately, I'd decided it didn't feel right to put my quaint—and loveable—town in the spotlight for such a gruesome event. I was young. There would be plenty of time to write a book (or two) later.

Not surprisingly, Chester grumbled at this news. "Still playing at that paper like a kid," he said. "Wasting her talent."

God, could he get some new material? He'd been saying this for years. I chose not to respond and perused the dinner specials. Ooh, the butternut ravioli in brown butter cream sauce with spiced walnuts sounded delicious. But the slow-roasted short ribs in red wine were the type of satisfying comfort food I could use right then.

"So, what's the news on Roy?" Teddy asked, after I'd

ordered the short ribs. I knew they'd go well with the merlot I'd brought with me from the bar.

While my brother didn't share my predilection for talking about town news—and in this case, police business—Teddy loved it. I filled him in on the mystery surrounding Harry Trott and the off-the-record theory that Roy was poisoned through his champagne.

"Well, he had a way of rubbing people the wrong way," Teddy said, "but I still can't believe someone went through with it.".

Chester opened his mouth like he was going to say something but stopped.

"Yes?" I prompted, knowing him too well, even if we didn't get along.

"Well, you didn't hear this from me," he said. "But if I was you, Little Miss Busybody, I'd look into how he came to acquire the majority ownership of that property."

He clamped his mouth shut, as if regretting his words already.

"Any reason why?" I asked.

He shook his head. "I shouldn't have even told you that."

I finished my short ribs, which were so tender I didn't even need a knife to cut them, and headed out without any more tidbits from Chester. He had picked up the dinner bill, always welcome on my reporter's salary. But later that night, I kept thinking about what he had told me about the property ownership. My brother wasn't exactly known for helping me out, especially when it came to my job. So why had he given me a tip now? And, considering our history, could I even trust him?

CHAPTER 6

I put in a call to Fiona Carmichael from the office the next day, ostensibly to do a story about plans for Roy's funeral. The truth was, I really wanted to slip in a question about how Roy got the majority stake in the property. She didn't answer, so I left a message with my office number and cell phone. Then I decided to head over to the Exeter Historical Society.

Todd looked up from his desk as I passed by on my way out. "What's happening Greene?" he asked. In recent weeks, he'd taken to calling me by my last name like I was one of the guys.

I shook my head. "Not much, Tisden. You?"

He spun around in his chair and leaned back, folding his arms behind his head. "The advance team members from the television network are coming in today to scope out the area for their taping. Figured I'd follow along. You know, drum up some excitement and all."

Todd seemed to create excitement almost without trying, and at times, I found myself going on his outings just to observe them for my own personal amusement. He was a bit like a little mosquito, always buzzing around and irritating me, but at the same time, I found myself drawn into his antics. But not today. I already had plans that I needed to stick with.

In the reception area I waved goodbye to Clara, who was on the phone, and then I set out on foot toward the Exeter Historical Society. I needed to see Winnie Smart, town historian, murder buff, and cutthroat poker player. Buttercup, her cat, was sitting in the hallway when I entered, like an ancient Egyptian emissary welcoming the lowly humans to her domain. I found Winnie in the back, her office-slash-kitchen space, with her head pressed up close to her old computer monitor and a cup of tea beside her.

"Oh, I was hoping you'd stop by," she said. "What's new?"

Now with anyone else, that might mean, "How's life? Your significant other? Your health?" But with Winnie, that meant, "What's the status of the murder investigation?"

"Not much," I said, sitting down in her side chair. "Waiting for the medical examiner to get his toxicology report back on what, if anything, poisoned Roy. Sounds like it could take a while. Things are kind of backed up at the state lab from what I heard."

I clued her in on the tip I'd received about looking into Roy's ownership. I also discussed my idea for a story looking back at the last big police investigation on this property, the fire nearly 50 years ago. We had covered some of the history in the stories we had published after the various Historic District Commission meetings, but I hadn't gone too deep into the arson angle. I had a gut feeling that two suspicious events on the same property meant something, but what? If nothing else, maybe writing about the old case would bring people out of the sidelines and lead to information that might be helpful now.

Winnie took a sip of her tea before using both hands to push herself out of her deep upholstered armchair, which served as her desk chair. I glanced at her desk, which was covered in papers as usual, and noticed a colorful travel brochure that said "Visit Exeter, England" on the top.

"Planning a trip?" I asked.

She smiled and looked positively giddy. "If all goes as planned, I'll be there in the spring," she said. "Saving up my wins from poker." She winked at me. "Not that I'd take advantage of anyone," she said. "But all's fair in history and poker."

She leaned down to pick up Buttercup, who was rubbing up against her ankles and weaving a figure eight through her legs—an accident in the making, if you asked me—and then made her way to the front room of the building. Still holding the cat, who looked absolutely pleased with its human servant, she used her foot to slide a cardboard file box out from under the table. It had the words *Murder Box* on the top in black marker.

"What happened to the murder files?" I asked her.

Winnie was known to keep tabs on the living and the dead, including those who had died under suspicious circumstances. She laughed. "Well, given the way bodies keep showing up in town, I decided to be proactive and just get the box."

God, that was both morbid and fantastic at the same time.

She set the cat down, lifted the top, and held up a manilla folder marked *Murder File #2*, which she handed to me. I sat down at the thick wooden table that served as the research area and began flipping through.

Winnie was nothing if not punctual. The folder already had the latest news articles about Roy's death, printed out from the newspaper's website. I moved past those, finding some old, yellowed newspaper clippings. I was careful to slow down and hold them gently so as not to damage them. I didn't want to become the inspiration for Murder File #3.

I looked at the first clipping, which had a black-and-white picture of a firefighter holding a hose in front of the burning playhouse. I leaned over to read the caption. "Firefighter Eddie Smart mounts an external attack with hose to stop the fire from spreading."

"I didn't know your husband was there," I called to her.

She looked up. "Oh yes, his first big fire. Some guys on his shift almost went through the floor inside. He said they almost lost the whole block. Apparently, the fire had a good head start on them before they even got there."

Winnie returned to her file, and I settled in to read the article. It had been written by a reporter I'd never heard of, which wasn't that unusual given how many years ago the fire had happened.

FIRE DESTROYS EXETER PLAYHOUSE; ARSON SUSPECTED

By Daniel Pendexter

EXETER__A *fast-moving fire leveled the Exeter Playhouse on Friday night, just hours after the opening night of* Bye Bye Birdie.

No one was injured in the fire, but it is considered suspicious in nature. Exeter Police are investigating in conjunction with the state fire marshal, Police Chief Rick Sinclair said.Playhouse owner Virginia Carmichael thanked the fire department for their quick response and vowed to rebuild. "There has been a theater on that site for as long as I can remember," she said. "And as long as a Carmichael owns it, a theater will remain."

Duncan McTavish, who was cast as Conrad Birdie in the play, said the loss was devastating. "It is just such a tragedy," he said. "The theater really gave me my start, and I credit that with helping me land a role in Boston."

McTavish said he was moving south for the new role but would always remember his time in town.

Fire Chief Jim Toland thanked the area towns who responded with mutual aid to assist in fighting the fire, with a ladder truck from Amesbury, Mass., on scene.

Hmm, I thought. There were a few more articles about the investigation, and reading between the lines, I realized there was some speculation about the fire being an inside job, but no arrest for the fire was ever made, and it all seemed to fade out of the news cycle. Then, every five or ten years, someone wrote an article about the now-vacant lot, with a question to Virginia Carmichael about when something would be built there. She was evasive but hinted that some of the family members didn't agree with the plan to rebuild. I knew that already because of the brief interview that I'd done with Fiona for my first article after Roy's death.

Finally, I flipped to the recent articles, mostly my coverage of the Historic District Commission meeting where its chairman, Tripp Bolton, insisted that the plan for the arcade would never see the light of day. I didn't have to read those again. Sit through any local zoning meeting like that and it is burned in your brain, not because of the excitement but due to the sheer monotony of hours of dry drivel on ordinances and regulations. I recalled seeing an older reporter painting her nails during a meeting when I was an intern during high school.

A few times during these meetings, Tripp had looked like he might spontaneously implode, particularly when Roy had unveiled the artist's rendering of the tacky neon sign. And there was that meeting where Tripp had jumped out from behind the table and looked like he might come to blows with Roy. Frankly, I would have loved to see an actual knockdown, drag-out fight at a boring town meeting, and I still wasn't completely convinced I was in the minority.

"What do you make of Tripp Bolton?" I asked Winnie now. "I don't really know him, but he was a force at those meetings."

Winnie clucked in sympathy. "You've got to pity anyone who has to live with Pansy," she replied.

She didn't have to say that again. Pansy was a grade-A pain in the you-know-what. She was always tsk-tsking when the newspaper covered anything controversial, as if we were on some sort of vendetta against good news and could control what happened in town. Just a few weeks ago, she'd cornered Hap at brunch to complain about my coverage of a Labor Day block party that had escalated into a neighborhood brawl after too much sangria was consumed. According to my boss, she'd whined, "Really, Hap, does Piper need to take every chance to make our town look bad?" Of course, Hap had politely but firmly told her the paper reported *all* of the news.

Bringing my thoughts back to the present again, I checked my watch and realized I needed to get going. Todd was handling the beer and chili article, but I still had to cover a town budget meeting that night. Though townspeople wouldn't vote until March, a group of volunteers and department heads began a line-by-line review in the fall. These meetings were also painful at times, as some of the thriftier members of the board spent agonizing hours debating the merits of street sweepers, new fire trucks, or even whether to repaint the crosswalks downtown. I wanted to make a stop at home before the meeting and get a bite to eat to sustain me through what I feared would be hours of monotony. I quickly snapped some photos of the old articles on my phone and said goodbye to Winnie.

By the time I reached the driveway of Gladys's house, I was ready to sit down. I couldn't wait until Todd got his scooter fixed so I could start driving Walter the Wagon once again. The Volvo was nowhere to be seen, but a red Toyota Prius I recognized as Tootie Wentworth's car was parked out front. She popped her head out of the window and waved me over when she saw me.

"Oh, Piper, glad you're here. I had a dish to return to Gladys, but it was you I wanted to see. I thought you'd want to know that Harry Trott got home today. And boy does he have a humdinger of a story about where he was! I'm late for tennis, but I'm sure he'll tell you all about it himself."

I could hardly wait, although the last time I'd heard someone use the word *humdinger*, they were describing a record-breaking bass pulled from the river by old Georgie Pottle. Still, I could only hope Harry's story wasn't one of those fish tales that are better in the retelling than reality.

CHAPTER 7

I didn't have time to track down Harry before my meeting, but it was the top item on my list the next day. I was dying to know where he had shot off to that morning like his pants were on fire; I just had to check in briefly at the office first.

Right after I walked in, a fax came through from the state police. Clara, who was working on the week's obituaries, let out a dramatic "Oh my! Oh my!" as she read it. She then called out to me, "You've got a live one here, Piper."

I grabbed the paper from her and scanned it as fast as I could. It was a press release with new details from the medical examiner's report about Roy's death. In typical "police speak," as I called their clinically written releases, the details were not extensive. Roy had been poisoned. Of course, I knew that already from my off-the-record conversation with the medical examiner, but at least I could report it now. However, given that this was my first poisoning death, I knew I would have to do some additional research. As a result, I spent most of the morning putting out phone calls and gathering as many supplemental tidbits as I could find to put together an article for the website.

Poison. God, it sounded like something straight out of *Arsenic and Old Lace*. I couldn't help but feel like the entire scene around Roy's murder was staged like a play in which we were all the audience getting ready for a big finale. I stopped myself there. That would take a lot of planning and effort, and honestly, this was Exeter, not a real-life Hollywood-style murder mystery production. Still, poison felt like the weapon of a specific kind of murderer: someone who was strategic, who was intelligent, who did their homework—but, mostly, who was cold-blooded.

I thought it would help if I knew what kind of poison it was, especially because some things could be bought easily over the counter while others, like poisons used in chemical warfare, were incredibly hard to source. I looked at the list of potential poisons I'd scribbled on a notepad on my desk— antifreeze, rat poison, arsenic, and cyanide—curious as to whether one of them would be the culprit. Then I put in a call to my new pal, the chatty medical examiner. Once I got some on-the-record comments from him, I fired up my computer to write a story.

POISONING SUSPECTED IN DEATH OF
ARCADE OWNER

By Piper Greene

EXETER__*The state medical examiner, Leland Flynn, says a preliminary autopsy points to poison as the likely cause of death for downtown property owner Roy Carmichael.*

"Specifics won't be known until we complete toxicology testing," Flynn said. "But given the visible appearance of some

swelling and regurgitation of partially digested food, it would appear that he did in fact consume something very lethal."

Flynn confirmed that a champagne flute found by Carmichael's body is being analyzed and tested to determine if traces of a poison remain. While the specific poison isn't known, the medical examiner went on to state that based on the condition of Carmichael's body, he could safely estimate that he died between 10:00 p.m. and midnight.

The family will hold a public visitation at the Cronin Funeral home, but the funeral and burial will be private, according to his sister.

I finished up and pondered the time-of-death information. It meant that Roy had been out in his chair all night before I found him. I was sure the police were asking various people where they were during that window and could only hope Richie would tell me if someone didn't have an alibi.

With my story done, it was finally time to follow up on Tootie's tidbit: Harry Trott's big humdinger of a story. Todd still had the Volvo, so I headed out on foot yet again, this time careful to avoid the section of rotten wood on Harry's deck as I walked up to knock on the door. I thumped the rusted metal knocker a few times and waited. A blue town recycling container now sat next to his giant bag of birdseed. It was filled with the cardboard boxes from what appeared to be endless microwave dinners. I guess when you spent your money on industrial-size quantities of birdseed, you had to economize at home. It looked like Salisbury steak and fried chicken with gravy were the current favorites.

Eventually the door opened, and Harry stood before me. I'd heard him described as a sprite by some people in town and a little gnome by others. He barely topped five feet and was lucky if he weighed over a hundred pounds. His gray hair was ruffled, with a section sticking up in the back that reminded me of a cockatiel.

"Harry, it's Piper Greene," I said, putting my hand out to greet him. "We met a few times recently during the town meetings about the arcade plan."

A look of recognition crossed his face. "Oh, I'm so sorry, I never got back to you," he said.

I smiled, hoping it might put him at ease. "That's okay," I said. "I hope you'll forgive Tootie, but she told me you were home and had quite a story."

He nodded, dare I say with some excitement. "Yes, yes, why don't you come in."

He turned and shuffled back inside. I followed, trying to hide my shock at the narrow goat path he took me on to navigate several large cardboard boxes.

"Moving?" I asked.

He looked perplexed, and I gestured to the boxes. He said, "Oh no, just organizing some of my treasures, that's all."

God, it was a fire hazard if I ever saw one. Once we finally reached the kitchen, I saw that it was quite small, the black-and-white linoleum chipped in places. However, although the hallways were cluttered, his counter was reasonably tidy, with what looked like a plate from breakfast next to the sink and a stack of mail on the other side. An actual rotary phone with a cord was mounted to the wall. Boy, what would that fetch on eBay? You didn't see them much anymore. He sat down at one of two chairs at a small worn table, and I eased myself into the other chair and looked at him expectantly.

Instead of speaking, he picked up a coffee cup, tipped it back, and drained it. There was a large container of Folgers instant coffee on the counter, and I hoped he wouldn't offer me a cup. I had a strict real coffee rule: unless it was a complete emergency, like I was trapped in the wilderness miles from civilization and my choices were instant coffee or cannibalism, I wouldn't drink it. This situation certainly didn't qualify.

It seemed like I'd have to speak first.

He put the cup down and said, "Yes, I apologize again for not getting back to you. Something came up."

It didn't seem possible, but even more enthusiasm crept into his voice. He went on. "A report of a Steller's sea eagle, which is native to eastern Russia, was spotted on the mid-coast of Maine."

So, while he didn't have a cell phone, apparently, he did use email. He told me he began every morning on the computer on the New England Birders message board. The morning I discovered Roy's body, birders from around the region "were flocking"—his words, not mine—up I-95 to catch a glimpse of the Steller's sea eagle. He knew the bird might not stay around long, so, like his fellow birders, he hopped in his car and took off immediately. Sadly, by the time he got to the spot, the bird was gone.

"I met up with a birder friend and decided to stay over that night, so we could return to the site first thing the next morning," he said. "But by then, the bird was crisscrossing the area, with a report that it was in Bangor."

In my mind I heard my late uncle Walter's voice say, *Bang her? I don't even know her!* He never failed to insert this off-color expression whenever he heard the name of the infamous Maine town. And each and every time, Gladys would wince and roll her eyes.

Quickly returning my mind to the present, I asked, "So, you never saw it?"

He shook his head. "It hasn't been spotted again. It was disappointing, but I needed to get back here, for my birds."

God, that was anticlimactic. Tootie's preview of his escapade had certainly not lived up to reality, though to be fair it had probably felt like an electrifying excursion in Harry's solitary world. I was reminded again of fish stories. Maybe the details of the Steller's sea eagle would get better after multiple retelling among the birders.

Now that I had the full scoop—or nonscoop—I stood up to leave. I had promised to take Glady's to Roy's public visitation at the funeral home, and I didn't want to be late. Todd had even promised to drop the car back at the house so that I could drive her there.

Harry gingerly walked me to the door, and I found myself speculating about just what was in all those boxes, but I didn't want to ask and make him even more uncomfortable. I noticed that a few had handwritten address labels on top. Perhaps he was passing his treasures on to someone else? Something else was tugging at my subconscious, too, and when I realized what it was, I turned back as he prepared to close the door behind me.

"Say, who fed your birds when you were gone?" I asked. Though I hadn't noticed anyone else filling his shoes downtown, I had a hunch that he wouldn't have allowed his beloved birds to go hungry in his absence.

"A friend," he said. "But leave her alone. I don't think she wants to talk about this with you."

My curiosity was piqued, but I knew I'd reached my limit.

"Well, thanks Harry. I appreciate your time," I said. "And good luck with the Russian eagle."

I raced home with just enough time to take a quick shower, change, and dash to Glady's back door to pick her up at our arranged time. She appeared like some sort of classic Hollywood mourner, complete with a black velvet shawl, dark glasses, and a scarf over her hair. Her timeless look was completed by a pair of shiny black silk gloves, which went up to her elbows. By contrast, I looked like I was going to a Catholic school assembly in a uniform with my basic navy skirt and white blouse.

"Oh, my dear, you look tired," she said, as she placed her hand on my cheek. "Why don't we have a nice dinner at the Terrace after this messiness."

The Terrace was an upscale spot my brother, Chester, preferred. Gladys also enjoyed the occasional Sunday brunch at the Terrace with Stanley, although he wouldn't be eating there anytime soon per the latest report from Gladys. He expected to be in rehab at least three to four weeks as the therapists worked to get him walking on his own.

I smiled at Gladys. "That would be lovely," I said. "It's been a day."

I eased Walter through downtown, where the yellow crime scene tape still surrounded the Exeter Playhouse lot, and up one of the side streets. I parked near the Tuck Tavern, and we walked the final block to the Cronin Funeral Home. There was a line of people out the door by the time we arrived. *Not necessarily mourners,* I thought, *perhaps the curious, like the people who rubberneck at an accident scene.* I recognized a veritable "who's who" of the local business community, from select board members to the old townies and even Pansy and

Tripp Bolton.

Gladys was standing next to me, silent in her funeral ensemble, when she suddenly faltered. I grabbed her arm to steady her.

"Oh, good heavens!" she exclaimed.

Something was clearly wrong.

"Are you okay?" I whispered, truly concerned. She looked like she'd seen a ghost. In the old days, they had called it a case of the vapors.

"It's Duncan McTavish," she gasped. "I haven't seen him since he stood me up for our last date almost fifty years ago."

CHAPTER 8

As the line shuffled forward, I tried to contain my surprise that Gladys had dated anyone besides her beloved late husband, Walter. But while patience is a virtue, it wasn't one I possessed, and it was less than ten seconds before I lost that battle and blurted out, "Wait, what?"

"A long story, my dear, and one I've not thought of in many years."

I studied the man she'd identified as Duncan McTavish. He looked like a leading man from the golden era of movies. He was tall with a chiseled face; his full head of silver hair was combed back without a piece out of place. His suit fit so perfectly, even Stanley, a retired tailor, would have found no issue with the cut. To top it off, he had on an impeccably tied crimson ascot.

Gladys took a deep breath. "God, he's as dashing as ever!"

At that moment, Dashing Duncan looked over and noticed us. I saw a look of recognition and an almost imperceptible widening of his smile as he strolled our way. He held out his hands, took Gladys's face in them, and kissed both cheeks.

"You're as stunning as ever, Glady," he said, dropping the

"s" from her name. A nickname? If so, I'd never heard it. "And I am an idiot."

God, he was like an aging libertine in both dress and demeanor. Gladys was about as flustered as I'd ever seen her. She took a moment to respond. "Well, Duncan, how unexpected to meet you here," she said. "I thought you forgot all of us when you went off to Broadway."

Yes, that was where I knew his name from: the old article about the fire and the theater. Duncan was the one who credited the theater with giving him his start before leaving to take the role in Boston. He'd been Conrad Birdie in the last play in Exeter.

Duncan put his hand on her arm with a little too much familiarity for me, especially given what Gladys had just said about being stood up 50 years prior.

He crooned, "Now how could one ever forget someone like you, Glady? It would be impossible."

Boy, he was really laying it on heavy. She smiled at him, and for a moment I could see what she might have been like as a young woman. She said, "How long are you here?"

He shrugged. "Long enough to make up for lost time with you." Then he stopped and looked at me as if only realizing I was there.

"Oh," Gladys said, as if she had also forgotten I was next to her. "My niece, Piper Greene."

He took my hand, held it up, and kissed it. "Enchanted."

Really? I thought. *Is this guy for real?*

We took a few steps forward in line. Gladys was gripping my hand so tightly I thought I might lose a finger or two. She said to him, "Piper and I are going to the Terrace for dinner after this. Why don't you join us?"

He smiled, showing a line of flawlessly straight white teeth that were most definitely not his own. As I pushed away a snarky thought that he'd be the perfect spokesman for denture cream, he responded, "I wouldn't miss it for the world."

We finally made our way through the line, where we shook hands with Fiona and some of the relatives, and then looked at a few photos of Roy and his trademark jet-black dyed hair. In some of the photos, he looked like an aspiring Elvis impersonator.

"Boy, he sure liked to gamble," I whispered to Gladys, as we viewed several photos of Roy in casinos. In one he was standing by a slot machine with a bucketful of coins; in another he was posing in front of a giant waterfall in Vegas.

Gladys frowned and spoke quietly so only I could hear her. "Did you expect anything else, my dear? I mean really, look at that dreadful arcade he was trying to build. Who does that in Exeter?"

She had a point.

There were also a few photos of a much younger Roy with Fiona and his mother, Virginia, who wasn't present.

"With the dementia it's just too much for her," Gladys whispered to us sadly.

To my dismay, Duncan stuck to us like a cheap suit as we stepped onto the back porch of the funeral home. I spotted Todd Tisden in the parking lot, and he waved and made his way toward us.

"Hap wanted some local color and thought you could use some help," he said, as he slid a reporter's notebook into his shirt pocket.

"Oh, Todd, do join us," Gladys insisted. She explained our dinner plans.

Todd, never one to turn down a free meal, shrugged and said, "Well, what the heck. If Greene's going, you know I'm in."

Gladys swatted his arm at the use of my last name, a social faux pas in her book, and the four of us set out for the Terrace. Where the Tuck Tavern had the comfortable feel of your own living room—or, at least, a place you could really relax in their old worn booths—the Terrace had crisp white tablecloths and overzealous waitstaff who refilled your drink of water as soon as you took a sip. The feeling of style with a side of old money pretentiousness was obvious from the moment we walked into the dining room.

"Swanky," Todd remarked. He was in his dress-up clothes, which consisted of khakis and an only slightly rumpled blue button-down shirt.

Todd and I kept pace with the hostess, who briskly led us to a table as Gladys and Duncan slowly trailed behind. Before they caught up, Todd leaned over and whispered, "What's the story on the stiff?"

"Old flame," I told him.

Duncan doted upon Gladys as he pulled her chair out, helped her in, and handed her a menu.

"Quite the Casanova, huh," Todd said, whispering again. "Let's pen a poem about them. I'll call it 'Under the Disco Ball.'"

I bit my lip to keep from laughing. Duncan did have the routine down, and I was surprised that Gladys didn't see through it. But perhaps the shock of seeing Duncan all these years later had thrown her for more of a loop than I realized.

We put in our drink orders and Duncan ordered the raw bar sampler, which appeared on our table on a tiered stand like something in a luxury cruise on the South Pacific. I had to wonder if they were bumping things up a notch with the actual Food Network show coming to town for the Beer and Chili Fest.

"Now, Duncan, dear, do tell us what you've been up to," Gladys said.

I noticed she didn't ask him why he stood her up for their last date five decades ago.

"Well, I'm in the city, near Hell's Kitchen, and I'm between productions right now," he said, stopping to slide an oyster down his throat in one gulp.

Yuck. I couldn't stomach oysters. To me they seemed like the loogies the boys used to spit in junior high, but I knew oysters were rumored to have aphrodisiac qualities. Given the zest with which he was consuming them, perhaps that's what he had in mind.

He grimaced as he continued. "They want to cast me in utterly awful roles now. Aging isn't for the faint of heart, my dear, but then, you haven't aged a day since I last laid eyes on you."

Gladys smiled politely at the compliment, and he recounted his career. "I've picked up some musical work, playing piano at a ritzy hotel. Tickling the ivories has always been a passion of mine," he said. He reached inside his jacket, pulled out a CD, and handed it to Gladys. "A compilation of my work."

I held back from smirking as I leaned over to get a look at the CD, titled "Melodies by McTavish," complete with a glamour shot of Duncan and his pearly whites front and center. The cover looked like it had been made on an inkjet printer in the 1980s.

"The hotel's lounge closed for renovations at the end of the summer," Duncan told us, "so I'm on a little break. Then I heard about Roy's death. Since Virginia gave me a start in my career, I decided to come pay my respects."

According to Duncan, although Virginia Carmichael was challenged by dementia when it came to current events, she had recognized him when he had stopped by the assisted living facility earlier in the day. I noticed he didn't elaborate about how long he planned to stay in town or if there was anything else that had brought him to the area.

"Piper and Todd both write for the *Exeter Independent*," Gladys said, like a proud parent on recital night. "Top-notch, quite accomplished, both of them. And Piper is even chasing down Roy's killer!"

Duncan looked at us and raised his eyebrows in interest. "Any leads so far?"

I chewed a piece of shrimp before I answered. No Old Bay seasoning on these, but the horseradish in the cocktail sauce was clearly freshly grated and had quite a kick. I could tell the shrimp had been poached with peppercorns before they were chilled. I took a sip of water to clear my throat before I responded.

"Not yet," I told him. "It's early still, but they did just release the cause of death as poisoning."

Gladys sat up a little straighter. She loved to play along as I investigated cases, and she could often be quite helpful with her knowledge of the history in town and beyond.

She said, "Well, that is something, isn't it. Kind of like that show I saw on PBS recently about some long-ago king being poisoned. Remember that one, Piper?"

I nodded at her. We'd watched the show together and I'd been intrigued by the theory that an unassuming plant slipped in his wine had caused his death. I had been even more troubled by the details of the poison, which would leave someone conscious but unable to move right up until they died. What a terrifying way to go. Despite his issues in town, I hoped Roy's final moments had been quicker than that.

Duncan popped a maraschino cherry from his Manhattan into his mouth and took a sip of the caramel-colored drink.

"Well, it's just unpleasant all around," he said. "Let's order. Shall I order for you, Glady?"

Now that was where I'd draw the line, but Gladys demurred and let him order for her. I was tempted to go over and bust Stanley out of the rehab right then and there if it would put Mr. Pearly Whites off the scent.

Duncan requested two orders of rare roast beef. *Gladys doesn't even like rare beef,* I wanted to tell him, but she smiled and nodded at him like he could do no wrong. The two of them bent their heads toward each other, reminiscing about old times at the theater and friends from those days. Todd and I listened in, making subtle faces at each other at the particularly amusing parts of their conversation. He whispered, "And their eyes met, under the spinning lights of the disco ball, and as they shone upon his pearly teeth, her heart spun too."

I held my napkin in front of my mouth as I struggled to hold back a laugh. When our entrees arrived, I glanced at my miniscule piece of lemon caper haddock, about the size a toddler might eat, while Todd made a face at his equally minute chicken cordon bleu.

"Guess they don't expect you to have an appetite here, huh?" he said.

He wasn't wrong. The food was carefully arranged, but it

was more like a piece of art than something that would sustain you. Tasty, but only whetting the appetite. I was definitely going to need a midnight snack.

Gladys and Duncan's conversation waned as they cut into their petite portions of beef, surrounded by some artful swirls of what I presumed was gravy or pureed vegetables. The rest of dinner was uneventful, and before long we found ourselves standing on the granite steps outside, ready to head home. The word *canoodling* came to mind as I watched the old loves say goodnight to each other. Todd and I glanced at each other in amusement as we patiently waited to give Gladys a ride home in Walter the Wagon.

"Hey, Greene, isn't that your friend the detective?" Todd asked suddenly.

I looked up and saw Richie Collins. He was sitting in his unmarked cruiser in front of the Terrace. He looked from Todd to me, then at Gladys and Duncan. He gave a little wave to me, but it wasn't what you'd call keen, and then he scowled before driving off abruptly without stopping to say hello. If I hadn't known better, I'd have said he was jealous. But of Todd, really?

CHAPTER 9

Todd and I alternated weekend duty coverage at the newspaper on Saturdays, but there was no sleeping in for me this weekend. I'd offered to help Jenny with her preparations for the Beer and Chili Fest. She was teaming up with Emily Athens at the Tuck Tavern on an entry: Emily's chili with Jenny's cornbread or another yet-to-be-discovered accompaniment. They were meeting in the kitchen at the Tavern later that morning to try several combinations as they decided upon their entry. I was not so secretly lobbying to be their main taste tester.

I'd arranged to meet up with Jenny at the Morning Musket so we could go to the Tavern together. At the Musket I plunked down on a stool in the kitchen as she bustled about. While she flitted around the kitchen, I filled her in on my latest encounter with Richie. Though I was pressing on with coverage of Roy's murder, I couldn't stop thinking about how Richie had driven off the night before without saying hello. It really bothered me.

I said, "I don't know, Jen, he seemed almost jealous—like really, how could he think Todd is a threat? I mean, he is a character and all, but definitely not my type."

Jenny looked up from a sheet pan, where she was slicing today's test: a jalapeno cornbread cooked in the pan with a local honey butter.

"Well, look on the bright side Miss Glass Is Half Empty. If he's jealous, he's really into you, right?"

I popped a piece of cornbread in my mouth and savored the combination of spicy flavors with a crunchy and mildly sweet crust.I said, "We're getting together tonight, so maybe I should try to feel him out. But I don't want to come across as needy or paranoid, you know?"

She transferred some of the tiny squares into a to-go box to bring to the Tuck Tavern so that she could make up small samples for the taste-testing process. She was momentarily quiet as she worked to line them up without breaking the pieces, which I knew were prone to crumble. Eventually, she said, "So, what's he got planned for you?"

She looked at me expectantly and I filled her in. "He's invited me over. Said he's going to cook for me, and he has a movie picked out."

She giggled. "Sounds like Netflix and chill to me."

We always told each other everything, so she knew I hadn't yet stayed over at his place. She added, "And maybe you might get some inside intel on the murder, right?"

I held my hands up in mock protest. "Who, me? I'd never do such a thing." But we both knew that it was part of the dynamic between me and Richie. She still laughed about our big date last month, which had transpired after we'd seen each other at a big fire and he'd taken me aside to say, "Want to get Chinese food and come over to talk about the fire?"

Jenny had moved on to boxing up some mini corn tortillas

made with a mixture of a local Monterey Jack cheese and roasted green chilis. Quickly, I filled her in on Gladys's love life.

"I've never seen her so giddy," I said. "It's really not like her at all, especially since that guy stood her up and left town without even saying goodbye when he moved to Boston for a role." I went on to share my twinge of sadness for Stanley's predicament, over in the rehab, unable to talk sense into her.

As we loaded up Jenny's little Volkswagen Beetle with the samples to take over to Emily's, I slid her tall black riding boots to the side to make way for the last box.

"I'm so glad you're going to the barn again," I told her.

She nodded. "Me too. It's hard to get back into it, but I'm hoping to get out with the fox hunt this fall if I can fit it in."

I smirked at the mention of the local fox hunt, recalling the story Todd had written about them recently. He had included an exclusive behind-the-scenes interview with the woman who was "the fox," as they no longer hunted real foxes. The woman went out several hours ahead of the pack, dribbling fox scent from a dish soap bottle around the territory.

"She's really into making it authentic," Todd had reported to me. He had been impressed at her preplanning and the number of times she crossed her own path to keep the hunt lively. "We should go to their post-hunt party, Greene; it sounds like quite the spread."

I hadn't gone but had later regretted it when he reported back on the types of food and drink the foxhunters had shared at what they inaccurately described as a little tea party. There'd been smoked salmon with capers, dill, and crème fraîche; French champagne; and an enormous charcuterie and cheese display on a carved wooden board shaped like a fox. The foxhunters' tea sounded more like an upscale cocktail party if you asked me. And I never said no to a good spread at one of those.

The Tuck Tavern didn't open until lunchtime on Saturdays, so Jenny and I went through the back door into the kitchen. Emily and the chef were huddled over an enormous pot, heads bent together, deep in conversation.

"I did detect the chipotle," she said. "And it's got a good kick, but that sweet potato is a good balance. Maybe add some black beans too. What do you think?"

The chef nodded and headed for the pantry area.

Emily smiled when she saw Jenny. "Good, you're here! I got word the Terrace is now even thinking of entering, but there's no way their accompaniments will be as good as yours, my amazing baker lady."

Jenny blushed. "It's just a little cornbread, nothing too crazy," she said. She was beaming at the compliment.

We settled onto the stools at the vast stainless steel work counter and got to the business of sampling the different combinations. Emily leaned toward me and smiled conspiratorially. "Anything new?"

I knew she was referring to Roy's murder and shook my head no.

She said, "Well, I had a thought after I saw you last." She laughed and quickly added, "Yes, I know, a miracle. But I wanted to tell you. You know Becky, from the business group? She was in here with Roy a few times. Had that look." She paused and batted her eyes in a completely over-the-top way. "You know—all doe-eyed."

Hmm, interesting. I had a hard time envisioning the young PR woman having a thing for Roy, who was in his late-sixties, but I guess there was someone for everyone. I made a note to investigate that later and returned to the sampling. It was a tough job, but someone had to do it.

We all agreed that the jalapeno honey bread, not the cheesy chili corn tortillas, was the winner. The tortillas were delicious, but the corn bread was unique and went perfectly with the spicy and mildly sweet chili. Emily decided to put it on the day's specials to test it on a crowd, almost like a focus group. She'd already ruled out the original moose meat chili after learning that she couldn't serve wild game to customers without a special license. Apparently, wild game had to be USDA certified to be legally served at restaurants, or so the health officer had told her.

She laughed as she explained what he'd said. "Too many people in the northern reaches of the state trying to pass off roadkill as farm to table." Based on my past travels, I thought this made sense.

Our work done, we stood around chatting for a bit longer before we said our goodbyes.

"Well, thanks, ladies," Emily eventually said, as Jenny and I headed out a while later. "I have a good feeling about our partnership."

Jenny gave her a little wave before we climbed back into her car and headed for my place on High Street.

"See you later, Jenny," I said, when we reached my carriage house. "Todd's still working, so I'm going to take Gladys over to visit Stanley at the rehab."

I make a quick stop inside to brush my teeth. I had loved the cornbread but did not want to taste jalapenos all afternoon. Then I headed over the path to the big house.

"Gladys," I called out, as I walked into the side entrance to her kitchen. No answer. I finally found her bent over an old photo album in her study. As I moved to join her, she looked up with a melancholy expression.

"Oh, dear, I forgot the time," she said. "I was just looking at these old photos, back when the Playhouse was in its prime."

I glanced down and took in a black-and-white photo, a group on stage, probably the cast of something. I spotted Duncan's gleaming whites immediately. Perhaps they were real after all? Either way, his reappearance was really throwing my aunt for a loop. She was normally so confident and assured on her own, and I felt like Duncan was causing her to relive the turmoil of being abandoned by him with no explanation all those years ago. She collected herself, wrapped up in a gray fox stole (this one named Sophia), and made her way outside.

We settled into Walter's comfortable front seats and headed for the rehab, which was on the other side of a local retirement home. I'd done a story over the summer about the trend of renovating rehabs because insurance companies paid more for that than for other types of care. No longer was it just God's waiting room. This place was like a hotel now, complete with a concierge and daily Wii bowling on their big-screen TV. I half expected to discover they put chocolates on the pillows.

Stanley was in a private room watching *The Lawrence Welk Show* on PBS. He was in a leisure suit sans bow tie, and it may have been the first time I'd seen him without one. He beamed when he saw Gladys, and I had that same twinge of unease from earlier. I hoped she didn't forget him while she was caught up with Duncan's return.

"God," he said to her, "for all the newfangled stuff they

have here, they can't even get you a decent martini."

Gladys patted him on the arm. "Don't worry, I'll see what I can do, Stanley, dear. I heard from my friend Agatha that you need a doctor's note, but we'll make sure we get that for you."

Stanley nodded approvingly, then turned to me and asked, "How's the big murder? Anything new?"

It turned out that Stanley had designed costumes at the Exeter Playhouse in its heyday, so he was quite interested in the whole affair. He'd been keeping tabs on the situation from his rehab bed, and he even had some news to share with us.

"You'll never believe who lives on the assisted living side of this place. Roy's mother, Virginia Carmichael. I heard her daughter—the commanding one, Fiona—talking to one of the nurses from that side. Fiona demanded to know which staff members were on the roster when Roy came to see her mother a few months back. Sounds like she thinks there was some funny business with how he got the majority ownership in the property."

Hadn't Chester hinted at the same thing? Hearing something once might be a coincidence, but twice—and this time from Stanley, who had produced credible tips in the past— meant I needed to follow up. But would Fiona confide in me, aka the nosiest reporter in town? There was only one way to find out. After my date with Richie, of course.

CHAPTER 10

I'd opted to walk over to Richie's that night, not wanting the recognizable Walter the Wagon spotted by anyone in town. Though we were heading toward being a couple behind closed doors, we needed to be careful about who knew about our romance, for the sake of both of our jobs.

As I walked, I found myself wondering if it would diminish some of the thrill when we were no longer sneaking around. I had to admit there was something kind of exciting about a clandestine affair when I only went to his place after dark. Richie lived on one of the main roads heading out of town, in a single-level apartment that they had called a condo when he had bought it, no doubt to charge a little more. It had once been a healthcare building, and I teased him about being next to the town skate park, the last place I could see the clean-cut Irish boy hanging out, but he seemed to have a soft spot for the skaters, who he felt were maligned. Most were good kids, he told me, just a little rough around the edges and in need of decent haircuts.

I mulled over Stanley's tidbit about Fiona Carmichael as I continued up Clifford Street, past the police department, and down Court Street. His words kept whirring around in my thoughts like a gnat that I couldn't quite swat away.

Had Roy coerced his mother, as Fiona seemed to suspect? Again, I recalled that Chester had hinted at the same thing. Being scammed out of your inheritance was a classic motive for murder. But Fiona was the last type of person I could envision killing someone. From her perch on the preservation alliance in town, she always looked like she had just stepped from the pages of a Talbots catalogue, with her tailored shirts, her flawlessly coiffed hair, and her expensive ballet flats. I was fairly confident that she wouldn't get her own hands dirty in a murder. Still, that didn't mean she hadn't persuaded someone else to do it for her.

I was so caught up in running over the information from Stanley that before I knew it, I was outside Richie's condo. He'd already put a pot of mums out front, a homey touch, and I found myself sensing that he was more domestic than me. I gave a little knock, and he opened the door. He had a white apron around his waist and was wearing jeans with a light-blue polo shirt.

"Hey, Scoop," he said with a wink, before he slid his arm around my waist and pulled me in for a long, slow kiss. I guessed he wasn't too upset about the Todd thing after all. Then he kissed me again and whispered, "Now that's more like it."

The twitter of the early romance hadn't died down yet, and I came back for round three. "Well then," he said. "What's gotten into you?"

I didn't say anything, only enjoyed the moment. When we finally broke apart, he smiled at me and pointed to an open seat at his kitchen island. I noticed he had already poured me a glass of wine. We usually ate at the island, because he didn't have space for an actual table in the tight kitchen.

I settled into my seat and looked over. It was like my own little cooking show. I took a small sip of the white wine. Not too sweet, with a hint of lemon and pear. Not as good as what Gladys kept in stock, but not bad. I appreciated his effort, knowing he was more of an IPA beer guy.

Richie returned to chopping and laying out ingredients on a large cutting board. He had a shallot, some mushrooms, a lemon, and a plate of uncooked chicken before him. He added a swirl of olive oil to a sauté pan, tossed in some diced shallots, and gave them a quick stir around the pan with a wooden spoon. Next up, he added the mushrooms and pieces of chicken, again giving a quick stir.

"So, what's the latest on the case?" I began. I didn't want to exploit our budding romance but was unable to hold back.

He looked up and responded, "Well, we're still waiting for the full tox screen. We need that testing to independently verify the type of poison. And the state cops are bringing in some witnesses who, if you ask me, could be suspects."

I blurted out, "Like his sister?"

He laughed. "I should have known you'd picked up on that already. Yes, it sounds like she was quite vocal about questioning how he came to get the majority share away from their mother."

I lowered my voice conspiratorially. "Stanley reports that she was making a real scene over at the nursing home the other day, but I don't know why it would matter anymore. I mean, with Roy out of the way, it's kind of a moot point."

Richie nodded and went on. "Yes, unless she's just one of those people who can't let something go, even when she's won. Or …" he paused for effect, "Roy's will is making things difficult."

I couldn't hide my surprise. "Don't leave me hanging. What's happening?"

He turned toward me from the sink, where he had some romaine lettuce in a colander. "Well, he left his estate to Anastasia Rose, a retired showgirl from Las Vegas—if you can believe it. Sounds like they had an ongoing fling for quite some time."

Of course, Roy had a lady friend from Vegas with a name like Anastasia Rose. It fit perfectly with his Elvis-like hair and polyester pants and would explain the plethora of photos from Sin City at his calling hours.

"Please tell me she's coming back to Exeter to collect," I said. "No one mentioned her at the wake, but I would love to see the exchange in a court battle between Fiona and Anastasia."

Richie shrugged and said, "Who knows. You'll probably be able to find something over at the court in his estate paperwork though."

I'd need to make sure to follow up on this possibility when I was at my office again.

As I watched, Richie pulled some of the lettuce out of the colander, shook off the water, and set to work giving it a rough chop. I was curious about where he had learned to cook, but just in case his skills came from an old girlfriend I still wasn't ready to hear about, I decided not to ask. I hoped he wouldn't be expecting something similar from me in the near future, given that my idea of cooking was going to Gladys's for cocktail hour and eating her food.

"Just between you and me," he said, "Fiona is coming down for a full interview tomorrow. Now that the funeral is over and all, it's time to fill in a few of the missing pieces."

Richie took a sip of a Michelob Ultra, something he'd switched to as part of his effort to cut calories while he trained for an upcoming police relay run across the state. The thought of him running through town and looking all fit was enticing, but I still had the murder on my mind.

"I mean, I'm surprised Fiona's allegations didn't come out in the endless Historic District Commission meetings," I said. "Let's be honest: everything else did. Tripp Bolton held nothing back. Why wouldn't she had come forward then with this information?"

He shrugged. "Maybe she was trying to fix it behind the scenes?"

Or maybe she struck out with that and just had him killed instead, I thought. It would certainly solve the ownership issue and allow her to do whatever she wanted with the property. But why continue to draw attention to it now when Roy was already dead? Unless she hadn't known about her brother's Vegas lady love. Would his majority share pass over to Anastasia? Again, I would need to find out.

I said, "Chester mentioned something about the majority ownership question too. Do you think his firm was somehow involved in the case?"

He shrugged and didn't offer a response, instead walking over to my side of the island and placing two salads on the counter. We were momentarily silent as we chewed. Our salads weren't fancy, just the romaine lettuce, but he'd gotten the fresh herb salad dressing from my favorite organic juice bar in town, a place that was now selling some of their dressings and sauces on the side. That he'd remembered I had mentioned it and gone out to get the dressing, as Gladys would say, made me swoon.

I mulled over my brother's rare tip as Richie headed back around the island to plate up our pasta. He'd finished it off with some white wine and chicken stock in the pan, and I was honestly surprised at how good it was. By the time we finished, I was stuffed, and we moved to the couch. We were still in the early stages of figuring out how to get comfortable with each other in a spot like this without going too far. I leaned back and curled my feet under myself on his couch, something I knew was okay, as he told me over and over to make myself comfortable. He turned on *Dexter,* which was being replayed and was something he insisted we should watch together. The serial killer angle in the show was a bit much for me, but let's be real, it gave me an excuse to lean over and hide my face in his chest when it got gory. Richie settled into the couch and put his arm around me. He jumped up abruptly as a Colgate commercial came on.

"I almost forgot!" he said when he returned. "I got you something!" Then he handed me a still-packaged toothbrush

God, is he saying I have bad breath? How romantic … not!

He must have seen the horror in my expression because he immediately said, "No! No! I just thought if you ever wanted to stay over …" He paused and looked away for a moment. "You could have this here, that's all."

Wow, he was moving things right along. I wasn't sure I was ready for that, but I didn't say anything right away.

He didn't seem to notice my hesitation. He said, "I wanted to ask. What *were* you all doing at the Terrace the other night?"

I filled him in on Duncan's return to town and Gladys's temporary break from reality, even for her, when she saw him. He frowned and said, "Well, I know that Todd lives with your aunt and all, but I don't like the way he looks at you."

Really? Was he really going to go all manly man on me? Ugh, just when I thought he was different.

"Come on," I said, trying to keep my voice light. "He's totally not my type, and Gladys invited him."

I leaned into him then. "And besides, I'm taken, right?"

He smiled, and I swooned again. Those darn dimples got me every time.

"You got that right," he said. And that was the last I saw of Dexter and his murderous face that night.

CHAPTER 11

As much as I was tempted to have my first official overnight at Richie's after our evening of canoodling, I knew I had an early morning at the paper ahead of me the next day. The toothbrush would just have to stay in its packaging for a while. Ever the gentleman, Richie insisted on driving me home so I wouldn't have to walk, even though Exeter was still the type of place you could walk alone without worry.

After one last kiss as we said our goodbyes in the car, I headed across the lawn toward my carriage house. I was surprised to see that Todd's red scooter wasn't back, and I wondered what adventure could be keeping him out.

The next day I was up at the crack of dawn. My early start wasn't something Hap had insisted on, but I knew a self-imposed workday was necessary if I wanted to keep up with my efforts to chase down leads in Roy's murder. The deadline for the *Seacoast Seniors* magazine, which came out quarterly, was set for the end of the week. After that, I needed to write a preview of the Halloween Howl, a benefit 5K run and walk to help a local homeless shelter.

Gladys always had plenty to say when she received her copy

of the senior's magazine. "Oh, Piper, dear, really that makes old age sound like nothing more than fiber supplements and bus trips to the casino."

This, of course, was the exact opposite of her own escapades in her eighties, which included daring adventures like an African safari, where a lion had climbed onto the top of their Range Rover, forcing them to sleep in the vehicle until the animal wandered off. "Oh, it was just thrilling being that close to such a majestic creature," she'd said when she returned. "Though I had a crick in my neck the rest of the trip from sleeping in that vehicle." She also made regular visits to both her reiki master and a new rainbow light therapist. I still didn't quite understand what the rainbow therapist did, but Gladys went twice a month and claimed the different colors that were shone into her veins did wonders for her energy.

I stopped to say good morning to her on my way to work. She was already dressed and was completely engrossed in the pages of a new British whodunnit set in an assisted living facility. She briefly raised her head to explain, "It's that author who was so clever in his last one, with the story within a story." Then she wished me a good day and dove right back into the book.

I was surprised to see Todd bent over his computer when I arrived at the newsroom.

"Little early for you, isn't it," I said.

A 32-ounce ice coffee sat next to him. *Well, that might get him to first gear,* I thought, *but he'll need a shot in the you know what to get to second.*

He was good-natured, albeit half asleep, as he lifted his head to look at me. "Greene, you've got to save me from this mundane existence. Let's run away on an adventure," he said.

"Let's elope."

I rolled my eyes at him, and he added, with a groan, "I've got to interview the chamber of commerce president about the boon to the town's hotels from the food network program coming to town."

I was still curious about his whereabouts last night. Knowing Todd, it could have been anything, so I dug right into that line of questioning.

"You came in late last night. Big goings on?"

"Well, kinda," he said. "I was at rehearsal for the *Thriller* dance on Halloween."

I nearly spit my coffee out at that disclosure.

He went on. "I ended up going out afterward with some of the volunteer dancers. I'm writing a first-person, behind-the-scenes account of what it's like to become a zombie."

This event was something I wasn't going to miss. A local exercise instructor taught people the dance each year and then held a performance as a benefit for the food pantry. People brought cans of food and dry goods for their admission. I made a mental note to cancel all other plans immediately. I could hardly wait to see Todd in full zombie makeup. Gladys was going to be gaga when I told her about this latest exploit by her favorite adventurer.

"Oh boy, Tripp is at it again!" Clara called out from her perch at the front. She frequently regaled us with dramatic readings of submissions for letters to the editor, which arrived on her desk before they were entered into the system.

Tripp's letter began by expressing sympathy for Roy's death before quickly moving on to say he hoped the family would realize the arcade plan was just wrong for Exeter's historic district and gem of a downtown.

"Glory be," Clara said. "This is in such bad taste, I'm not even sure I feel right publishing it."

That might be an understatement, I thought. If it was too much even for Clara's well-developed sense of gallows humor, what would readers say? And honestly, wasn't it time for Tripp to take a hiatus from his crusade to stop the Carmichael's Arcade in Arms? Roy was still adjusting to his new digs six feet under, and even the family wasn't announcing the next step for the property.

I turned back to my computer and started writing.

BENEFIT RUN A HOWLING GOOD CAUSE

By Piper Greene

EXETER__*When they run through town this Halloween, a pack of ghouls, goblins, and ghosts will have a different mission than scaring up screams. They're hoping to scare up money for those in need.*

The runners are raising money for a new homeless shelter on the Seacoast, which was founded by a trio of Exeter activists. The first annual 5K Halloween Howl on October 31 will raise money for the shelter's new space.

"We are thrilled with the response so far and look forward to runners, and walkers, getting in the spirit of the season by wearing a costume," said Anita Crowe, one of the organizers. "As the issue of homelessness has become more serious in our area, we are eager to open our doors to help those in need as soon as possible."

Tim Spillane, a member of a run club in town, has entered an entire team in the Halloween Howl and said he can't wait for people to see their costumes. "We're all in for the cause. Our group is going as the Addams Family, which some think was filmed in Exeter, but I know Winnie Smart says that it's just an urban legend," he said. "Either way, it's going to be quite a sight."

Entries are being accepted now for the benefit race, which will begin on Swasey Parkway and wind through the downtown.

I sent the story over to Hap, who was still standing in as both owner and editor. His brother, Dick, had returned to town from his summer home in the Lake's Region but had opted to step away from the day-to-day duties at the paper. Dick was a jovial guy, always out in town shaking hands with the locals, engaging with groups like the Rotary, and taking part in business roundtables. To me, Hap had always seemed like the more serious of the two—until I heard a story about him driving a race car, with an alias, while he was still in high school.

Todd leaned back in his chair, put his feet on his desk, and opened a plastic bag of croissants. It looked like he had bought the bulk package from Jenny's day-old goodies at the Morning Musket. Crumbs surrounded him like a Bat Signal for all the rats in town. For weeks, Clara had been threatening to put a mousetrap under his desk to prove to him that his habits would attract critters, and not the kind he wanted.

"Todd, I know you like the strays, but stick with women, not rats! If I see another one, I'm going to bring out the machete in my desk! Slice and dice, bye, bye mice," she'd told him the other day.

Todd wheeled around and stuffed a huge chunk of croissant in his mouth. It was amazing he didn't choke. But as soon as he swallowed, he leaned over, eager for news.

"So, what's the word on the murder?" he asked, stuffing another half a croissant in his mouth.

Nothing like stopping to savor your food, I thought.

His words were a bit garbled as he said, "You think it's the bird guy or what?"

I used my feet to wheel my chair a little closer to his desk.

"Honestly, I think it's the sister, Fiona. It sounds like she thinks there was some funny business with the way Roy got the majority shares signed over to him by their mother, and now with news that Roy's mystery showgirl inherited his share, I just have a feeling."

Todd didn't even flinch at the words *mystery showgirl*. Maybe the rumor had already gotten around. Instead, he paused, opened a container of cookie butter on his desk, and dipped another of the croissants into it. Don't get me wrong, that cookie butter was like crack, but I much preferred Jenny's homemade caramel filling.

"Funny you should say that," he said, between bites. "Because I saw Fiona going into the police station on my way in today."

And he only just now thought to tell me! Todd time was not in alignment with Piper time. I wondered how he got anything done. "What time was that?" I asked him.

He shrugged. "I dunno, a while ago. Maybe an hour or so."

I grabbed my bag and jumped up from my chair. Richie had given me the heads up that she'd be going in for an interview, *but come on Todd, when you work in a newsroom, share the news!*

"I'm heading over to the PD to follow up on something," I told Clara, as I bolted out the front door. "If Hap asks, tell him I'll fill him in later."

I made record time to the police department and plopped down on a bench in the Town House Common Park across the street. The park was so named because the historic Town House of Exeter had once stood there. Winnie was fond of recounting how in 1776 the Provincial Congress adopted and signed the first state constitution—establishing an independent state government, and the first of the thirteen colonies—at the spot. The park was now home to the occasional yoga class and a decorated and illuminated tree during the holidays, but it mostly served as a cut-through area for people on foot who had parked in the free downtown parking lot, which was right nearby.

From my spot on the bench, I had a direct view of the front entrance to the police station. Fiona's car, a sleek silver Audi SUV, was still out front, so I surmised she was still there. I hadn't thought through my plan other than getting over there as fast as I could, so I simply sat, caught my breath, and waited.

I didn't have to wait long. Fiona strode out, immaculate as always, in a red tartan plaid scarf, black pants, and ballet flats. She looked like she should be hosting a PBS show about Scotland.

I stood up to catch her eye. "Fiona!" I called out. "I was hoping for a few minutes of your time."

She stopped and glanced at her watch. "Okay, but I've got another appointment, so just a few."

I slid my ever-present reporter's notebook from my bag and clicked my pen open.

"Well, we're working on a story with any updates on your brother's case," I began, then took a breath and reminded myself to ease in. "I'm not sure if I've told you how very sorry I am."

She nodded in acknowledgement. "I don't think I asked you when you last saw him," I said.

She shook her head. "Well, it's no secret that we disagreed on the plan for this property, so I hadn't seen him in a few days," she said. "I'd been at a friend's the night before and then, well, you were there when I found out."

Oh yes, Piper Greene, always walking into murders. "You have an unusual talent," Gladys had told me that night. I walked closer to Fiona and pushed ahead.

"So, anything we can report about the property and the plan?" I asked.

"This is so fresh, our family is just trying to come to terms with it," she said. To me, this sounded a bit rehearsed. "But obviously, with everything that is going on, we're going to pause until things calm down a little."

At this point, the urge to ask what I wanted to know over-ruled my attempts to be subtle. I plowed ahead.

"Well, we got a tip in the newsroom," I said, taking care not to mention Stanley, "that you might be challenging own-ership status of the land."

She pinched her lips together and narrowed her eyes. "I'd rather not comment on that now," she said. "And really, you can take it up with my lawyer. I know you know him: Chester Greene."

You've got to be kidding, I thought. And knowing Ches-ter, I'd get nothing other than a strong serving of disapproval with a side of distain.

CHAPTER 12

As much as it pained me, I knew my next stop was going to be a trip to see my brother, Chester. We'd never been close, given how much older he was than me, but after my parents' deaths, the divide had only grown. He'd gone back to law school, and I had moved in with our aunt, Gladys. To top it off, he was what Gladys and I nicely called a stick in the mud. Seriously, if the guy enjoyed anything in life, it was news to me—aside, of course, from running the family law firm and being part of the who's who circle of the old establishment in town. We didn't travel in the same crowds, if you catch my drift.

Still, his uncharacteristic tip, combined with the news from Fiona that the firm was handling her affairs, meant that this was a necessary evil. I imagined this was how Gladys had felt as a child when she had been forced to take a spoonful of cod liver oil each morning to fend off whatever her parents had worried might ail her. I might even have chosen eating the dreaded anchovies in her famous Caesar dressing over approaching Chester, but my desire to get to the bottom of the story overruled, and I set out for his office.

The firm was in one of the old blocks on Water Street,

a building called Odd Fellows Hall, which was a tall brick structure with a full view of Water Street on one side and the Squamscott River on the other. It was a few doors down from the Morning Musket, so I made a quick detour and fortified myself with a pumpkin butterscotch scone on the way over.

Chester's receptionist was a neat older woman with glasses that still had the little points on the side, reminding me of an episode of the show *Mad Men*. She looked up as I walked in.

"Oh, hello," she said, no doubt hiding her surprise. "Are you looking for your brother?"

I nodded. "I am," I said. "I need to check with him about something I'm working on."

She picked up the phone to buzz him, but before he answered, Teddy, his partner at the firm, walked in.

"Hey," he said, with a genuine smile. Teddy was such a decent guy, not the least stuck up like Chester, and I had no idea why he liked working for him. But he was a legal genius and somehow had the ability to be impervious to Chester's pretentious ways.

"Hey, yourself," I said. He gestured for me to walk toward the offices in the back with him.

"Let me guess. After our dinner, you couldn't take the suspense, so now you're looking to talk with Chester about the Carmichael estate?"

I nodded, not feeling the need to tell him about my conversation with Fiona. He headed toward the offices past the waiting room, and I quickly glanced at the portraits of my mother and father, who had both worked as lawyers at the firm before their fatal accident. I missed them. They now looked over visitors in the waiting room, a gentle reminder of the firm's long tenure in Exeter.

Teddy knocked on Chester's door and cracked it open when he heard a grunt from inside.

"Hey, Barbara Walters is here," he said, giving me a wink. He may have been unaffected by Chester's arrogance, but he wasn't averse to a little good-natured ribbing.

Chester looked up and frowned, his normal expression, and beckoned me in. He was a grade A snob, but he was still an impressive man by most standards, clad today in a perfectly pressed pinstripe shirt with a red tie that no doubt cost more than my entire wardrobe.

I sat in one of the mahogany-colored leather armchairs opposite his desk.

"Fiona said you might be in," he said. "So, let's get this over with."

Geez, did she have a direct line to him or what?

In the past, I'd done enough interviews with lawyers as a reporter at the big metro paper in the city to know the drill. They didn't say anything on the record that wasn't in a court document or that hadn't been okayed by their client. There were also a lot of ethical rules about what they could and could not say, and God knows Chester was a rule follower. And I knew he was well aware of the fate of a local lawyer with a beaver fur hat who, after her client was convicted of murder, enjoyed a few too many cocktails at the Tuck Tavern and told reporters that she had always known he was guilty. Instead of practicing law, she was now practicing needlepoint in her early retirement.

God knows Chester would never make a mistake like that with a reporter, so I wasn't expecting much. But even so,

I held my pen at the ready above my reporter's notebook. "So, what can you tell me for print?" I asked him.

He shuffled some papers on his desk and began.

"Not much yet," he said. "I can confirm that our firm has been retained by Fiona Carmichael to protect her interests in the ongoing questions about the ownership of the former Exeter Playhouse property and that there may be more information available soon."

God, he was frustrating. I needed a little bit more. "Can you confirm that she is challenging the majority ownership by Roy?"

He shook his head. "No," he said, then lowered his voice. "Off the record, we are in contact with this beneficiary in Las Vegas, and I'm confident she will do the right thing."

Boy, if that didn't sound like a veiled threat, I didn't know what did. And how interesting. I'd just learned about Roy's lady love from Richie, and now she was already the focus of legal wrangling. I was more than a little curious about Anastasia Rose, but I didn't think Chester would tell me, so I forged ahead.

"Anything else?" I asked.

He stood up and started edging toward the door. "Nope, that's all you'll get out of me," he said. "But if I were you, I might swing by the courthouse at the end of the month."

A rare olive branch from Chester. So, they were filing a suit. But I'd have to wait for the details until it was official. He walked me toward the door, clearly ready for me to leave so that he could get back to billable hours. In addition to the prestige, it was all about the money. I stopped and looked at him before I left.

"One more thing," I said. "Any idea who Fiona's friend was that she was visiting the night of the murder? I bet the police are going to want to talk to her. You know, to confirm timelines and all."

To say he looked annoyed was an understatement. "I'm not sure how that's relevant," he said. "She has nothing to hide."

And yet, I thought, *whenever people said they had nothing to hide, they usually did. Was he was being deliberately cagey about where Fiona had been the night of Roy's murder?* I mean, really, that did not seem like a coincidence.

CHAPTER 13

I hoped to see Richie again that week, but he was working nonstop as he helped the state police major crimes people with the investigation. Jenny rolled her eyes at me when I confided that I was still feeling a little anxious after his jealously about Todd.

"He's busy on a murder investigation," she told me. "You should know what that's like."

She was right, but all of this did make me think twice when Todd invited me to go along with him on a mission to the Tuck Tavern later in the week.

"Come on, Greene, it will be like a stakeout. Becky the PR lady is avoiding me," he said. "You know you love being my wingman, admit it. I'll buy you a drink."

I'd believe that when I saw it. Todd was notoriously cheap, but with Richie working, I decided to go. Todd had heard that Becky had been hanging at the Tavern a lot since arriving in town. It was just across the street from the short-term rental she had booked: a nicely updated historical home that was vacant while the prep school teacher who lived there spent a semester overseas on an exchange.

Todd continued, "So this way I can accidentally on purpose see her, and she'll come around." He smirked. "You know, the ladies always come around."

There were times as Todd talked when all I could picture was a California surfer circa 1970s with a harem of women around him. He really did fancy himself the ladies' man, and while I was not falling for his ways, I couldn't resist going along, mostly to watch how he managed to pull this off. We walked over to the Tavern from High Street, stopping to look at the bandstand in the center of town, which was surrounded by orange and red mums.

"Boy, this town takes its holidays seriously, huh?" Todd said.

I laughed. "Well, if you think this is a lot, wait until the town's elves put up the lights downtown for the Christmas holidays."

We kept walking, up Front Street and then down a narrow side street toward the Tuck Tavern. While the rest of Exeter looked like something out a Hallmark fall festival, the Tuck Tavern still looked the same. Old white colonial with tall brick chimneys, black shutters, and tiny candle lights in the upstairs windows. To be fair, my last trip had been off the side street and through the back door to the kitchen, so I'd missed their lack of autumn spirit out front.

Inside, they had added some seasonal specials to the regular menu, starting with cocktails.

"Ooh, I'll try the pumpkin martini," I said to Emily, who was still tending bar while she looked for a new bartender.

Todd didn't look impressed by my order. "Pabst Blue Ribbon," he said. "And how about some actual chow?" He eyed the tiny bowl of bar snacks next to us with distain.

We settled in at the bar while we waited for our drinks. Grayson Adams, of the select board, was in his regular seat on the other side of the room. He gave a slight acknowledgement to me, though he was much more subdued than he had been in years past. Not only had he been wrongfully accused of murder a few months ago, but in his eyes a worse fate had befallen him: thanks to the wonders of at-home DNA kits, he had confirmed local rumors that he wasn't actually a descendant of the founder of Exeter. Still, despite that fall from grace, he was keeping up his regular nights at the Tavern with his high school friend, Brian. Brian's loyalty to his pal seemed almost inspiring—if Grayson wasn't such a prat.

Stanley's bar stool, noted by the brass nameplate on the back, was vacant. I wondered if Gladys had managed to get his doctor to give him the okay for a martini each night at the rehab. I meant to tell her what I'd remembered about drinks being served from the medicine cart in paper cups that I'd learned when I wrote an article about rehab facilities a few months ago. I knew she'd want to bring Stanley a real martini glass. The thought of him drinking from a Dixie cup was enough to make them both break out in hives.

Emily placed our drinks in front of us along with some menus.

"Happy hour specials are good for another thirty minutes," she said.

I paused briefly to peruse the most appealing listings: a roasted butternut, prosciutto, and goat cheese flatbread and a kale salad with caramelized apples, blue cheese, and maple walnut vinaigrette.

Todd swigged a gulp of beer and took in the room. "So, this is where it all happens, huh? Funny, I don't see much happening here at all."

He hadn't yet come to appreciate the stoic Yankee way of life.

"Trust me," I said. "This is where I find out most of the news in town."

I didn't tell him that a lot of that came directly via Emily. I was never one to reveal my sources, even to fellow journalists.

"Huh," he said, then popped a miniature pretzel in his mouth. "Well, so we wait for this Becky, and then it's go time."

I sipped my pumpkin martini, which was like a dessert in a glass, complete with a cinnamon sugar rim. These were the type of drinks that could sneak up on you because they were so sweet.

"You know, it reminds me of the time I was in east Texas, and I was hot on the trail of an alleged smuggling operation when I heard about this place, the Broken Spoke Saloon. So, I went in and got stuck in the middle of a real-life gunfight."

I swear, Todd had a story for everything, and half of them seemed so far-fetched that I questioned how they had all happened. Were they simply more exaggerated fishing tales? Even so, another part of me found the never-ending adventures kind of appealing.

"Hey," I said, interrupting him and giving his arm a little bump toward the right. "Isn't that her?"

He paused and looked across the bar where Becky was standing. She was short, in good shape, like someone who did a lot of yoga or Pilates classes, and had long chestnut hair.

"Wow, she has good hair," I said quietly, envious because my flat black hair would never have the body and shape of Becky's. She looked over and spotted Todd. She clearly recognized him, and after a brief blip on her face from irritation to acceptance, she headed our way. She was a pro in more ways than one.

"Todd," she said, cozying up next to him. "I'm so sorry we've missed each other this week. Things have just been beyond busy to say the least."

He shrugged, nonchalant, as if it was the last thing on his mind, despite the way he had orchestrated this whole meeting. He gestured to the stool next to him and said, "Hey, I know how it is. Take a load off, have a drink, and we can just talk off the record."

I watched as she considered his invite. I hadn't seen her come in with anyone, and it seemed like she was alone. She hesitated only briefly before she climbed onto the stool and joined us. She had on black leather boots with narrow heels, which on me would have been a broken ankle in the making, given my inability to walk in anything but flats.

"I'm Piper, by the way," I said, and she reached over to shake my hand. "We talked on the phone after Roy's death."

Becky looked back at me. "You're the one who found poor Roy, right?"

My reputation as the grim reaper of Exeter was getting out.

I nodded. "Yes, and thanks for the comment you gave for my article about the work you were doing for him."

She looked like that was the last thing she wanted to reminisce about. She said, "My work with Roy was just informal. The festival is my top priority right now." She paused and ran a hand through her perfect hair. "It's really why I came to town, although I had been speaking with Roy about sticking around to help with the PR for the arcade. He really needed a marketing plan if that project was ever going to get through."

Emily sidled up to our group and looked at Becky, "What

can I get you?" Becky didn't even look at the menu. "Hendricks and grapefruit. Sprig of rosemary if you have it."

Todd grabbed another handful of nuts and pretzels, clearly hoping to make a meal out of the complimentary bar snacks. I was still mulling over the flatbread special.

"So, Becks," he said, leaning back and putting one arm on the back of his stool. "Can I call you Becks?"

She smiled at him in a way that floored me. Now granted, I knew it was part of his master plan, but it did surprise me that she bought into it so quickly. Or perhaps it was part of her repertoire.

He went on. "I thought it would be a nice human-interest story to include a little about you: how you got into the field and all. It would add to the excitement of the event."

She flipped her shiny brown mane over her shoulder and smiled at him again. "Well, it's really a crazy story. I started this PR business out of a closet in my basement that I converted to a home office space," she said. She explained that she had expanded her client base, developed a following, and before long was one of the most sought-after PR women in New York City.

In that case, why she was in our tiny New England town hawking a Beer and Chili Fest was well beyond me. Why would a hotshot PR lady from New York spend so much time with something that should have been relegated to her underlings? So, I asked.

She replied, "Honestly, the only reason I took this gig is because my daughter is at the prep school, and this gave me a chance to see a little more of her during the school year."

Finally, this made sense. I knew that some wealthy parents even bought homes in town for the years their kids studied at the prep school.

Todd and Becky each ordered another drink. They were already leaning closer together as they talked. I excused myself to use the ladies' room. Emily, who was coming out of the doorway as I approached, leaned over and whispered, "Keep your eye on that one. I think there was more going on with her and Roy than she's letting on."

I guess like any savvy bartender she'd been listening to our conversation at the bar. "Like what?" I asked.

She lowered her voice even further, so much I had to strain to hear her.

"Between us, I happened to see Roy leaving her rental next door very early one morning if you catch my drift."

Hmm. So, an early morning probably meant a late night. I didn't say anything to Becky about it when I returned to the bar area, but as I half-listened to their flirtatious chatter, I kept mulling over what Emily had shared. I decided to skip the flatbread, and I think they barely noticed when I left.

I zipped up my jacket to block out the chill as I walked back to my carriage house, still rolling over what I knew about the murder and now about Becky. Something just wasn't right about the idea of her and Roy being romantically linked. She was young, good looking, and accomplished, and he was the equivalent of a washed-up Elvis impersonator at the Jersey Shore. But I was really stuck on one part of this possibility. If they had been involved, why didn't she seem more upset when she talked about his death?

CHAPTER 14

When Todd rolled into the newsroom late the next morning, he was unusually tight-lipped when I asked how the rest of his evening with Becky had gone. He shrugged and winked at me but didn't elaborate. I did notice that he had added a feature story about Becky to the story budget for that week's paper, so my guess was he had gotten to see the inside of her rental, or that at least he had gotten enough information for a story after that second cocktail. But my doubts remained: if she was so quick to sidle up to Todd, could she really have had a fling with Roy as Emily suspected?

I didn't have time to dwell on that. Dick Henderson was making a habit of stopping by with story suggestions, even though he wasn't technically working at the paper. He had been waiting at my desk upon my arrival to suggest that I do an in-depth look back at the Exeter Playhouse's heyday for this week's paper.

"A real deep dive, if you know what I mean," he had said, and despite my desire to focus on the present day, Hap had agreed. People loved their history in this town, he had reminded me, and I knew he was right. My first stop, as usual, would be the Exeter Historical Society for some research, and of course I was eager to see Winnie to find out what juicy tidbits she had to share. Those who thought she was a sweet little old lady completely underestimated her, but that was part of her superpower.

I walked up the hill on Spring Street to the historical society, glancing down in the quad at the prep school, where the students were back on campus and playing ultimate frisbee. I continued past the red brick Baptist church, which had striking stained-glass windows. A local real estate agent had recently discovered a hand-dug well in the basement that was nearly two hundred years old. Apparently, there were all sorts of pieces of history under the church, including a pile of bricks left when the building that had originally been located at that site before the church was taken down.

I continued past the church and then turned right onto Front Street toward my destination. The heavy wooden door to the historical society was cracked open—though to be fair, it was so heavy I could see the sense in not closing it all the way. It always felt like a workout. And they wondered why more people didn't visit the society? Some of the older people might not even have the arm strength to open that door.

I stopped before entering when I heard a familiar male voice, although I couldn't immediately identify who it belonged to.

"I just need a few more days, that's all. I'll take care of it."

Winnie's voice cut in next. "Well, just this once, because I'm not totally heartless," she said.

What on earth was going on in there? I couldn't resist, so I pushed the big door in a bit further. As I walked inside, I narrowly missed getting knocked over by Tripp Bolton, who was making a hasty exit. I opened my mouth to say hello, but he didn't even stop as he scurried down the front steps. Hmm. Winnie looked flustered when I walked into the front room.

"What did *he* want?" I asked.

"Oh, nothing, just a bit of Historic District Commission business and something I need from him."

Well, she did like to keep her files current. I mean, she had started the murder file #2 before Roy's body was even cold, and now she had an entire box. But of course murder was a little more exciting than the Historic District Commission, a necessary body to keep the historical nature of the town, but a bit dull to say the least. Sure, there were people who could talk about authentic wooden siding options for hours, but I was not one of them.

Winnie's cat, Buttercup, was sitting on the top of a bookshelf, exhibiting the normal pose of distain for anyone other than her personal human servant.

"So, what can I do for you," Winnie asked.

I plunked my bag down on the able and slid my notebook out.

"Well, while I wait for the police to release their next tidbit, Dick suggested—and Hap agreed—that I do a big in-depth piece on the halcyon days of the playhouse. You know, look back and tie that to what's going on now."

Winnie nodded, well versed at providing research assistance for my regular articles. We had a routine and knew our roles by heart at this point.

"Well, you know Exeter was the cultural hub of the region for a while," she began, as she pulled a big file box nearly half her size from a shelf and plopped it on the table. "We had the Exeter Playhouse, but we also had the opera house, and of course you know the Ioka Theater."

Oh, did I ever. The Ioka, now defunct (much to the sadness of longtime residents), had been the site of many a first date and first kiss for several generations of Exeter's youth since it first opened in 1915. I hadn't gotten a kiss, but rather the even more awkward hand on the thigh and graze hands with your crush episode. I remember being thankful we were in the dark so no one could see the amount of blushing I did during that moment. Even thinking about it now made me flush slightly.

After years of decline, at one point including a tree growing out of the roof, the Ioka was shuttered, but many still fondly recalled its glory days as a theater. The words "Mayer Building" on the top were one of the permanent reminders of the theater's birth way back when Edward Mayer, a lawyer and traffic court judge, spotted a prospect in the land next to the town hall. He announced an idea to build the theater and persuaded townspeople to invest in his new project.

Buttercup gave a loud meow at Winnie, who picked her up, clearly in tune with the cat's requests for attention.

"The playhouse had cachet," she said, as she scratched the cat's chin. "It was really a place for talent to develop before they went off to bigger things."

Like Dashing Duncan, who was out on another excursion with Gladys today up to a luncheon show at a theater in Maine. I felt another twinge of regret for Stanley, long loyal companion, unable to compete from the rehab facility, where he was still walking with assistance as he recovered from the snafu with Scarlett the red scooter.

"So, that box has all the files, old clippings, cast photos, and anything else we took in from the family over the years,"

Winnie said.

I pulled off the top and looked at the hard wooden chair at the table. Oh, the price of snooping into local history. A sore behind. I should really take a lesson from some of the people I saw at the high school football games, who showed up with portable chairs and cushions to make the bleacher seats less numbing. I picked up a news clipping from the *Exeter Independent*, which had a photo of two people shaking hands and a short blurb. It looked like something submitted by the theater as a press release.

MAY 15, 1964

PLAYHOUSE PREMIERS NEW DIRECTOR

EXETER__*The Exeter Playhouse is pleased to announce that Martin Henley of the East End Theatre in NYC has accepted the role of director for this year's summer production of* Our Town.

Henley has been a long-time fixture in the NYC theater scene and was drawn to the town after driving through the general area on his ride to Maine one summer. "I not only saw this quaint downtown and beautiful school campus, but the playhouse, a feisty little theater with a track record of turning out some big names." He said he wanted to get out of the city for a while and have a change of scenery. "And being able to bring a production like Our Town, *which pays tribute to the qualities that make a town special, seemed an ideal fit for my time in Exeter."*

Virginia Carmichael, owner of the theater, said she was thrilled to bring in someone of Henley's stature for the summer production. "Our family loves being the caretakers of this theater and look forward to it being here for generations to come."

Next up, a few stories about shows, including cast photos. This time I took a closer look and realized why Gladys was so enamored with Duncan back then. He looked like Cary Grant in the photos, and the leading lady, with platinum blonde hair, was equally striking. Standing off to the side in one picture was Stanley, looking remarkably like he did now—right down to the bow tie—when he served as the costume designer. Even Tootie appeared as an assistant director in one of the shows.

Under the early stacks I found a whole file on the fire, although most of the major details were things I already knew and some I didn't, like the fact that some old theater memorabilia had been reported missing before the fire. The fire broke out after the opening night of *Bye Bye Birdie* and happened late enough that it had a big head start by the time the fire department arrived on scene. The whole building was razed because it was unsafe to leave it standing, but parts of the original foundation were left intact. They never did find the missing mementos from the theater, including old cast photos autographed by thespians who went on to Hollywood or Broadway. It was classified as suspicious in nature, but no arrest was ever made. A later story, one of those 10-year lookback pieces, quoted Chief Sinclair's father, then the chief, as saying, "We do hope as time passes that someone who knows what happened will come forward with information. We know there is someone out there who knows who did this."

Interesting. I had to wonder if anyone who knew what happened to the theater was even still alive or in Exeter. And if they were, did they have information about why Roy was killed? My mind was gathering momentum and I took a leap: What if Roy knew about the fire? And if he did know, what if someone had killed him to keep him quiet? It was a long shot, but I filed it away in my mental Rolodex. Old secrets did have a way of turning deadly.

CHAPTER 15

I was sitting at my desk in the newsroom the next day, trying to get over the inertia that sometimes took hold when I stared at a blank screen. So far, instead of writing my story about the Exeter Playhouse, I had managed to clean out my in-box, scroll through the other area newspapers online, and clear off my desk. Oh yes, and I'd sampled Jenny's latest creation, a cross between a croissant and a cinnamon bun, which had involved baking croissant dough, rolled into a bun, and topping it with a maple cream frosting. I didn't want to tell Richie, but it was almost better than kissing him—just not quite.

Todd wasn't in yet and Clara was on the phone with Horace, one of the town's three funeral directors. She'd been taking breaks from the call to make faces at me, part of her regular routine when he called to talk up the size of certain funerals he was overseeing.

"Oh, really, well that *is* quite prominent," she said, nodding her head and rolling her eyes at me. It was part of our inside joke; this local funeral director always liked to give Clara the behind-the-scenes scoop of the town's dead. "Standing room only" was one of his favorite expressions to convey a big turnout at a funeral. You would have thought he was putting on a theatrical production for the pomp and circumstance that went into his retellings of the affairs.

"What do you think he'll say about yours?" I had asked Clara one day, and she had laughed. "God help me when I'm laid out at Horace's funeral home and he's had a chance to do my makeup!"

Clara continued to nod and make appropriate "hmm" responses through the phone. After several more moments, she cleared her throat as if to get his attention. She confirmed this by saying, "Hold on, Horace. I've got someone in the lobby."

I looked toward the front, where I could barely see the diminutive Harry Trott walking through the newspaper's front door. I sat up a little straighter. Lately he'd fallen off my radar, so I was curious to know what had brought him in today. Given his resistance to the arcade proposal and his absence at the time of Roy's murder, I also wondered if he had been questioned by police as a suspect. I didn't see him in that role, but stranger things had happened.

He walked toward Clara and eyed her statue of St. Francis warily. It was an office joke that this statue was our first line of defense in the event of a disgruntled reader attacking the newsroom. It had sharp edges and easily weighed ten pounds. Harry looked around warily and cleared his throat.

"I'm looking for Miss Greene. It's important."

Clara held her pointer finger up toward him and wheeled around so that she could see me, but I was already standing. What was he doing at the paper? It must be big because people rarely saw him out around town, and if they did, he was friendly but didn't seek out conversation. His appearances at the historic district meetings and his letters to the editor about Roy's plan had been the most many people had heard from him in years.

I opened the office door and stepped into the lobby. "Mr. Trott, good to see you again. How can I help you?"

He held up his hand, said, "Harry, please," and looked around. "Is there somewhere we could go talk? It's kind of delicate."

Ooh! I kept my face neutral, even though that sounded intriguing, and opened the door to the newsroom.

"Sure," I said, and led him to my desk. I pulled a spare chair over and offered him a seat. He lowered himself gently into the maroon office chair. He had on well-worn but clean denim pants, Merrell hiking boots, and a green plaid shirt, the epitome of fall—or really, any season—in New England.

He looked around the newsroom, where we were still the only people, before he said, "Listen, there's something you should know about Roy Carmichael."

I nodded, wanting to keep him at ease but clapping enthusiastically inside my head at the prospect of juicy intel. This wasn't the time to pull out my notebook, but rather to keep him comfortable with talking.

"Go on," I said, in what I hoped was a "no pressure" tone. Inside my voice was yelling, *Tell me everything—and I mean everything—right now!* However, I pushed that voice aside and looked at him with what I hoped was my most serene face.

"Well, there's no nice way to say this. I think he was trying to kill my birds."

Whoa! I didn't see that coming. He explained, "I went out to the lot just days after Roy's death, even though the police tape was up, because the birds are used to me feeding them every day. I know it was wrong, but they depend on me. They're almost like my children."

He paused, and I nodded at him to continue.

He said, "One of the seagulls was wobbling around, clearly not well. I managed to get it into a box and rushed it to the vet, where it died."

I immediately rearranged my expression to look sad, although it didn't take much because this really did seem sad.

"They took some blood tests, but it took a while for the results to come back, which is why I didn't come see you until now." He lowered his voice to a whisper and said, "It was poisoned."

What! I felt like I'd gotten an electric shock. "Have you shared this with the police?" I asked.

He shook his head vigorously. "Oh yes, I went there first, but you know how they never tell you anything ..."

I tuned him out for a brief moment. My mind was racing. Roy had died by poison, though the medical examiner was still waiting on the test results to say what type, and now a bird had also died of poison. It didn't take a detective to know this was an unlikely coincidence.

I said, "So, Harry, just curious. Why did you also want to tell me?"

"You know Tootie," he said. "She tells me you have a knack for this kind of thing. Actually, she said you could investigate circles around those police." He paused before adding, "And quite frankly, I don't want any more birds to die. Someone has to speak for them."

I was glad he didn't mention my questionable journalistic practice of getting involved behind the scenes to help people. It was something that locals appreciated, but the big metro paper would have fired me over.

He said, "I'm especially worried about the Ross's gull that is with the local flock. It's so rare in these parts, and I'm sure my regular feedings have been keeping it healthy."

Unburdened with this news, he started to twist in the chair. He was clearly getting antsy, and I sensed I had only a short window of time before he got up and moved on. The time for soft-pedaling was over.

"So, Harry, I want to chase this down, but to do so I need something on the record. Can I quote you on some of this?"

"Absolutely, that's why I came here. I'm sure the cops will do something at some point, but a dead bird during a murder case isn't going to take priority."

Unless, I thought, *they were connected,* which did seem entirely plausible. I scribbled down a few notes about the bird's symptoms, the vet's office, and the fact that he had reported the situation to the police. Then I gently showed him out of the newsroom.

As we said goodbye, I assured him I'd let him know when I had something to share. Though I was most focused on Roy's murder, I did feel sympathy for Harry and his attachment to his beloved birds. He was right; someone had to speak up for them, and I'd always had a soft spot for the underdog. I watched as he made his way to his car, which was one of the all-wheel-drive Subaru station wagons that might as well have been the official town car considering how many people drove one in Exeter. He signaled responsibly as he left the parking lot and drove off.

Back inside the office, I stopped at Clara's desk.

"Well, what do you make of him?" Clara asked, and I was certain she had eavesdropped on the whole conversation.

She was certainly getting her money's worth with those new hearing aids. Perhaps she'd let me borrow them for my next stakeout.

"Hard to say," I said. "But I'm going to put a call in to the police and see what they have to say."

By "police" I meant Richie, who picked up on the second ring. He said, "You missed me, right?"

It had been a few days since we'd seen each other, but my need for news temporarily overshadowed my need for romance. I got right to the point.

"So, Harry Trott just came to see me. What do you know about a dead bird being poisoned?"

He lowered his voice. "This has to come from the official spokesperson," he said, and I knew he meant the state police major crimes people.

"Uh huh," I said.

Richie cleared his throat and went on. "So, the old guy is on to something. Turns out the poison used to kill that bird was the same kind used to kill Roy."

Whoa, that was dark to say the least. I saw a glimmer of an Alfred Hitchcock horror movie.

"When are they going to release that publicly?" I asked him.

He paused, then answered, "Hopefully later this week. They want to do some interviews before that's made public. See what, if anything, people volunteer on their own."

I had so many questions. Top of the list was, *If Roy poisoned the birds, why did he ingest the poison? Was Roy's death simply an accidental death that occurred because his champagne flute came into contact with poison for the birds? Or did someone come up with a clever way to kill two birds—so to say—with one poison?*

I still couldn't see Harry doing something like that—and if he had, why would he have come to me with the news about the dead bird? But what about his mystery friend who fed the birds when he was away? Perhaps they weren't as kind as Harry and took matters into their own hands, especially if they caught someone jeopardizing the gulls. If only I knew who that friend was.

CHAPTER 16

Gladys rapped on my door of my carriage house early the next morning. "Do come over for dinner tonight, dear," she said. "Duncan and Tootie are coming, and I think you'll enjoy their stories of the old days."

The old days, per Gladys, were the good days: the ones when women dressed, *really dressed*, when they went out in town. There had been a nightclub owned by a former hockey star where we now had a pharmacy, and of course, the Exeter Playhouse. Gladys had been in her early days of being discovered as a mature lady model, following her dancing career, which had included being short-listed for the Rockettes. I assured her I'd see her later and set off for work.

I was still pondering who Harry's birding friend might be, but I had other more immediate leads to chase on the case. I spent the day in the newsroom trying to get the state police to return my phone calls. When I finally got the spokesperson—who had no comment—I had to bring him around by telling him I had permission to quote Harry Trott's side of things and it would look like the police weren't being forthcoming if they didn't at least confirm it.

"Fine," the spokesperson said. "You can say police confirmed his account but could not comment further at this time."

I typed up my story and sent it over to Hap for his review. He suggested I do a follow-up story, getting one of the state agricultural lab people on the phone to talk about the uptick in the accidental poisoning of birds, including owls, by people who put out rat poison. I made the calls, left some messages, and sent some emails. Then I left the newsroom a little early. My schedule had started as part-time, but after a few months, with additional duties, the hours were climbing. So, whenever I had a chance to take a few hours off, I did. I'd seen far too many journalists burned out young by not taking a break until they dropped from a heart attack. A little dramatic, I know, but the job could wear you down if you weren't careful.

I slipped home unseen and tucked myself into my little carriage house, where I decided to take a long bath in the antique clawfoot tub Gladys had put in when she renovated. Even she admitted that it was terribly impractical, but it was a real escape when I had time to use it for its original purpose. An hour later, relaxed and smelling like the lavender bath salts I'd added to my tub, I slipped on a comfortable dress and arrived on her doorstep promptly at five for the traditional cocktail hour.

With the change in seasons, Gladys had moved to her fall and winter entertaining spot, an elegantly decorated round sunroom off the side of her house. She leapt up when I walked in.

"Oh, Piper! We've been waiting for you; everyone wants to know the latest on poor Roy's demise."

She was decked out in a deep-purple velvet pantsuit with

a neat belt around her tiny waist and a gorgeous blue stone necklace that I hadn't seen before. She caught me staring at it.

"Isn't it gorgeous? A gift from Duncan. It's a special blue topaz from Brazil."

Boy, Duncan was really laying it on strong. But Gladys seemed to bask in his attention, so I'd keep quiet for now. He was sitting in an armchair, martini in hand, while Tootie sat on the other side. She was wearing beige corduroys and a green Fair Isle–patterned sweater, the stereotypical image of a new England prep schoolteacher. I accepted a glass of white wine from Gladys and made myself a little plate of snacks—I'd missed lunch—before I found a seat near one of the windows. Given their eager expressions, I knew I had to get right to the business of the murder.

"Well," I began. "The big news is that Roy might have been poisoning the birds, and at least one bird died from the same type of poison he ingested, which doesn't make any sense to me."

They all leaned forward, eyes wide, eager for more details. There was nothing I loved more than a rapt audience when I had inside information to share. I told them about my follow-up story about the birds, explaining how owls can be accidentally poisoned if they eat mice that have ingested poison set out by people trying to get rid of rodents in barns and other areas.

"Ooh," Tootie piped up, "you know, owls can be quite dangerous. I just watched a documentary where a man was accused of throwing his wife down some stairs, but he claims an owl attacked her head."

I knew the documentary about the infamous Michael Peterson case but was surprised that Tootie had watched it.

"Well, Roy always was a bit of a chit," Duncan told me. Then he turned to Gladys and Tootie and said, "Remember when we had that infestation of mice at the Playhouse, and it turned out Roy was the cause?"

He looked back at me and explained, "Roy was using the dressing room as a sort of teenage bachelor pad. Snack crumbs and leftovers everywhere. Eventually, his mother discovered his lair by following the mice to the source of their food. Roy got an earful, I'll tell you! We could hear her all the way up on the stage during rehearsal."

I popped a puff pastry bite with Brie and apple chutney into my mouth. Yum. It had the perfect amount of spice in the chutney, and the pastry was soft inside and crunchy on the outside, just how I liked them. There'd be no crumbs left for mice to snack on in this house.

"So, you all were in the theater when Roy was young," I said. I never missed a chance to collect background information, even if I couldn't use it in an official story. I had a dossier on everyone in town in my head at this point.

I asked them, "What was he liked then? I'm quite curious, especially about how he and Fiona got along."

Tootie jumped right in. "Honestly, he was kind of a rotten apple from the get-go. Always in trouble, and just looking out for himself. But he was just a teenager at that time, barely out of high school, and I think his mother always hoped it might be a phase he'd outgrow. Too bad that didn't turn out to be true."

Duncan and Gladys nodded in agreement.

"Still," Gladys said, "it's a shame to see anyone murdered, even someone like him."

I wasn't so sure the others agreed, but they didn't contradict her. Duncan finished off his martini and put an olive into his mouth.

"Fiona always understood the historic value of the theater: its history, its place in town," he said. "Roy, obviously, did not."

Gladys stood up from her seat with the energy of someone half her age and started circulating with the tray of appetizers again. "Oh, Duncan, do tell Piper about the time you played Curly McLain in *Oklahoma!*" She smiled at him. "He was the talk of the town."

Tootie looked like she had something to say but held her tongue. Duncan, on the other hand, curled forward in his seat like a cat getting his back scratched. "Well, you know I was the leading man in every production that year," he said, pausing to show off his sparkling teeth again. "Some people would let that go to their head, would rest on their laurels, but ..."

He shrugged, and I held back from rolling my eyes. At the rate he was going, his head wasn't going to fit out the door when he left Gladys's place. "That was of course the year I was launched to Broadway, and if you'll allow me to indulge my ego for a moment, it was really like playing myself."

God, if I managed to hold my tongue and not say something sarcastic to this guy, I would deserve a medal. I knew Curly McLain in *Oklahoma!* was known for his swagger and for being the most handsome man in town, but yuck. How could Gladys stomach him? Honestly, I looked over again and cringed. He'd taken his expensive loafers off and was stretching out his feet. I could see the outline of his toes straining against his argyle socks. Who does that?

I noticed Tootie was focused on something on the other side of the room. No doubt she was also done with his prattle.

To my dismay, Duncan took another sip of his drink and went on.

"When I got the call about auditioning in Boston, I left without a second thought."

Or, I thought, *without telling Gladys and standing her up for your date.*

Gladys, normally one of the first to call out BS, was basking in the glow of his shiny white teeth. Her dearly departed husband, Walter, who died when was I was in elementary school, was a strong, quiet type but totally devoted to her—and I dare say a lot less boastful than Duncan. I'd had enough of his grandstanding.

"Back to the Carmichaels," I interjected. "Apparently, Fiona is going to challenge the ownership stake Roy acquired. Sounds like he might have pushed the boundaries when he had Virginia sign her shares over to him at the nursing home, and now apparently there's a Vegas showgirl he dated who gets his share."

Gladys clapped her hands together with glee. "Oh boy, I hope she comes to town. Now that would shake up our little Puritan village, wouldn't it?"

They all nodded knowingly; our town's reputation was firmly established when it came to upholding proper New England decorum, which was the main reason Grayson had been so devasted recently about his DNA test results.

After a beat, Tootie perked up. "I did wonder how Roy got the majority. A friend who lives in that same home as Virginia Carmichael told me Roy's mother doesn't even know what year it is most of the time. And she was always so determined to rebuild the playhouse, bring it back for the town."

That had been my thought, too, but it was no secret Roy,

who already owned a string of tacky arcades, had a certain outrageous style. Even his mother must have known that. Something else was also bugging me about Fiona.

"So," I told the group, "Fiona has commented for my articles, but she's been a little cagey about identifying the friend she was visiting the night her brother was murdered."

Duncan and Gladys looked at each other in confusion, while Tootie practically leapt out of her seat in her haste to refill her martini glass from the pitcher Gladys had on the rolling bar cart. She downed half the glass and turned to me.

"I probably shouldn't tell you this, but I can blame it on Gladys's martinis," she said, and took another healthy sip. "There I was, taking my morning constitutional as I do every morning." She paused, sipped, then added, "It takes me a little longer now, you know."

She was 92 after all, but that didn't stop her from her daily 5:00 a.m. walkabout. On the rare days I was up early enough to spot Tootie, I always thought that a little pace car wouldn't be a bad safety measure for her.

"Go on," I said.

"Well, I walked through the back of the academy fields and up that little cut-through to High Street. I'm not one to tell tales, but I saw her coming out the back door of a house we all know, wearing what I'm sure was the previous evening's dress. The 'walk of shame,' I think you kids call it."

I had no idea where she was going with this, but it certainly sounded juicy. "So, Tootie, don't leave us hanging," I said. "Whose house was it?"

She paused, clearly relishing the look of anticipation on our faces. "Well, someone you all know: your dear brother, Chester Greene."

CHAPTER 17

I closed my eyes to block the images from my mind. Yuck. It was hard for me to imagine anyone finding Chester attractive in a romantic way. Perhaps there was another explanation for why Fiona was coming out of his house in the wee hours of the morning. Honestly, I hoped she was just there signing a last-minute paper for her court case or something ordinary.

Gladys seemed stunned as well and brought it up again later after she said goodnight to Tootie and Duncan.

"Maybe I'll pay him a little auntly visit," she told me, once we were alone. "Though to be honest, I did wonder if he'd ever find someone, given how much he works. And if I'm not mistaken, Fiona's a bit older than him, too."

I followed after her as she carried a tray of empty glasses to the kitchen. She stopped suddenly and added, "But it might have to wait. Duncan wants to go visit that hotel on the cliff in Maine, which is hosting a big band evening with a saxophone player from New York City."

Inwardly, I groaned. She hadn't mentioned Stanley all evening, and she had been hanging upon Duncan's every word with what I could only describe as lovestruck eyes. Now she was being lured by the promise of an oceanside view and some music, complete with a hotel right on a cliff.

"Separate rooms of course, Piper," she told me, as she rinsed the martini glasses. "I may be in my eighties, but there is such a thing as propriety you know."

I helped Gladys finish the dishes and went back to my carriage house. Later, as I tried to fall asleep, I replayed the whole scene in my head. I knew Dashing Duncan always tried to put on a good show, but I was still put off by the way he'd removed his shoes. It was a little too familiar, if you know what I mean, like he was settling in for the long haul. Eventually, I tried to push my qualms about Duncan aside, knowing if I allowed myself to really think about the situation, I'd never get to sleep.

As it was, I was up way too early the next morning. Hap had asked me to cover the Rotary Club's annual apple sale by the bandstand, and he wanted me there at opening apple. Every fall, the cheerful men and women of the club pitched their tables and stood waving down cars, eager to sell them freshly picked apples and homemade pies. I was not looking forward to seeing Pansy Bolton, chairperson of the Rotary, with her motionless blonde hair and supercilious distain for me, but Jenny was involved this year, so I knew I'd have an ally.

As I slipped out on the little path from my carriage house to High Street, Oscar, the feral cat, even followed me a few steps. Perhaps he wouldn't kill me in my sleep after all. In fact, it seemed like I had a much better chance at being taken out by one of the heavy minivans that were zipping along High Street toward the town's recreation fields, where soccer games would dominate most of the day, a regular fall scene in town. By the time I got to the bandstand, I was ready for a seat, but the apple sale was in full swing. Gah, hadn't these people ever heard of a lazy weekend morning?

"Hey, you," Jenny said, as I arrived. "I feel like I haven't seen you forever."

I gave her a quick hug and glanced around at the apple ambassadors, a mix of business owners and some retirees. Right at the center, in a pair of tailored jeans and a crisp button-down shirt with an apple pattern, was Pansy. She was standing next to some cornstalks and pumpkins, where she resembled the lead from a Metamucil ad on TV.

"Piper," she said, when she saw me, "I hope this won't be one of your little exposés like the last time. This is a charity after all. Do remember that."

She still hadn't gotten over the humiliation of falling into the river during a charity rubber duck race over the summer. The photo of her soaking wet was one of my best snaps to date, but she had been furious when it ran on the front page of the paper.

I pushed aside all the sardonic comments that I wanted to blurt out and instead replied, "Oh, Pansy, I'm just here to take a few photos for the community page. No need to worry."

She sniffed, as was her habit, and looked around for her next target, but I couldn't resist a little snooping while she was still next to me. I said, "Boy, sounds like Tripp's been busy with that historical society project for the Historic District Commission. Winnie was really hounding him."

She narrowed her eyes as she looked at me. "I'm not sure what you're talking about. He's not doing anything there now."

Hmm. That didn't make sense, Winnie had clearly told me it was some business they were working on, but come to think of it, he had been quite flustered that day. I forged ahead. "Bet he's relieved that whole hubbub with the arcade proposal is on pause for a bit."

She smoothed her hair, though I questioned the necessity since a flyover by an F-16 jet wouldn't have even caused a stray wisp. She visibly regrouped. "Well, yes," she said. "Roy's death was quite unfortunate, but I dare say, the town will be better off without that eyesore there. Really, Tripp was just speaking for most of the town at those meetings."

She immediately looked away, and I could sense she didn't have much more tolerance for my questions, so I excused myself to go stand with Jenny. She was busy hawking pies to passing motorists.

"So," she said. "What's the latest in the love life?"

Her guess was as good as mine. After our late-night dinner and Dexter session, Richie and I had both been too busy to meet up again.

"Well," I told her, "he did present me with a toothbrush when I was at his place."

Her eyes widened and she let out a little shriek. "Sooo, did you need to use it? Say, in the morning hours, you know, to combat that morning breath situation."

I swatted her arm. "Jenny!" and she laughed. I went on. "I'm not ready for that step. And honestly, he's been strange about Todd living with Gladys, like he actually thinks Todd's a threat."

Jenny rolled her eyes. "A threat to what, your hot water bill?"

We laughed again. She thought it was hysterical how Todd kept asking to use my clawfoot tub. He'd been in there for over an hour one time, which had caused me to raise my eyebrows until I'd discovered he'd fallen asleep in the bath.

With my dating update out of the way, we moved on to more important things: the murder. I asked, "So, what are you hearing at the bakery?"

She shook her head and replied, "Not much really. The word on the street is that Fiona is challenging the estate for control." Then she winked at me, inclined her head toward Pansy, and said, "And plenty of folks wouldn't mind seeing a certain Rotary president's husband go down on a murder charge."

Tripp certainly had been the most vocal critic of Roy's arcade proposal, and I dare say those were the liveliest town meetings I'd ever covered, especially the time he banged his gavel so hard it split in half. But a murderer? He didn't seem like the type of person to get his hands dirty. The fact that people were rooting for him to be one said a lot about how his haughty attitude rubbed folks the wrong way.

"What makes you say that?" I asked her.

Jenny looked around to make sure we were out of earshot of anyone else, then said quietly, "Well, I overheard our dear cranky Myrna going on and on about how simply dreadful it was that Roy had tried to take out a restraining order against Tripp after that meeting where they almost came to blows."

My eyes widened. "Wait, what? And you're just telling me about it now?"

Jenny smiled and shrugged. "I just figured that you had the inside line on that from you-know-who."

She was right, and I couldn't believe Richie hadn't told me about this restraining order. That was huge. Jenny gave me a gentle nudge and said, "Well, well, well, look what we have here?"

I glanced over. My brother, Chester, was walking in the crosswalk by the town offices, and he was heading toward us. He was dressed down—for him—in jeans with his trademark blue blazer and tie. He acknowledged me only briefly before turning to Jenny. "What types of pies do you have left? I've got a special occasion tonight."

She opened the lids on the boxes behind her before rattling off the lineup. "Traditional apple pie made with Pat Nixon's recipe, which was one of my grandmother's favorites, plus an open-faced apple tart with caramel sauce and a few apple-cranberry turnovers."

Wow, she really took the same-old, same-old apple pie sale to a new level this year.

"How about the caramel," he said, handing a twenty-dollar bill to her. "Keep the change."

Ooh, big spender. He turned to me, and I was struck as usual by the lack of sibling connection between us. But, given what I'd heard last night, and the fact that he was right in front of me, it seemed like fate. Plus, I couldn't wait to see his reaction when I called him out for his potential clandestine coupling. It would be a nice turn of the tables in our dynamic.

I leaned toward him and spoke softly so only he could hear me. "So, I thought you might want to know, we got an anonymous tip, a witness of sorts." I created a little white lie to protect my source. "They called the anonymous tip line and said that Fiona Carmichael was seen coming out of your place quite early in the morning." I paused for effect as his glare grew ominous. "In what looked like the previous evening's clothes."

His face was beet red—not the embarrassment red, but the anger red like Yosemite Sam from Looney Toons. He gritted his teeth as he replied to me.

"What two friends do on their own time is none of your business," he said. "And I certainly hope that if not because of our relationship, then because of your journalistic training, you will not repeat that in any of your stories, because for all you know it was a professional legal appointment."

Boy, I hadn't seen Chester this steamed up since the time someone beat his course record during the annual chamber of commerce golf tournament.

"So, it's true, you're coupling?" I asked.

He turned to leave, still muttering at me as he went. "I'm not going to dignify that with a response."

Bingo. Given his reaction, I'd say they were more than just friends as he'd claimed. More to the point, if she was with him all night, then she probably wasn't out at the vacant lot poisoning her brother. But who did that leave?

CHAPTER 18

Gladys called me while I was standing there digesting the information about Chester and Fiona. She asked me to bring home some baked goods, and she invited me to join her and Todd around 5:00 for a drink. As an extra incentive, she promised me a tantalizing story.

"Oh, Piper, you have to come over for cocktail hour so Todd and I can tell you about the senior belly dancing class. You won't believe the things we saw."

Todd was writing a series of feature stories about unique senior exercise options as part of a plan to recharge the *Seacoast Seniors* magazine, of which I was now in charge. Gladys had volunteered to be his assistant, and they were working their way through belly dancing to tai chi to laughter yoga. I could only imagine what she would report. Whenever she used the "things we saw" expression, the listener was in for a doozy of a tale. In the past, this had included reports of scandalous key parties in the 1970s, and more recently the time she'd seen a dachshund riding shotgun on a scooter complete with a helmet, goggles, and leather jacket.

I headed home from the apple sale with a box of Jenny's

new apple-cranberry turnovers for Gladys and some cinnamon buns with a white chocolate glaze for myself. I decided to make a pit stop to relax at my carriage house for a while, and as I leaned into the old armchair in my living room, I texted Richie to find out if he might be freed up enough on the case to come over later. I usually went to his place, but I thought it was time for him to start to come to my place too. I knew I was committed to drinks with Gladys, but I figured I'd be home early enough to have dinner with him afterward. His work schedule was such that an early dinner was not often in the cards, and his positive replied confirmed that this day would be no exception. He promised to swing by around 7:30 if he wasn't delayed.

Though I knew Gladys would serve appetizers during her traditional cocktail hour, my stomach was growling, and I couldn't resist sampling one of the cinnamon buns. As the sweet icing melted in my mouth, I pondered what I knew so far. Roy had been poisoned. He'd probably wrenched the majority control from Fiona by getting his mother's signature in a dubious way. He may have been poisoning the birds. He was possibly having a tryst with the PR maven Becky Bean.

As I considered this last possibility, I knew that a little late-night love was not a motive for murder, but Becky's connection to Roy gnawed at me. If they'd been spending time together, she might have heard if someone was bothering him or upset with him. There was always the chance that she knew something that could be a clue.

The sound of Middle Eastern instrumental music, heavy on the flute, drifted over from the main house, bringing me back to the task at hand. *Dear me,* I thought, *were they actually listening to that now? And how loud had they turned it up if I could hear it at my place?* Though the show tunes could get repetitive, I would take them over this music any day. Reluctantly, I collected the turnovers and headed up, unsure of what I might find.

Todd and Gladys were in the round sunroom, where Gladys had gathered our small group the other night. She had her hair piled in a bun on top of her head, with a pink scarf twisted artfully around it, conjuring up a very Barbara-Eden-in-"I-Dream-of-Jeannie" vibe. Todd, meanwhile, was in his regular at-home attire: tie-dyed shirt with the Grateful Dead teddy bears, wrinkled chino shorts, and Birkenstocks with gray wool socks.

"Oh, Piper, dear," Gladys said, plunging right in as she hopped to her feet, "like I said on the phone, you won't believe the things Todd and I saw on our field trip today!"

She turned to him and said, "Isn't that right, Todd, darling?"

He shrugged and laughed. "Unbelievable is one way to describe it."

I poured a seltzer with lime, made a little plate of cheese with apple slices, and sat down.

"Do tell," I said. Then I leaned in to hear their dramatic recounting of the class.

"First off," Gladys began, "someone was wearing a white dress. After Labor Day. Good heavens!"

I shared a brief eye roll with Todd as she continued.

"Then, the instructor started talking about sex, if you can believe that. With a group of eighty- and ninety-year-olds! She told us to swivel one hip, swivel another, and really, Piper, most of those people have titanium hips, if you know what I mean."

She was really fired up now. "It got even more outrageous,"

she said. "She told us to push our lady parts forward like we meant it. Can you imagine!" Then, pointing at Todd, she said, "And that one, he showed us all up, like he had been doing it for years."

Todd stood up and swiveled his hips in a way that made me blush. He winked and said, "I dated a master belly dancer for a while when I was in Turkey, so I did learn a thing or two about the technique—if you know what I mean."

Gladys swatted his arm. "Now, Todd, don't ruin my impression of you with crass talk like that."

Entertained by their banter, I sipped my seltzer. Then I asked, "So, will you go back to the class?"

Gladys smiled and nodded. "Well, for all of that, it did remind me of the time in the burlesque dance troupe. Now those were the days."

She seemed to be gathering steam again. She popped back up, reaching out to hold Todd's arm, and said, "Oh, Todd, let's show Piper our little routine."

Oh boy. I held my face in a neutral gaze because I feared I'd burst out laughing.

"Okay, Todd, places, places!" she commanded.

He ambled over next to her, and she turned toward the bar cart, where her new speaker sat. She said, "Alexa, turn on belly dancing music."

The little speaker started bouncing on the table as the sound of drums and a flute floated out. Todd did a little half hip pop while Gladys gracefully raised her arms above her head, weaving them around like flames. For an octogenarian, she had moves. For a brief second, I wondered where Dashing Duncan was, though to be honest, it was nice to have a night without him.

Gladys continued, really getting into the dance moves by twirling the pink scarf around in her hands. Todd, for all his boasting, did have good rhythm as he moved in time to the eerie music, and I wondered if his story about the girlfriend in Turkey was actually true. The two went on for a few more minutes, slowly swiveling and twisting, with Gladys laughing again as she said, "All I can hear is that woman saying to push those lady parts forward. Oh, I can't wipe it from my mind."

They finished their routine with a flourish, and I clapped. "Bravo!" Then I said, "Oh, Gladys, I wish Stanley was here to see this. He'd love it!"

She nodded sadly. "I talked with him today, and he said they think he'll be another two weeks. Maybe Todd and I can take our show on the road. It would certainly distract Stanley from being stuck in that place—give him a little entertainment."

It was hard to imagine this and keep a straight face, but thankfully, my phone pinged and excused me from having to answer her. Richie had arrived.

"Well, as much as I'd like to stay and see the encore performance, I have a date," I said.

Gladys clapped her hands together. "Oh, that nice little Irish boy. He was always such a darling." I nodded but didn't say anything, working to keep the flush down on my cheeks as I anticipated our meeting. I gave Todd a little wave and then headed out the side door, which led directly to the back yard.

"Hey, Scoop," Richie said, and I jumped. I hadn't seen him right outside the door.

"Hey, yourself."

He was holding a brown paper bag with handles. "Dinner,"

he said. "I got Thai from the new place downtown. Cindy from work says it's amazing."

"Sounds good to me." I was still starving, and it smelled delicious. I detected curry, lemongrass, and cumin wafting up from the takeaway containers.

Richie followed me inside my carriage house, waiting until we were out of view before he leaned in for a real welcome. If I hadn't been so hungry, I might have forgone dinner at that point, but the little growl from my stomach convinced me otherwise.

"Hold that thought," I told him, and he stepped back. I pulled out some plates and arranged the food in serving bowls. I knew Gladys always gasped in horror at the thought of eating takeout straight from the container, so I guess her habits were finally influencing me too.

Richie had arrived with a good assortment. He had my favorite, the traditional pad thai, some spring rolls, and to start, the spicy tom yum soup. We sat at the butcher block island and ate in comfortable silence for a few minutes. The soup was complex with layers of flavor: the lemongrass, garlic, lime juice, and fish sauce, with the bright spice.

"So, what's the word?" I asked.

He winked at me. "What, I don't see you for days and all you want is to get information. I see how it is."

I held both hands out and shrugged, before smiling suggestively at him. He grinned back and gave in. "Well, funny you should ask," he said. "We followed up on that lead about the birds being poisoned and it was true, but here's the kicker."

He paused and ate a shrimp from the soup before he responded, no doubt to torture me and my heightened curiosity. He said, "You'll never believe where we found some of the very same poison."

I swatted his thigh. "Come on, you're killing me here. Spill it!"

He leaned toward me, so close I could smell his cologne: spicy with a hint of cedar and tobacco. He said, "What do I get if I tell you?"

I played along. "Your wildest dreams come true."

"Well in that case," he said, "it was in Harry Trott's garage."

CHAPTER 19

I was up early the next morning, and while I should have been thinking of my romantic evening with Richie, I was fixated on the intel that Harry Trott had the same type of poison that had killed Roy. Richie had also let it slip that it was rat poison—specifically, arsenic. Apparently, Harry had claimed he found it near the Carmichael lot and brought it to his garage for safekeeping because of its potential to poison birds, before calling the police to report his suspicions about Roy targeting his birds. Richie said they couldn't even trace the date of the packaging because Harry had poured it into an old cat litter bucket. I couldn't help rolling it over in my mind; why hadn't the police found the poison during their initial search of the lot? Was it possible that there was another explanation for how the same type of poison that had killed Roy was in Harry's garage?

I knew I shouldn't interfere with the police investigation, but I was going to burst if I didn't go over to Harry's house to do some light sleuthing. I had kept my end of the bargain for the intel, and Richie had left my carriage house rather late. Now I hoped that the memory of our extended make-out session would cancel out any irritation he might feel later if he ever discovered I went to Harry's.

As I planned out my day, I realized that I would have to wait until the afternoon before I could swing by Harry's place. First I needed to edit the *Seacoast Seniors* special section insert, and I must admit, I was looking forward to reading Todd's account of the senior belly dancing class he and Gladys had attended.

"Morning, Clara," I said, as I walked into the lobby. "Anything big happening that I need to know about?"

She looked up from Facebook, following her grandchildren as usual, and said, "Well, not really. Except Pansy Bolton stopped by to tell Hap she didn't want any of 'Piper's exposés' about the apple sale. I mean, what does she think you're going to expose, that they used store-bought applies instead of the ones from the orchard or something?"

She stopped and held a finger up in the air, as if she'd just remembered something else. "And if you can believe it, Todd is out in Brentwood, where there's a police chase underway to capture an escaped emu that's blocking traffic. It almost got hit by a school bus full of kids this morning."

I shrieked, not from fear but from the hilarity of that statement. "What! Are you kidding me?"

She chuckled. "I know. He heard it over the police scanner and moved about as fast as I've seen him go to get over there."

Boy, Todd certainly had a knack for finding unusual stories. I could only imagine the tale he'd regale us with when he returned. I sat down at my desk and booted up my computer, where his story on the belly dance class was waiting for me.

SENIORS SIZZLE AT BELLY DANCING

By Todd Tisden

EXETER__*Gone are the days of chair yoga at the Exeter recreation department's senior exercise program.*

Caroline Tursi recently started teaching belly dancing for seniors as a way to help hip mobility and have fun at the same time.

"So many senior exercise classes make folks feel like they're just biding their time until their number is up," she said. "This class is silly, sexy, and shows that seniors can still have some sizzle in their life."

The new class joins other offerings such as tai chi, disco groove, and Jazzercize, which are all open to residents who visit the center.

This reporter attended a class with an unnamed research assistant, an active octogenarian who once was a professional dancer, and she admitted she was skeptical at first.

"Honestly, half of the people don't have hips healthy enough to swivel anymore," she told me. "But it certainly was a lot more enjoyable than the last program I attended there. I say two thumbs, or hips, up."

The class meets twice a week and spaces can be reserved ahead of time as it's been selling out. Caroline asks that dancers be prepared to shake their booty and bring their own scarves. The town of Exeter suggests getting approval from your physician before starting any new exercise program.

That last line killed me, like the town was afraid they might be held liable if some elderly belly dancer had a heart attack while doing too much swiveling. I mean, they'd go out happy, right? I also never thought I'd use the headline *senior sizzle* in anything not related to an early bird special at a chain steakhouse, and yet I opted to keep Todd's suggested headline.

I made my way through the other stories in this issue: an estate-planning event at the library, a bus trip to a Loretta LaRoche comedy show in Boston, and a Thanksgiving cornucopia centerpiece course at the senior center. Todd came strolling into the newsroom just as I was finishing up.

I said, "So, what's the story? Did they get the emu?"

He sat down and didn't say anything for a minute. Clearly, he was going to draw this story out for full impact. Any poker face I had failed me when Todd leaned back and took off his Birkenstocks, revealing his thick gray wool socks. I cringed and covered my nose with my hand. God, you'd think he lived in a campsite or something. It was even worse than Duncan's gold-toed argyles.

"Well, it's a good thing I was there," he said. "I basically saved its life."

He went on to tell me how the police had tried to lasso the poor bird before Todd stepped in, worried they might strangle it if the emu decided to run. "Didn't want them to be labeled as emu murderers or anything."

God, that would have been a headline. Cops accidentally choke emu to death. All of the animal rights advocates would picket them for sure.

"So," I prompted him. "Did they get it?"

He shrugged, nonchalantly smiled, and said, "They didn't, but I did."

Talk about getting involved in the news. Apparently, Todd

had once worked on an alpaca farm in Vermont where they'd also had a few emus, so he fancied himself a bit of a bird whisperer. He'd used a technique where they surrounded the emu with ropes and gradually moved closer until someone could get ahold of it.

Hap walked into the newsroom as Todd finished the story. Hap said, "Well, write it up. You know how people love an animal story in the paper."

Then Hap turned to me. "What's new on the murder? Anything?"

I filled him in on what I said was a tip about the poison at Harry Trott's garage, and I explained my plans for the rest of the day. I told him, "I just sent you the *Seacoast Seniors*. It's ready to go, so I'm about to head over to Harry's to see what I can find out."

He nodded his head in agreement. "Good, good, keep me posted."

I'd taken Walter the Wagon to work given that Todd finally had Scarlett the Scooter back to operational shape, and I was glad to be able to drive to Harry's. Not that I minded a good walk, but at times like this I just wanted to get somewhere quickly, especially after thinking about it all day. Harry's Subaru was in his driveway, so it looked like he was home, a good sign. I picked my way over the old porch, now well versed in all the trouble spots, and knocked on the door. No answer. Huh. I rapped again.

"He should be home," a voice called out, and I turned to see Tootie, who was planting red mums in her side garden. "His car's been there all day."

Well, that was strange, unless he was working on something inside and couldn't hear me. Now, I could have just left a note on his door and headed back to the office, but my curiosity was too great, so I peered into the front windows. I didn't see anything other than stacks of newspapers and some recycling in a brown grocery bag. I glanced at the side of the house. This time, I decided to walk around the back. Maybe he was in the kitchen.

I picked my way along the side of the house, which was a no-frills landscaping job compared to Tootie's gardens. Tootie's yard looked like she was entering a *Yankee Magazine* fall house-decorating contest, complete with mums, pumpkins, and freshly raked mulch. In contrast, Harry only had some crushed stone under the roof drip line and some bare patches of grass on his lawn, although there were so many bird feeders around the yard, it looked like he might be selling them.

I rounded the corner and came upon his rear steps, a common thing in older New Englander houses around town, which had little stoops out back. I climbed the steps, going slowly given the condition of the front porch, and peered in the window of the back door. Nothing.

I picked my way around the perimeter of the building until I got to his one-car garage. Maybe he was working on project in there. But as I peered through the window, my heart sank. Oh no. Not again. There on the cement floor was Harry Trott. He was laid out like a bird in a museum display case. And it didn't look like he was there of his own free will, if you know what I mean.

CHAPTER 20

Tootie and I were relegated to her yard after the police and ambulance arrived on the scene. Her mums were immediately forgotten as we watched the paramedics wheel Harry out on a stretcher. He had an oxygen mask over his nose and mouth, and I hoped this meant he would be okay. I knew from off-the-record conversations I'd had in the past with local paramedics that sometimes for appearances they left the mask on even when it was clear the person was gone—more to make observers feel better than for actual medical value.

"I'm starting to get a complex," I told Tootie. "People keep dropping around me."

Tootie patted my arm. "Sometimes life isn't for everyone," she said. "But I don't think it's his time. Probably just a fainting spell or something."

I guess, but it seemed more than a little suspicious given the recent developments about the rat poison in his garage and his proximity to Roy's murder.

Tootie rambled on about what she knew about him as we watched the response next door. She said, "Harry lives alone. He ran the projector at the Ioka Theater many years back. He never married, but his older sister lives over in the county nursing home. Really, it's just him and the birds."

Before I could reply, she pulled off her gardening gloves and continued. "And if you get a look at his recycling, which I may or may not have seen on my morning constitutional, he likes a little nip here and there. But oh my, he could stand to eat something other than microwave dinners."

Clearly, nothing got by Tootie, and I was lucky she was on my side in this mystery. I had to wonder what else she'd discovered about people in town from those early morning walks. The only person who probably knew more was our regular UPS driver, John, and—as he liked to remind me—he wasn't sharing.

Chief Sinclair's unmarked cruiser pulled up in front of us. He opened the door, looked over, and shook his head when he saw me.

"Miss Greene, really? If I didn't know any better, I'd say you were a bad omen. What exactly are you doing here?"

I wanted to ask him the same question. It seemed a little odd that the police were responding to a medical call. Usually, it was just the paramedics from the fire department who showed up, stabilized the patients, and transported them to our local hospital.

I thought about how I might answer him. Finally, I said, "Just coming over to see him for a follow-up story." I left out the details of what that story was. "When he didn't answer the front door, I went around back. And ... " I paused for a breath, "that's when I saw him on the garage floor."

He nodded and looked temporarily mollified, although he still didn't seem pleased at my presence there. Then, before we could continue, his attention shifted. A detective—not

Richie—arrived on scene, and the chief held his hand up to me.

"I'll talk with you in a few. I've got to handle this," he said. He quickly turned and walked away from us.

Tootie had pulled out two folding camp chairs, which she set up facing Harry's house to observe the ongoing events. "Would you like some cider?" she asked me. "I just got some from the orchard over in Hampton Falls. It's fresh from the press."

Clearly, nothing said "It's sad to see my neighbor almost die and take a trip to the hospital" than a nice autumn drink and a view of an ambulance. All I needed was a pumpkin butterscotch scone and my life would be complete.

I decided to text Hap to let him know that I'd stay at the scene until we could get an official comment from the police or fire department. We didn't typically write about medical events like this, but given Harry's connection to the ongoing murder investigation, it just felt like I should stick around. I'd already managed to snap a few photos on my phone, making sure not to show Harry's face on the stretcher. Done with that, I surreptitiously took a few more photos as the police walked in and out of Harry's garage.

Something was up, but whether Chief Sinclair would actually spill anything was a long shot. Just the same, I edged over to his spot by the command car and let him know I would need some sort of official comment about the police being on the scene, to which he responded with a deep long sigh. Eventually he said, "Give me a few minutes."

I returned to my position with Tootie, where we sipped our cider and continued to watch the show. Small-town life seemed to get more exciting by the day.

Richie eventually arrived on the scene, but he didn't come over to talk with us. Instead, he joined a handful of police officers who were still walking in and out of the tiny garage. It was hard to imagine there was much inside, given the size of the building, but they were clearly interested in something.

A few minutes later, I heard the squelch and beep of a police radio nearby. A voice came through. "Chief, you need to come in here."

Tootie and I looked at each other and raised our eyebrows. What had they found in there?

My need to know what was transpiring was killing me. I said, "Tootie, what do you think it could be?"

She shook her head. "You got me. Knowing Harry, it could be anything. Old birds, gold bullion, lost treasure."

I swatted her arm. "Tootie, you know you can't tease me like that. I would be so excited if someone found lost treasure in there."

She laughed. "Oh, I know, my dear, but alas, it's probably only old license plates or perhaps something those old guys on *Car Talk* would be excited to have."

Finally, just when I thought I'd burst from the anticipation of a hot scoop, Chief Sinclair reemerged. Impulse control was a thing of the past, and I pounced as soon as he reached his cruiser.

"Chief, I know you're busy, but could you just give me something short on the record, please?"

He stopped with a look of resignation. The poor guy was probably wondering what had happened to his tranquil days of outreach at the elementary school and leisurely lunches with the elderly at the senior center. I had to wonder if two murders in town this year would send him to an early retirement.

"Okay, but then will you and Miss Marple over there give us some space to work?" He eyed Tootie on her chair.

I nodded and held two fingers up. "Scouts honor," I said.

He took a breath and began. "So, here's what I can say on the record. At this time, we do not believe this is a suspicious event. The word from the hospital is that he fell off his ladder and had a heart attack."

Hmm. Well, on a positive, Harry was living, which meant Exeter wouldn't be the murder capital of the northeast just yet.

"What about what you found inside," I said, taking a chance.

He looked at me, surprised, and I responded, "I heard the scanner chatter."

He looked around, checking to see if we were out of earshot of the others. Then he lowered his voice and said, "This is off the record, okay?"

I nodded, and he went on. "I'm probably going to regret telling you this, but it's the craziest thing. He had a bunch of stuff up in the rafters of his garage, hence why he was climbing that ladder, but it wasn't any old stuff, it was old theater memorabilia. Things not only from the Ioka but—even more shocking—the Exeter Playhouse. As you may or may not know, these items were said to have been taken out before the fire, somewhat suspiciously."

Wow! I remembered the old articles in the paper about the missing items from the Playhouse, but why would Harry have them? And what were the police looking for in his garage prior to the unexpected discovery of the theater relics. The chief said, "Given the poison he brought home from the Carmichael lot, we wanted to make sure he hadn't ingested or inhaled anything that caused a blackout." He paused, then added, "We did a quick check of any potential poisons or hazards throughout the garage." Again, he reminded me that these details were totally off the record, strictly for background. It was unusual for him to be this forthcoming, and I was not about to look a gift horse in the mouth. Still, I had a few more questions to try.

Not really expecting answers, I said, "But why would Harry have things from the Exeter Playhouse like that? Especially when he worked at the Ioka, not the Playhouse?"

The chief said, "Between you and me, I think he had a little side business these past few years, selling old memorabilia through online auction sites. We found some of the receipts. But there is a lot that doesn't add up."

You don't say, I thought. Then I couldn't contain myself. "So, are you going to ask him about it? Why he had so much there?"

He nodded. "We will. When he makes a recovery. But ..." He stopped, raised his eyebrows, and looked right at me the way my dad used to when making an important point. "I won't be sharing any personal information he provides if it compromises our case. You'll just have to be patient."

It was like he didn't know me at all. There was no way I would be satisfied until I found out exactly where Harry had gotten those theater mementos from—and why he had them squirreled away in his garage.

CHAPTER 21

I headed back to the newsroom buzzing with the excitement of off-the-record material. There was nothing so thrilling as possessing a tidbit that I wasn't supposed to have, and as a reporter I admit it was an intoxicating feeling. Of course, it also came with responsibility, especially in a small town, and I knew I'd have to wait until I could independently confirm the information and not burn my source. Still, the thought of Harry Trott with a garage full of relics from the Exeter Playhouse and the Ioka was beyond titillating; I would just need to be tactful as I asked around about how he came into possession of these treasures.

In the meantime, I had enough public information for a brief preliminary story on the medical emergency and ambulance call at Harry's house. Hap was in his office, wearing a rare solid-blue shirt—no plaid today—so I gave him the sixty-second elevator pitch of the piece and then headed over to my computer. This was one of those times when the approach was to tap out a quick story to get the initial news released quickly, with the intention that I'd update it and refresh the story online as more information was released.

POLICE MUM ON MEDICAL CALL AT HOUSE OF LOCAL BIRD MAN

By Piper Greene

EXETER__*Police say a medical emergency that sent local bird enthusiast Harry Trott to the hospital today is not suspicious, despite his ties to a recent murder inquiry.*

Trott was found unresponsive in the garage of his home on Court Street early this morning by a visitor. "At this time, the medical professionals say this was likely a natural medical event," Police Chief Frank Sinclair said. "I am able to confirm that Mr. Trott is stable at the hospital and expected to make a full recovery."

Trott's neighbor, Tootie Wentworth, expressed concern for the older man. "He does live alone, and I'm just so thankful that he was found when he was," she said. "Honestly, it could have saved his life."

Trott has been in the news lately as one of the most vocal critics of the proposed Carmichael's Arcade in Arms, a Revolutionary War–themed arcade and fun house. He'd been feeding a rare Ross's gull there this year and feared construction would displace the finicky avian native to the Arctic region of the world. This story will be updated as more information is available.

I sent the story over to Hap directly and decided to put in a call to Richie. Given what the chief had told me about the case, I was pretty sure Richie would no longer be on the scene. He picked up on the second ring.

"Hey, Scoop. Let me guess—you're just dying to know why the old guy had all of those theater pieces in the garage, aren't you?"

Boy, he knew me too well. But that wasn't necessarily a bad thing.

"You got me," I said. I lowered my voice, as I was known to do when asking about a juicy tidbit. "But, seriously, isn't it more than a bit suspicious, especially since some of the things from the Playhouse were taken out before the fire?"

"We're all under strict orders not to let that intel out," he said. "Unless there's a really good reason."

He was holding back on purpose. I was going to have to work for it. I said, "Couldn't you just give me a little hint? Like, do you think he set the fire? Was he working with someone who did? Or was he just a kleptomaniac with a penchant for unusual items?"

"Simmer down there, Nancy Drew," he said, then laughed at his little joke before adding, "but honestly, we don't really know anything more than you do at this point."

I found myself wondering again not only how Harry got the paraphernalia from the playhouse and theater but why he'd kept them all these years. Did he see himself as the guardian of their history? Or did he just want to possess them for his own personal collection? The chief had seemed to think Harry was selling some of them online. None of it made sense to me.

Still, while I had Richie's attention, I decided to move on, curious if there was anything I could report now on the case. I said, "Do you have any updates that might be public?"

Richie cleared his throat before responding. "Well, we're bringing Tripp Bolton back in for another interview. He can't really account for his whereabouts during the window of time the medical examiner estimates that Roy died between ten and midnight. Says he was out for a walk, but no one saw him."

Honestly, I can't say I wouldn't take a walk after dark to get some alone time if I lived with Pansy. Still, he had been the most vocal opponent of the arcade plan, so what's to say he didn't go out to talk with Roy late at night and get carried away? There was also the tidbit I'd heard from Jenny about the restraining order, and after a brief hesitation, I decided to pose the question.

"And of course with the restraining order Roy was seeking after Tripp went after him at that meeting … well, that must make you wonder, right?" Richie paused on the other end of the line, and I worried I'd pushed too much. But then he said. "So, you know about that! I should have known. Yes, that's a bad fact for Tripp, to put it mildly."

You don't say, I thought, but I held back to keep my response low key. I simply said, "I can't wait to hear how that goes."

Richie lowered his voice, and I had to strain to hear him. "Don't get me in trouble with all of this, Scoop, okay?"

If I hadn't known better, I'd have said he sounded a little nervous.

"I never reveal my sources," I said. "For real."

In the background I heard a voice call his name. He said, "I have to get back to work, but we'll talk again soon. Let's make plans for this weekend, maybe an outing to Newburyport or dinner again at my place?"

"Sounds good," I said. I was a bit surprised he was willing to go out in public, but perhaps he thought the trendy city over the border in Massachusetts was far enough from prying eyes. I added, "Thanks for your help."

After we hung up, I decided it was time to go see Winnie. Given the fact that Tripp was being questioned by the police, who had the restraining order paperwork Roy had filled out claiming he felt threatened by Tripp, I couldn't help but be suspicious of the man. I mean, why had Tripp really stopped by the historical society? Pansy had denied any knowledge of Tripp's "project." And Winnie's voice had sounded more demanding than I had ever heard it before when she told him she'd give him more time. Just what was going on, and who was telling the truth?

Todd was off working on a story about an elderly man named Henry who walked to see his wife in a local nursing home each day, a real feel-good story, particularly given the man's age of 92 years old. Exeter seemed to have no shortage of inspirational nonagenarians, Tootie and Stanley among them. Todd had decided to walk with Henry to get the behind-the-scenes details.

"Could be a while," Todd had said, as he had headed out. "I've seen him walk, and while he's determined, there are times I fear he might not make it." Maybe my pace car idea for elderly walkers in town wasn't so far-fetched after all.

I waved to Clara, who had the phone against her ear, and slipped out the front door in the lobby. It was less than a five-minute walk, and I found Winnie on her computer in her little office kitchen room at the back of the historical society.

"Oh, Piper, come take a look at this, it's really something," she said, beckoning me toward her computer monitor. I walked around where she had the Exeter, England, tourism page displayed.

"Still planning that trip, huh?" I asked.

She nodded enthusiastically. "I had a fabulous call with the historian over there, and we're looking to do a program for next summer."

She went on to regale me with some of her newfound knowledge of our sister city, which dated back to the Roman era. "And there are walls around the center and a Gothic cathedral that sounds just stunning," she said. It was as if she were already there. "And then she told me about these vaulted, medieval underground passages, and I was all in. You know how I love a good hidden tunnel in a historic village."

Oh, did I ever. Winnie had been consumed for years with a project that aimed to document alleged hidden tunnels under our local Exeter. There were actual tunnels at the prep school, once used to transport food from a central kitchen to the dormitories, but locals had been sharing tales of other tunnels in the town forest. Those tunnels were rumored to be a hiding spot dating back to the early history of town, when relations with some of the Native Americans were not always friendly; some of the tunnels were even believed to date back to the Revolutionary War.

One lifelong resident, Richard Manix, loved to recount the time he and his brother had fallen into one of the tunnels near a spot known as the Ledges. Winnie and her walking group actually took a hike into the town forest one day to track down these tunnels, but after walking in circles for three hours, she now feared they got destroyed when the highway was built.

Winnie pointed back at the computer screen. "I'm even talking with my colleague across the pond about establishing an exchange program where we have residents of our Exeter go visit their Exeter and likewise."

Now that was a trip I'd love to go on, but I knew it would never be in the budget of the *Exeter Independent*. Maybe I'd need to start saving my pennies—or pence. We looked at a few more images and maps, and then I got down to the business of my visit.

"So, I just got a tip about the investigation into Roy's murder," I said. "Apparently, they have some questions for Tripp Bolton."

Winnie's surprise was evident.

"They're bringing him back in for questioning," I said. Then I filled her in about his late-night Exeter walkabout that he had no witnesses for. "I mean, he doesn't seem like the kind of person who'd kill someone, but honestly, he was quite enraged at some of those meetings. And there was the time he broke the gavel."

Winnie looked conflicted, as if she wanted to tell me something but wasn't sure she should. I decided it was time to drop the rest of the information. "They also found paperwork in which Roy was preparing to file a restraining order against Tripp," I said. "And given that his walkabout was at the same time they say Roy was killed, it doesn't look good."

Winnie squirmed in her seat, and I could tell she had information. I looked at her pointedly and said, "Time to fess up."

She sat still for a minute, pursing her lips together. Then she took a deep breath. "Here's all I can say," she told me. "I know where he was that night. I can't tell you how I know, but honestly, Piper, he's most definitely not the murderer."

I blurted out, "Come again?"

She shook her head decisively. "That's all I can say right now. I'm sorry."

I'd never known her to be so cagy, and I had a sneaking suspicion that it had to do with her poker games. Still, while the list of attendees was not public, wouldn't the ability to produce a watertight alibi for a murder suspect surpass any oath of secrecy?

I tried to figure out the best way to approach this.

"Well, if you won't tell me," I finally said, "you should at least tell the police. If he's actually innocent, they need to know."

She sighed heavily. "I know," she said. "Give me a day or two and I'll work up my nerve."

I patted her arm and stood up to leave. What I wouldn't give to be a fly on the wall when she made that phone call. Or better yet when Tripp had to fess up to Pansy about where he'd actually been.

CHAPTER 22

Later that week, I headed over to the Tuck Tavern for a business-after-hours mixer, the last hurrah for the locals taking part in the Beer and Chili Fest. It was billed as a pep rally of sorts for the local restaurants and breweries that were taking part in the festival this year. I met up with Jenny to walk over. She had finally decided on her recipe with Emily, and the two were feeling good about their chances.

We passed by the open lawns of the prep school campus, where the lights of the library were blazing, and I assumed the students were burning the evening oil to finish the hours of homework they reportedly got every day. The library, which was designed by famed architect Louis Kahn, was renowned for its dramatic atrium with enormous circular openings into the book stacks. In the lives of Exeter townies, it was famous as a place teenagers snuck into and tried to make their way to the top floor as a dare. Not that it was closed to the public, but there was something about going into the enormous building that seemed off limits to those who weren't part of the student body.

A few moments later, we turned left down the little side

street, which was peppered with white colonials and led to the Tuck Tavern. I filled Jenny in on what I'd heard about Tripp Bolton.

"Honestly," I told her, "Winnie is acting so out of character. She's never been one to cover for people, but I can't help but feel that's what's happening here. I really hope she goes forward with her plan to talk to the police about what she knows."

Jenny, decked out in black pants that hugged all the right places and a green sweater, shrugged. "You never know. It could be anything, and let's be real, if it was something totally illegal or related to the murder, you know she'd tell you."

She was right. Winnie was not one to condone anything that might harm someone, but the question remained: where was Tripp on the night of Roy's murder? My gut still said he was at the poker game, but whether she'd tell me that officially was unknown. There'd been rumors that the minister's wife was part of the group too, and that remained unsubstantiated as well.

We approached the Tavern, where the front steps were now lined with pumpkins and cornstalks for fall. Apparently, they decided to catch up with the decorations around town and get in the spirit. I got a slight whiff of wood smoke. They must have started up the fireplace to take the chill out of the old, drafty building.

Emily gave a big wave to Jenny as we arrived, and Jenny returned a shy smile to her teammate. Then Jenny turned to me and said, "I'll catch up with you. I need to ask Emily something."

She crossed the room, and the two women gave each other a hug before leaning in to begin an animated conversation.

It looked like their friendship was evolving into a closer connection. I'd have to ask Jenny about that when we were alone.

A server was circulating the room with a tray of hors d'oeuvres, and when she offered me the selection, I helped myself to a crostini topped with blue cheese, walnuts, and a fig. Just the right amount of each for the perfect bite.

I gave the room the once-over to get the lay of the land. Grayson Adams was in his regular seat, and his greeting to me was lukewarm at best. The woman from the bean-to-bar chocolate shop was also there. Word on the street was that for her entry, she was concocting a chocolate-inspired chili based on a Mexican mole sauce. Over on the far side of the bar, at a high-top table, Todd and Becky, the PR lady, sat with their heads together, and I got a feeling from general body language that they too were having a private conversation. I was still struggling to believe what Emily had told me about Becky and Roy. First, she was much younger and better looking than he was, and second, if they had been involved, wouldn't she be in mourning? Honestly, it seemed more likely to me that she was being overly friendly to land a job as his PR consultant. She was clearly flirting with Todd, who was actually dressed up: his mop of blonde shaggy hair had been trimmed, and he had on a collared shirt without missing buttons.

Hap had asked Todd to put together another feature story about the Beer and Chili Fest, complete with a few photos, as part of the press leading up to the event, which was now only a week away. I made my way toward them as I prepared to work the room for more food and informational tidbits. "Hey, Greene," Todd said, as I approached. "I was just telling Becky about my walk through the town with old Henry this morning. There's a lot more to him than meets the eye. Did you know he founded a society about some random cell's role in the body?"

Todd explained that it had to do with plants and their value to keeping this cell healthy, but as he went on, my mind wandered. It was just too technical and detailed for me. Apparently, old Henry credited his vegetarian diet with maintaining his ability to walk those long distances every day. Becky smiled, but I could tell she wasn't really engaged with his story either. Her eyes kept scanning the room, a trait I knew all too well. There were times I kept track of several conversations at once in a place like this.

"I'll be right back," she suddenly told Todd, leaping up and setting off. She was dressed to the nines with a low-cut, sparkling tunic, a pair of black leggings, and sleek leather boots that came to her knees.

"Looks like the two of you are still pretty friendly," I said to Todd, throwing out a feeler. He shrugged and answered, "For now," before taking a sip of his beer. *Typical Todd,* I thought.

I had decided to share what I was working on with him, so I filled him in about the situation with Tripp's unknown whereabouts that night and his interview with the police.

"Listen, I'm not telling you to do anything," I said, though we both knew I was, "but do you think you might feel out Chief Sinclair's secretary, Cindy, over there? See if there's any news she might part with?"

It was no secret that the old ladies loved Todd—Gladys being the chief octogenarian in point, as she loved it whenever he regaled her with stories of his world travels. Usually, Winnie was my line to Cindy, but in this case, I needed to get creative. As Todd moved closer to Cindy, I turned toward the bar, where I spotted Pansy and her sidekick, Myrna, known as the Cranky Yankee. Myrna, with her strict lifestyle and lack of joy, seemed more like a Puritan blast from the past than anyone I knew. Pansy's bottled blonde bob was as immaculate as ever, nary a hair out of place. She acknowledged me, but her facial expression didn't invite me to stop.

Emily and Jenny were laughing about something when I reached them. Emily looked over at me and asked, "Can I get you anything from the bar?"

"Sure, how about a Pinot Noir?" It was fall, after all—the time of the year when even Gladys added some hearty red wine to her repertoire. I took a small sip and detected cherry, raspberry, and something earthy with a hint of vanilla spice. Not bad, but a little dry for my taste.

I turned back to Jenny and Emily. "So, are you ladies ready for the main event?"

They both nodded, and Emily said, "I've tweaked the seasoning one more time, and Jenny added some creamed corn to her latest corn bread recipe, which really added another layer of flavor and helped with the tendency for it to crumble. I'd say we're a pretty good team."

Jenny beamed then quickly looked down, a faint blush on her cheeks at the compliment.

Before I could reply, I heard someone tapping a glass with a spoon to get the room's attention. Tom Stone, the head of the chamber of commerce, was standing at the side of the room. He stepped forward and put his hands up to ask the crowd to quiet down. I glanced around but didn't see Todd or Becky anymore. Perhaps they'd gone somewhere more private to chat?

Tom said, "Thank you so much for coming out tonight. It's just fantastic to see the business community coming together to reflect our town in such a positive way. We're just a week away, and I can't wait for the television viewers to see what makes Exeter so special."

The room erupted in enthusiastic applause. He made a few more canned remarks, the kind reporters tend to tune out because they don't seem authentic, before wrapping it up. The group returned to their drinks and conversations, and I spied Todd walking back into the room. "Where's Becky?" I asked him. "Did she already go home?"

He shook his head. "She went to the ladies' room. But you're not going to believe what I just found out."

"Yeees?" I said, dragging out my response in a way I hoped would encourage him to spill the details quickly.

He lowered his voice and said, "Well, Cindy told me she was at her desk at the police station when Tripp came out from his interview." He paused for a breath. "And you'll never guess what he said!"

He was right. "What?"

"I'd rather go to jail for a murder that I didn't commit than tell you where I was that night."

Yikes! That sounded a little extreme if he was just playing poker, but where else could he have been? This question echoed through my mind all the way home.

CHAPTER 23

My curiosity was still front and center as I got ready for work the next morning. Was Tripp Bolton afraid? And of what? The only answer I could think of was Pansy. Heck, I'd probably rather go to jail than face her myself. But was a harmless little poker game so bad that he feared Pansy more than he feared the police? It was time to address this one headfirst, despite Winnie's reluctance, and I decided to stop by the historical society before going into the office.

"Winnie," I called out, as I walked into the front lobby.

She popped out from her office, a cup of tea in hand. "Oh, Piper, this is a bit early for you, isn't it?"

I shrugged and got right to the point. "Winnie, I don't like Tripp either, but I fear that an innocent man may go to jail if you don't do something."

To highlight my point, I added, "The gig's up, Lady Maverick." I knew she'd get my reference to the prize-winning French American poker player. "Have you talked to the police yet?"

I let that sit and checked her expression. She looked almost sheepish.

She said, "I haven't, but I'll go over today." Then she sighed and continued, with a look of resignation on her face. "Yes, Tripp is part of the poker game, but he's the worst player I've ever encountered. He just keeps coming back, and at this rate, he's basically funding my whole trip to Exeter, England."

I knew it! But, my God, did Tripp really believe hiding his activity was worth letting the police think he was a murder suspect? I pushed Winnie a bit more on that angle.

"Well …" she said, slowly. Once again, she looked a bit guilty. "Pansy is adamant that he does not engage in any sort of gambling. Tripp told me it was a real issue early in their marriage."

I didn't know a lot about poker. Okay, I knew basically nothing other than the fact that strategy was a big part of the game. I said, "What makes Tripp such a bad player?"

"Well …" she began again, "any poker player worth their salt knows you should wait until the big blind comes before you post your blind, but he never does, and it gets him every time."

I must have looked as confused as I felt, because she said, "It's basically like paying your taxes twice, and as a frugal Yankee, you think he'd know better—or at least learn after the tenth time."

I still had no idea what she was talking about, so I moved back to more important matters. I said, "Winnie, do you want me to walk over to the police station with you? It's time to come clean. They seriously think he's a suspect at this point."

She sighed deeply. "I know, I know, but it's so hard to let go of the easy money. Tripp was a sure thing, and all of his poker losses were extra money for my big trip next year."

Not once had I ever imagined there were such high stakes

at the Historical Society's secret card games. Perhaps this explained the little red convertible the minister's wife drove around in all summer.

"Well, maybe you'll still make out with the other players," I suggested. Then I couldn't resist slipping in, "Who are the other players, by the way?"

She shook her head. "Sorry, that's still top secret. Let's just say they are all a tad bit better at the game than old Tripp."

Winnie promised to go to the police as soon as I left, so I finally headed for the office. It was deadline day after all, and I still had an article to write about the upcoming town budget process. It was a real snore story, but the proposal for a second street sweeper had resulted in a lively debate at the last meeting. Apparently, some people felt the streets and sidewalks were clean enough and viewed this as frivolous spending.

"Back in my day, the shop owners just swept them," one old timer had grumbled. "It's not like it's that hard."

As I walked downtown, I took the longer route past the Congregational Church. The maple tree out front was now a mix of orange and deep red leaves, almost the same shade as the church's three red doors, which the parish historian had once told me signified welcome and sanctuary. I cut through the church's side driveway and walked past the Independence Museum toward the newspaper offices by the river.

I felt like the investigation was stalling, though to be honest, I didn't know everything the police were following up on, despite my direct line to Richie. The confirmation that Tripp was out late playing poker, not murdering Roy, was good, but there was still that pesky restraining order paperwork. But setting Tripp aside for now, who did that leave as a suspect? Harry Trott, still in the hospital, could be a killer, but really that didn't seem likely to me, although I still had no explanation for the playhouse items found in his garage. Fiona, who had also made it onto my initial suspect list, had actually been with my own brother that night. And honestly, the less I had to think about what the two of them had been up to, the better. But who else could have wanted Roy out of the way? Gladys and I were still hoping Roy's showgirl from Vegas would show up one day, but would she have really arranged a poisoning from afar?

I made quick work of the last article and headed home. With the paper off to the press, there would be a natural pause in production until the next deadline started up again. I hunkered down in my carriage house for the afternoon, puttering about and using the time to catch up on laundry. Oscar, the feral cat, wandered over to my side door and sat in the sunshine, peering inside at me. Despite my skepticism of Todd's methods, the cat did seem to be mellowing.

I heard Gladys say to the cat, "Oh, hello there, you big handsome boy!" She really loved Oscar. I glanced outside, where she was teetering across the walkway from her large Victorian to my little sanctuary.

"Piper, dear," she called out, "I just picked up some tapas from that new restaurant by the bandstand. Duncan's coming for dinner, and I'd love for you to drop by."

I did love tapas, especially because it gave me a chance to sample several things at once. Plus, I'd missed lunch and was regretting my decision to survive on just the coffee and pastry I'd eaten in the morning. I could use a real meal. "Sure," I told her.

She smiled and clasped her hands together in her regular expression of excitement. "Good, and I do want to hear the latest about the goings-on with the big murder case and all."

Gladys loved to live vicariously through my job, but she was also a good source of information about the town's past and people. I told her I'd see her at five for the regular cocktail hour, and then I freshened up. Though she was my aunt and we were eating at her place, she still had pretty high standards. I changed out of the cozy sweatshirt I'd put on when I came home into a cranberry-colored sweater. I had on what I considered my good jeans, meaning they weren't faded or ripped, so I kept them on and headed over.

My aunt was in the large eat-in kitchen when I arrived.

"Oh, Piper, dear, you're here!" she said with great enthusiasm, as if we hadn't just seen each other a short time ago. "Duncan and I were just talking about the old days."

Duncan had on a blazer with a shiny silver handkerchief just barely visible from the pocket and a pair of dark-gray pants. This seemed to be his standard outfit the past few times I'd seen him. Perhaps he hadn't planned on staying in town long enough to bring a larger wardrobe?

"Yes," he said, breaking into my speculations. "My favorite role at the playhouse before I went to Boston—what a show!"

He explained that he'd been in *Carnival* as Marco the Magnificent with a real up-and-coming female lead, Vivian Hall, cast as Lili the orphan. "The voice of an angel," he said. "But, that role, it was like it was made for me."

He stood up and held his arms out with a flourish before he began singing. "In me you see a relic of a long-lamented age; When masculine behavior wrote a grand romantic page; With every man a lover like a hero on a stage; With a sword and a rose and a cape."

To my relief, Gladys quickly interjected. "Now, Duncan,

Piper didn't come for dinner and a show."

Though I did love a show, I wasn't sure how long I could keep a straight face if Duncan continued.

Gladys added, "Really, Vivian was extraordinary. I was more than a little envious of that platinum blonde hair of hers, a stunner."

Duncan nodded, and Gladys inclined her head toward him. She said, "Some people speculated that the two of them ran off together. Both of them left town for bigger and better things after the fire at the Playhouse."

Duncan ignored her suggestion that he had eloped with Vivian and instead stood up and helped himself to another of the bacon-wrapped dates. Gladys caught his eye and said, "So, what *do* you think became of her career after Exeter?"

Duncan shrugged. "I mean, I really wouldn't know." Then he added,

"I always thought she went to the West Coast. She talked about having a contact in California. I assumed that's where she landed."

Gladys looked skeptical, but given that he'd dumped her, it seemed like a good time to change the subject.

"So, Duncan," I said, "will you be staying in town much longer?"

He and Gladys looked at each other. "Well, that depends," he said, "if my leading lady here is willing to keep me around."

God, he was so over the top. Glady smiled impishly at him and then popped an olive from her martini in her mouth. She chewed slowly, and I noticed she didn't answer right away, which seemed like a good thing. I hated to see her rush into anything, especially given their history and with Stanley still at rehab.

"That depends," she said eventually. "Are you willing to help Piper and me track down a killer, or do you think we're too old for that kind of excitement?"

He stood up again and began another theatrical performance. I recognized the sonnet from my high school's unit on Shakespeare. "To me, fair friend, you never can be old; For as you were when first your eye I eyed; Such seems your beauty still."

Gladys smiled at his tribute, then waved him off, reminding him that we should finish the tapas before it got cold. The food was delicious, especially the grilled shrimp with a hearty romesco sauce, and I managed to eat my fill and get home without another solo performance. Honestly, if this was all Duncan had for talent, he might be better to focus on his career as a lounge pianist.

CHAPTER 24

When the bright sun streamed through my bedroom window the next day, I lay in bed for a bit and mulled over what I knew about the case. I pulled my down comforter over my eyes and concluded that it wasn't the right time yet to ask Harry Trott why he had theater relics and treasures packed up in his garage. He was still in the hospital, and while I wanted answers, I felt badly about approaching him in that condition. There would be time to talk to him when he was home and healthy. Instead, I decided to switch my immediate focus to how Roy got the majority shares from his mother and whether Anastasia Rose, his mystery lady friend from Las Vegas, would ever arrive in Exeter. If she did, how would the ownership of the property play out with Fiona, and their mother, Virginia?

Given my recent contact with Fiona, I didn't have high hopes that she'd spill anything, and Chester was a definite no. Instead, I decided to go over to the retirement community to see Roy's mother, Virginia Carmichael, under the guise of writing another story about the history of the Playhouse. Several people had told me that she struggled to recall recent events, but I also knew from a friend who worked with the elderly that the old memories were sometimes the last to remain. What happened five minutes ago might vanish from her thoughts very quickly, but she might recall a conversation from fifty years ago. Or so I hoped.

I slid into Walter the Wagon and headed toward the Orchard, a retirement community just outside of the downtown area that was known for their active and engaged residents and for dining options that were better than most restaurants. The rehab side of the place, where Stanley was recovering, was nicer than most hotels. I thought, *Virginia certainly must have done well for herself to buy into this community.*

I parked in a visitor spot and headed into a cream-colored lobby, which was dotted with watercolor paintings by local artists. I adjusted my purse over my shoulder as I approached the receptionist, an older woman in a pink knit sweater with stitched apples lining the collar.

"How can I help you?" she asked. She set down her book and I glanced at the cover, which featured a glamorous-looking woman in a long silky dress standing next to a handsome, bare-chested man with his hand on her shoulder It was called *The Duke's Mistress.* My, oh my.

Forcing my thoughts back to the present, I knew I was going to have to tell a little white lie. I said, "I'm here to see Virginia Carmichael. She told me to check in and go down to her room."

I was using my best girl-next-door voice, and she smiled warmly before responding. "Oh yes," she said, handing me a pen and a visitor's sticker. "You just need to sign in and wear this sticker someplace visible."

Then she gave me brief directions to the assisted living section of the facility—quite far from the section where Gladys and I had visited Stanley—and returned to her book. I was honestly a bit surprised at how easy it had been to get inside the place, though to be fair, I could have interrupted a racy scene with the duke that she wanted to finish.

The facility was immaculate, and I thought, *I would not mind living there.* I passed a library full of older people, including a woman in an armchair just inside the door who was reading the *New York Times.* Down the hallway, I saw a brick pizza oven and felt more like I'd stepped onto a Caribbean cruise than into a local retirement home. I could almost hear Gladys suggesting they add a pool boy serving fruity drinks with umbrellas.

I went a little further and eventually saw the number for Virginia's room. It seemed like a good sign to me that she was well enough to stay in the general assisted living section instead of the restricted dementia area. Perhaps I'd get lucky with information if I caught her on a good day.

I knocked, didn't hear a response, and knocked again. I looked both ways, saw there was no one around, gently opened the unlocked door, and called out, "Hello, Ms. Carmichael?"

A dignified older woman's voice responded, "Yes, in here." I considered that an invitation and walked in. The place was nicer than most apartments I'd ever lived in. It was tastefully decorated with pastel oriental rugs, and the living room furniture included embroidered cushions. A framed poster on the wall advertised a performance for Agatha Christie's *Murder on the Nile* at the Exeter Playhouse.

Virginia Carmichael was sitting in a recliner chair with a crocheted blanket over her lap, and she was watching an opera singer on television. She was tall and thin with long white hair that had been pulled back on either side with hairpins.

She had a commanding presence, even now. She flicked the television off when she saw me, her expression one of confusion. "Do I know you?" she asked.

I smiled, hoping to put her at ease. "I'm not sure. I'm Piper Greene, and I write for the *Exeter Independent*. I think you might know my aunt, Gladys?" I wasn't immune to dropping Gladys's name with a certain generation of residents in town to get myself an in.

"Now that's a classy lady," she said.

I sat on the edge of the love seat next to her. "Oh, she certainly is," I said.

Roy's mother didn't seem to be addled or out of it, but I knew that looks could be deceiving. I said, "Well, Ms. Carmichael, I'm working on a story about the old Exeter Playhouse, and I would love to hear some of your memories of those days. I'm sure you have lots of good stories you could tell me of what it was like back then."

She shifted her gaze and stared at the show poster I'd noticed on the way in. "Such a shame," she said. "That fire really came at a bad time."

She went on to tell me details that I already knew: the family had been divided over the lot's future; the insurance had not paid out because the arson case had never been solved, and she wanted the space to be used again for a theater someday. I was surprised she was offering so much information and hoped this meant she'd reveal something helpful to the case.

She said, "It was such a part of the town, truly. My Roy, he wants to fix it up and bring it back. Such a good boy, Roy."

I noticed she was using the present tense, and I decided not to delve into whether she knew, or remembered, that Roy was dead. That could derail the whole conversation.

"What about some of the regular performers," I asked. "Duncan McTavish and a young woman named Vivian Hall?"

She looked at me again as if she was trying to place me. "You said you're Gladys's niece?" I nodded, and she shook her head almost sadly before she said, "Poor Gladys. She was classy, smart, sophisticated, but she just couldn't compete with Vivian once Duncan saw her."

According to Virginia, Vivian was young, vivacious, talented, and completely out of Duncan's league. She said, "Honestly, I wasn't surprised when they left town at the same time. He had been pursuing her for months with talk of what the two of them could do on Broadway together."

Interesting, especially since Duncan had just told me and Gladys that Vivian had likely moved away to try her luck in Hollywood. Virginia added, "There was nothing keeping her here. It seemed like she was mostly on her own in the world."

Virginia's comment was more in line with what Gladys had heard years ago. So, who was telling the truth?

Roy's mother was clearly locked onto this period now, and I hoped she would go on. I asked, "Aside from Duncan, did Vivian have a boyfriend her own age?" Then I conjured up the expression her generation had used, and said, "A gentleman caller, perhaps?"

Virginia nodded. "Oh, she had many, right down to my Roy. He was just smitten with her. Embarrassing, really, the way he acted, given how young he was. He could have been her little brother. But she had that effect on people."

She paused and then added, "Fiona tried to convince Roy to lay off a bit, but there was no changing his feelings. It was a serious case of puppy love."

Virginia stopped and leaned her head back on her recliner. She closed her eyes and started breathing deeply. I was afraid she would drift off before I got to the real purpose of my visit.

"Ms. Carmichael," I said, urgently. She opened her eyes, but this time she looked as if she had no idea who I was. God, I hoped I hadn't missed the window for my final question. "What about a woman named Anastasia Rose, who had a relationship with Roy? Does she ever visit you?"

She quickly straightened her posture, and I prayed the window into her mind was still open. She looked at me sharply and said, "What? You must be mistaken. Roy took care of that years ago. He left that problem in Vegas."

Geez, talk about what happens in Vegas, stays in Vegas.

She shut her eyes again, and I stood up to go. I was curious, but I really didn't want to pester the poor woman, who had been nothing but gracious to me that morning. Still, her statement about Roy's girlfriend raised so many new questions. Why was Anastasia a problem, and what did Roy have to do to take care of her? I couldn't stand not knowing, but this was not the time or place to follow up on that.

In her sleep, Virginia sighed heavily, and I turned to go. As I reached for my purse, the door sprang open, and Fiona Carmichael burst in. She gasped when she saw me and hissed, "What are you doing here?"

I jumped up like I'd suddenly been caught shoplifting. My hands started shaking, and I said, "Just talking about the old days for a piece in the paper. But your mother just fell asleep."

Despite my quick response, which I thought sounded plausible, I knew I'd been shut down.

Fiona scowled. "Well, that's enough for today. She gets easily upset talking about those things, and really, Piper, don't you think you should have checked with me before you did this?"

I felt the hot flush of genuine shame creeping up my neck. Of course, I knew that, but it was nearly impossible to stop myself sometimes when the tantalizing potential of a hot scoop was so close.

I said, "So sorry, Fiona. I'll just be on my way."

I slid my purse over my arm and slipped out of the room, still wondering if Virginia Carmichael knew anything more about Anastasia Rose, the mysterious Vegas showgirl whom no one had met. I hoped I hadn't just ruined my only opportunity to find out. Could a trip to Las Vegas be in my future? God, Gladys would love it, wouldn't she?

CHAPTER 25

I was awakened the next morning by a persistent knocking on my door. I was still half asleep and certainly not ready to face anyone, but in case it was Gladys in the throes of an emergency, I forced myself to get up. I made it down from the loft and over to the side door, where the rapping continued as if my house was on fire. As it turned out, it was not an emergency at all, but Todd Tisden, holding a threadbare beach towel in one hand and a bar of Irish Spring in the other.

"Good morning, Sunshine!" he said. "Hey, I could really use a nice bath to start my day. Please, Greene, the tub up at the house isn't working. Gladys says it's something to do with the faucet, so she sent me over here."

And he couldn't take a shower, why? It wasn't like Gladys didn't have several completely functioning showers in the main house.

Todd smiled widely and persisted. "Come on, please Greene."

I tried to keep the irritation out of my voice but failed. What was he even doing up so early?

"Fine," I said. "But leave that soap outside. The smell is just too much for me. A boy in my middle school history class used to drench himself with hair gel that smelled just like that. I couldn't shake the smell for days."

When he raised his hands in surrender and dropped the soap onto my doorstep, I said, "And don't use all the hot water like you did the last time."

He shrugged and said, "Who, me?" Then he sauntered through my living room and made a turn into the bathroom, leaving the side door open. I noticed that Oscar, the feral cat, was sitting at the entrance like a watchdog waiting for his human to return. I bent down and managed to touch the top of Oscar's head before he turned and scurried over to the hydrangea bush next to my place. I went inside and shut the door.

As I climbed back up to the loft to get dressed, I tried to ignore Todd, who seemed to be missing the situational awareness gene as he belted out an Elvis Presley ballad from my bathroom. "Wise men say, only fools rush in, oh, but I can't help falling in love with you."

His voice wasn't half bad, but I was not in the frame of mind for a sing-along in my home. I settled in at the butcher block island with a stiff cup of coffee—extra cream, no sugar, and a sprinkle of cinnamon on top. As I sipped, I scrolled through the emails on my laptop, catching up on the daily national news briefing and checking for any work-related emails. The only message was a general press release announcement from the major crime unit saying they would hold another press conference tomorrow about the investigation into Roy's murder. They always seemed to schedule them on a Friday afternoon, which seemed too convenient to be a coincidence since it meant there was no one at their headquarters to answer any follow-up questions that arose after the news broke.

I drained my first cup of coffee and poured a second, starting to feel annoyed about Todd's leisurely bath. His Elvis impersonations continued as he belted out, "I'm just a hunk, a hunk of burning love; Just a hunk, a hunk of burning love," and I debated knocking loudly on the door and telling him to hush up and hurry up, the way we'd handled bad roommates in college. But before I could move toward the door, he strolled out, bare chested with his towel wrapped around his waist. Even from my spot across the room I could smell my lavender bath salts. Gah, I hoped he hadn't used all of them. They'd been pricey and I was trying to make them last.

"Hey, Greene, I'd love a cup of coffee," he said, as if he belonged in my kitchen. Seriously, I was not running a bed-and-breakfast. I was prepared to tell him exactly that when I heard a rap at the door, looked over, and saw Richie peering in. His face dropped when he saw Todd, then turned as stormy as a nor'easter blowing in from the Atlantic.

Todd actually strolled over and opened the door.

"Hey, man," Todd said, clearly oblivious to how this looked. He was such a buffoon sometimes. Richie did not respond and turned to leave.

I followed him out and called, "Wait up, please."

He stopped so short I almost ran into him. Then he turned to me and said, "You know, I'm not stupid, Piper, I've been seeing this for weeks."

I put my hands on his shoulders. "Rich, it's really not how it looks. Really! He was just using the tub because the one in the main house is broken. Gladys sent him over. I swear."

I silently cursed myself for not just sending Todd away. Richie was as mad as I'd ever seen him. "Whatever you say," he said. As he turned away, he added, "I know you resent me trying to keep you safe, and here he is offering this adventurous Indiana Jones spiel. I can't compete with that."

Tears started to well up in my eyes as he went on. "Piper, let's just cool things off while you think about what you really want."

He stalked over to his unmarked cruiser and left without another word or look back. I took a breath and wiped my eyes. Despite my best efforts to take things slowly, I'd started to want Richie around for more than just the inside scoop.

When I went back inside, I felt like I could have killed Todd, who had done nothing to help the situation. Instead, he had actually made himself comfortable at the island and was pouring himself a mug of coffee. Good grief, this was why I had sworn off men when I moved back to Exeter. Hopefully I could talk to Richie when he'd had time to calm down. I would need to help him see the real story: Todd was just like an unruly brother who was fun to have as a wingman on stories, but that was it.

Before I could tell Todd just how I felt about his clueless behavior, my phone pinged with an incoming text. It was Hap. A delivery truck was stuck under the narrow railroad bridge on Newfields Road, and he wanted me to go take a picture. This was a regular occurrence at the bridge, despite the multiple signs on either side that warned of its low height. There were always a few drivers who were sure they could just squeeze through. Some found themselves wedged under the bridge while others stopped just in time but then had to do what seemed like a 100-point turn to get back up the hill to the highway.

I made quick work of brushing my teeth and pulling my

hair back so I could get out to the scene. To my enormous relief, Todd was gone when I came out of the bathroom. I grabbed the car keys and headed toward the bridge.

When I arrived, the locals on the stretch of road beside the bridge were standing around watching the show. One had even pulled out a video camera as the excitement unfolded. No doubt they thought their camerawork would end up on the six o'clock news—and if the day's events were slow enough, they'd probably be right.

I parked at the driveway for the town's public works department, near the giant red salt shed, and got out to snap some photos while the truck was still stuck. Not only was it a big box truck, but it was fully wedged underneath. I could see the logo, which said *Hattie's Real English Crumpets.*

"Hey, you think we'll get some tea and crumpets today?" I said to one of the firefighters.

He laughed. "You never know. But they might be pressed like a panini by the time we see them."

A police officer was standing by a cruiser with the lights on, turning cars around before they got too close. Nearby, a giant tow truck, the kind they used for tractor trailer accidents on the highway, was hooking up a giant winch to pull the truck out.

"You'd think people would learn by now," I commented to the firefighter.

He shook his head. "It's just job security for the tow truck company." Then he laughed and said, "And us."

He wasn't wrong. As I watched the winch being tightened, I realized that the roof of the van was peeling off like the top of a tin can of tuna. I snapped photos as this happened, trying to keep my reaction neutral despite the ridiculous scene

I was observing. Eventually, the truck was pulled out and I did a few quick interviews for a story, deciding it was time to raise awareness of this ongoing bridge trap, rather than to just report on the accident.

TEA, BUT NO CRUMPETS, AFTER BRIDGE MISHAP

By Piper Greene

EXETER__*For the third time this month, a truck became lodged under the narrow railroad bridge on Newfields Road.*

The Hattie's Real English Crumpets truck driver said he thought he could skip the highway and get to his next delivery stop sooner with the shortcut. "As you can see, that didn't work out for me," he said. "It's only my second week on the job and now this. I just can't catch a break."

Safety officials say this is a good reminder for drivers to stay aware of road signs and their surroundings when driving through town. "There are signs on both sides of this bridge, clearly marked and painted yellow to give drivers fair warning of the low height," the town's fire chief, George Schreiber, said. "But for some reason, everyone thinks they can squeeze through."

I filed the story and decided to head back to my carriage house to get a shower and change before the rest of my day.

Gladys called just as I was headed out the back door to the parking lot. She said, "Oh, Piper, dear, could you make a stop at the fish pickup? I got word that our halibut has arrived. All you have to do is drive up, give my name to the man with a cooler, and take the bag he gives you. Simple as that."

To me, the "fish pickup" sounded more than a bit nefarious, like something out of an old-school gangster movie. I was intrigued as I headed back out toward Newfields Road in Walter the Wagon. Would I meet someone named Bugsy, get some intel, or maybe find some cash in the bag with my fish? I could only hope.

CHAPTER 26

I piloted Walter out of downtown and made a right turn down a long, narrow gravel driveway just before the railroad bridge. Talk about intrigue. Picking up fish had never been so thrilling. A large cedar-shingled house with a front-row view of the river sat at the end of the driveway. I'd heard that the neighbor across the street set up an ice-fishing shack in front of this house in the winter to fish for the tiny smelts native to these waters. The scuttlebutt about town was that more than one late-night party had happened in that smelt shack.

Navigating Walter down the narrow driveway toward the pickup spot was tricky at best, especially when I met a car trying to exit without enough space to pass. The other driver backed up and pulled to the side so I could get past. I was going to chalk this up as one of the "most New England" experiences ever. I parked and walked over to the opened garage, where a wiry old man with a white beard, who I recognized as an occasional house painter, sat with a clipboard and a cooler.

"Piper, right," he said.

I nodded and gave him Gladys's name on the order. He leaned down, opened the cooler, and said, "Looks like she has one pound each of halibut and scallops this time."

I agreed, not because I knew that was correct but because I had no idea what she had ordered other than the halibut she'd told me about during our short phone call. The man opened a plastic bag, pulled out some smaller bags inside, and handed them to me.

"Thanks," I said.

With the fish sorted out, he moved on to other more pressing topics. "You've been covering the whole business with Roy Carmichael, right?"

I nodded, and he smiled the way people do before they're about to share a juicy piece of gossip. He went on. "Well, I hear a lot here as you might imagine."

No lie—there was something about this whole experience that just screamed nefarious happenings. It made me want to sign up to be a fish pickup helper like him. I could only imagine the stories I'd hear.

After a brief pause, he continued. "Well, the dentist who lives next to Tripp and Pansy Bolton just came for his order: two lobsters, no fish." It seemed curious that he felt the need to share the details of their order. "And boy, it sounds like the Boltons are on the outs. A big fight in the driveway last night."

Ooh, boy! I leaned in, eager for whatever was to come next. According to my new informant, the dentist heard Pansy shouting about how much money Tripp had lost through poker games, and Tripp had fired back, pointing to the price Pansy had paid to import her latest hybrid rose strain and her white Mercedes gas-guzzler, not to mention what she had spent stocking their prized wine cellar.

"They went to France a few years ago to tour the vineyards there," the fish guy told me, rolling his eyes. "Personally, I can't tell the difference between a ten-dollar bottle of wine and a ten-thousand-dollar bottle of wine, but I guess it's their thing."

He paused again briefly and scratched the back of his neck. "Then Patsy kicked Tripp out. The dentist saw Tripp leave the house with a suitcase. Said that the next day he heard from a patient that Tripp's staying at the bed-and-breakfast downtown."

This was interesting, given Tripp's recent poker losses, because the boutique B&B catered to high-end visitors. Gladys and I had gone for brunch on their enclosed patio over the summer, and it had felt like we were in a private garden in Europe, complete with food styled with fresh flowers. Maybe Tripp had stashed some money under his mattress. In any case, it seemed like Tripp was making out okay. No Pansy and some plush accommodations.

"Well, thanks for that tip," I said. "I'll keep my eyes and ears open when I go to the historic district meeting tonight."

He gave me a little salute as I left and told me to keep up the good work.

I made a beeline for Gladys's purple Victorian, knowing the fish needed to get in the refrigerator sooner than later. Gladys was flitting about the kitchen in a dark-purple kimono with Frank Sinatra's "Fly Me to the Moon" crooning over on her Bluetooth speaker. I was relieved it wasn't the "Melodies of McTavish" CD that Duncan had been playing almost every time he was there. I could only take the lounge piano and his warbling baritone for so long, but even worse, he kept pushing for me to buy copies for all of my friends, offering a three percent bulk discount for orders of twelve or more.

I set the bag down on the new white marble counter she'd

had installed last winter.

"Oh, Piper, dear, thank you," she said. "This was caught fresh off the coast, out past the Isles of Shoals, they said. I do love the selection the fish pickup has at this time of the year."

That was a huge plus of living in the New Hampshire seacoast: the access to fresh seafood, direct from the fishermen— and in this case, fishermen's helpers who had gossip.

"No problem," I said. "It was definitely worth it. I heard an interesting story about Tripp and Pansy when I was there."

She clasped her hands together almost gleefully. We could repent later, but nearly all of us in town got a little buzz at the prospect of something, or someone, putting Pansy in her place.

Her eyes lit up, and she said, "Oh, do tell."

I filled her in on the fight and Tripp's temporary lodging at the bed-and-breakfast downtown.

She raised her eyebrows when I got to the part about the gambling debt. Then, at the end of my news, she said, "That bed-and-breakfast is such a lovely spot, you know. Maybe Duncan and I will go over for brunch this weekend to help you with your investigation and all." "Keep me posted," I said. "I've got to cover the Historic District Commission meeting tonight, so I need to go home and get ready. Apparently, Fiona is coming to the meeting with a new plan for the lot, but no one knows what it is yet."

Gladys looked surprised, and to be honest, I felt that way too. The police crime scene tape had only been down for a few weeks, but perhaps Fiona wanted to set the townspeople at ease with news that the tacky arcade was as dead as her brother.

I ate a handful of Jenny's maple vanilla granola, then

grabbed my laptop bag and headed toward the town offices, housed in an old brick building across from the town hall, where the official business of the town took place. I climbed the massive granite steps out front, holding onto the black wrought-iron railing as I did so to steady myself. I glanced over at the B&B next door—once the home of a jeweler in the early 1900s—and wondered if Tripp was indeed over there now.

Once inside, I set up shop before the meeting, taking my laptop out and situating myself close enough to an electrical outlet that I could charge up again if things dragged out too long—which often tended to be the case. Covering town meetings was a necessary part of being a local reporter, but the regulars were known to rehash the same points over and over without making any progress. It could feel like a trip to the dentist to get your teeth pulled out one by one. God, I missed having an intern to handle these duties. Hap's nephew Jimmy had covered many of the meetings during his time with us, but if his winter internship at the *Hartford Courant* worked out, I suspected that he'd probably stay there next summer instead. Maybe I could talk him into changing his mind if he stopped by during Thanksgiving break.

Fiona and my brother, Chester, took seats over on one side of the room. Some of the abutting property owners, whose opinion on any plan would be considered, sat opposite them. Chester acknowledged me with a nod but didn't look thrilled to see me there. What did he expect? This was the biggest news in Exeter right now.

I fired up my laptop and waited. Tripp walked in, looking like he always did: gray suit coat, burgundy tie, expensive Italian leather shoes, and no visible hint that he was on the outs with his wife. He banged his gavel and called the meeting to order, and I couldn't help but realize it was a new one. I hoped he'd gotten a stronger replacement than the one he'd smashed in half during that contentious meeting with Roy a few months prior.

"Ms. Carmichael, I understand you're here to provide an amended version of the plan we had before us. How would you like to proceed?"

Fiona stood, impressive as always, and walked to the microphone. "I'm going to defer to my attorney, Chester Greene, to take you through the proposal and the waivers we are requesting."

Tripp nodded and Chester stood up, a thick manilla file in his hand, and moved toward the podium. He took his time walking over, opening the folder deliberately, and adjusting his glasses. For crying out loud, did he think he was Perry Mason? Then he finally leaned toward the microphone and began.

"I'm here to take you through a plan to once again have the Exeter Playhouse on this lot, to bring back one of the town's downtown jewels for future generations."

Whoa! I didn't see that coming. As he droned on, rolling out the plans and explaining Fiona's hope for the property, I couldn't help but think she had really benefited from her brother's murder. But was that an unanticipated side effect of his death or—I hated to ask—proper and poisonous preplanning? And how was she making these plans if Roy's lady love, Anastasia Rose, was still in the mix?

CHAPTER 27

The next morning, I popped my head into Gladys's kitchen, where I found her sipping kombucha and reading the *Boston Globe.*

"It's finally Friday," I announced with a smile, and she beckoned me toward a seat at the island. She stood and poured me a juice-sized portion of the kombucha she'd been buying from a natural food store downtown.

"Oh, Piper," she said, then shook her head sadly. "I'm really worried about dear Stanley at that place. When Tootie and I stopped by this week, we both felt that he's letting himself go. I haven't seen him out of those awful flannel pajamas in days, and they're not even properly maintaining his hair."

She got up and returned momentarily with a bag bearing the logo I recognized from an expensive gentlemen's shop a few towns over. She opened it and pulled the contents out with a flourish. "And so, I got him these," she said, holding up a burgundy bundle of fabric.

I wasn't awake enough to understand what these were. "You got him a robe?" I asked.

She shook her head. "No, no, it's a two-piece silk leisure

suit, but it's sold as sleepwear, for men like our dear Stanley who aren't content to lounge around like a toad. I hope it will give him a little lift."

I took a closer look at the burgundy ensemble, which was trimmed with gold, and had a vision of Hugh Heffner in the Playboy Mansion. Stanley might end up with a line of ladies at the rehab in those silky duds. If I heard the word *grotto*, I'd break him out of the place myself.

I finished my kombucha and kissed her goodbye, because I was eager to make a stop at the Morning Musket on the way into work. The meeting had indeed ended late, and then I'd stayed up even later to write a story about it on deadline. While Gladys's new fermented drink was healthy, I needed an infusion of caffeine if I was going to string together a sentence that day. Plus, Jenny had recently started serving a high-test coffee that was guaranteed to power rocket ships, something I could use this morning to power my fingers on the keyboard.

"Hey, you," I called out to her, as I slipped in the side door of the bakery to the kitchen.

She smiled at me. "Hey, yourself." She wiped her flour-covered hands on her apron and came over to give me a hug. She was rolling out her trademark soft pretzels, which she'd been supplying to some of the local microbreweries for the Octoberfest events that seemed to happen all month long these days. I didn't like beer, but I'd eat those pretzels for all three meals if I could. Thankfully, she'd been making them all month so I could get my fill.

Jenny went on. "Any word from Richie?"

I shook my head. "Radio silence."

She gave my arm a gentle squeeze. "Give him time; he's reasonable. I think once he's had a chance to cool down, he'll realize that Todd is just Todd and not anything romantic."

I hoped she was right, but I wasn't feeling super-optimistic. Richie hadn't answered my text messages, so in addition to my love life drying up, so was my inside line to the case. I tried to muster a smile for her just the same.

"Want to meet up tonight?" I asked her. "Drown our sorrows together."

She shook her head ever so slightly and blushed. "Actually, I have plans."

That sounded like more than just plans, and I couldn't help myself from prodding a bit.

"Like a date? Do tell."

She responded, "Well, it's something new on many levels, but it kind of feels right." She paused for a moment, then said, "I'm going over to Emily's place for dinner."

"Like dinner? Or *dinner, dinner*?" I asked.

She blushed. "Dinner dinner."

Oh my! I hadn't seen that one coming. "Wait, what? Are you serious? How did this happen?"

She was silent for a moment as if choosing her words thoughtfully. "Well, we've been spending a lot of time together for the Beer and Chili Fest, and it just sort of happened." She pushed one of her tight red curls behind her ear. "You know, I'm just going to see where it takes me. I know I've only dated guys before, but something about Emily just feels right."

Her face almost matched the shade of her hair at this point, and although I was tempted to engage in a little good-natured teasing about the blush, I held back. Jenny had a rough past in the romance department, especially after following her prior partner to France. A little romance might be just what she needed going into the holiday season, and I was glad she was open to dating Emily. Maybe she'd spill the whole story when we could find time to sit and talk.

"Well, have fun," I said. "I'll plan to see you both at the festival tomorrow."

She nodded enthusiastically. "I can't believe it's finally here."

It did seem like we'd had months of buildup to this event, and I only hoped it lived up to the hype. Come to think of it, I hadn't heard a lot of hype lately, and I briefly wondered what Becky Bean was doing for the last big publicity blitz. I'd heard a rumor that someone was going to be roaming the downtown in a chili bean mascot suit but had yet to confirm that. I was dying to know which unlucky person at the Chamber of Commerce had picked that short straw. And would there be an accompanying corn bread mascot? A giant tortilla chip or even a beer can?

Jenny returned to her pretzel prep, expertly rolling, and twisting the dough, and I made my way to the front of the bakery. I poured some of the high-test coffee and asked the young girl working at the counter for a piece of the apple breakfast strudel—technically a regular apple strudel, but I told myself it was for breakfast and not dessert to justify the choice. It was the same approach I used after Thanksgiving when I ate apple pie for breakfast for an entire week. It was technically fruit. I found a seat in the corner where I could eat and look at that day's hard copy of the *Exeter Independent*.

PROPERTY OWNER ANNOUNCES PLAN TO BRING PLAYHOUSE BACK

By Piper Greene

EXETER__*The owner of a vacant lot where her brother was only recently found murdered unveiled a new plan to restore the property to its former use.*

Fiona Carmichael, through her attorney Chester Greene, went before the town's Historic District Commission Thursday night with a new request. Her plan includes constructing an exact replica of the former Exeter Playhouse, destroyed decades ago by a suspicious fire, with the addition of an acting school and café. The commission stressed that siding and windows needed to be consistent with the nature of the historic district in town. "The plan is just the type of business we need in our historic downtown," she said after the meeting. "And I'm thrilled to be at a place where it's now possible to move forward with this exciting project."

Her late brother, Roy, was found dead under dubious circumstances on the lot earlier this month. He was previously the majority property owner and had been trying to bring Carmichael's Arcade in Arms, a Revolutionary War–themed arcade and funhouse, to the downtown. The plan had many locals up in arms, so much so that they planned a protest after hearing about the idea to have a replica of one of the town's founding fathers lit up in flashing red-white-and-blue neon at the entrance to downtown.

His sister said she decided to announce her plan so soon after his death to give the town something positive to focus on.

The HDC took the matter under advisement and will render a decision at their next meeting.

Police Chief Frank Sinclair said there is nothing new to release on the investigation into Roy Carmichael's murder. Any updates, he said, would come from the state police.

An abrasive voice interrupted my reading. "Well, haven't you stirred up a hornet's nest!" I looked up to see the Cranky Yankee walk into the bakery.

I smiled up at her. "I'm not sure what you mean, Ms. Smith," I replied, even though I knew full well she was referring to Tripp and Pansy, who was one of her closest friends.

She sniffed with disapproval. "Well, you and that little historical lady butting your noses in about Tripp like that. It's caused a lot of problems—more than you know."

I knew that Tripp had moved down to the bed-and-breakfast after his row with Pansy, but was Myrna hinting at something else? I also knew Winnie had finally gone to the police to give Tripp an alibi, because she was still mourning the loss of extra income for her trip. However, I knew not to get into that with Myrna, so I simply responded, "Just trying to keep him out of jail, which doesn't sound like a bad thing."

She harrumphed and stomped over to the counter, where she put in her order. Dry toast and black coffee. To be fair, I'd be cranky too if I ate that day after day for breakfast.

I flipped back to the paper and was taking in Todd's story on a local group of women organizing a yarn bombing of trees for charity when, speak of the devil, he walked in. He looked more animated than normal, especially given the early hour.

"Hey, Greene," he said. "The food TV people are here. They want to meet at our office in ten minutes. Come with me?"

I hadn't forgiven him for his oblivious behavior during the bathtub incident, but I couldn't resist the excitement of saying hello to the TV people. I had a lot of work to complete, but maybe I could shift my schedule.

"Sure," I said. "Let me clear my table and I'll be right there."

I dusted off the crumbs from my strudel and hopped up. I could only hope that as the beer flowed at the festival the next day, some information might also unfold and reveal some crumbs that could lead me to the killer.

CHAPTER 28

When I walked into the office behind Todd, Clara inclined her head toward the newsroom and gave me the same "lunatics on board" look she had favored in the past whenever the paper's last features writer, Sheila, had returned from her alien abduction support group. Given Clara's raised eyebrows, I suspected I would hear her opinions about the television crew as soon as they departed. Clara loved to share her reviews of people who passed through our doors, and they were often comical due to her sarcastic and no-nonsense demeanor.

Todd bounded ahead to greet the men I assumed were the television crew, one of whom called out, "Tisden! About time!"

Todd slapped a burly guy holding a camera bag on the back and said, "Man, I haven't seen you since that time at Gloucester. When was that, twenty years ago? Back when the crew was there to film for that movie with Clooney, right?"

Clara leaned toward me and whispered, "Quite the crew. If you ask me, they're got more than cameras in that bag, if you know what I mean."

I must have looked confused, because she said, "

"Well, the big guy, he's wearing that pachouli stuff, and you know about those people, right? Hippies, smoking the wacky tobaccy, and God knows what else!"

I nodded briefly and moved toward my desk. She did enjoy her conjectures.

Todd called out then, "Greene, come meet the guys."

He sounded like we were at a party and not in the newsroom, where I had a pile of work to get through that morning. First, I had to get through the annual Halloween coloring contest, the finals of which would be published in the next autumn special section before Thanksgiving. After that, I had my daily check-ins with the state police about the status of the investigation.

I deposited my bag and coffee on my desk and walked over to the group. Todd did the round of introductions. "Howie does the camera work, Patrick here produces, and Jason is the on-air talent."

The three gave me an enthusiastic wave as Todd went on, clearly eager to relive his glory days on the North Shore of Massachusetts.

"Yeah, Howie and I worked together way back when I covered Rockport. He was a local camera guy who got lucky when the film crew came in after that book about the fishing boat that went down during the hurricane of ninety-two," Todd continued. "So now he's making the big bucks."

Howie shrugged it off. "Hey, it pays the bills, I get to travel, and usually I get to avoid hooligans like you. Just kidding, man. It's good to see you again."

I piped up and asked, "So, are you all going down to do some preliminary shooting and interviews during the setup?" They nodded, and I said, pointedly, "I'd love to be there, but I need to make a dent in my desk or I'll be here all night."

I excused myself from the group as they moved back toward the front door, and then I settled in to get to work. My phone rang as soon as I sat down. The call was coming in on the direct line, which meant it was someone who had my number.

"*Exeter Independent,* this is Piper."

A man's voice that I knew—and barely tolerated—greeted me on the other end.

"Piper," he began. My brother Chester. "Fiona asked me to follow up with you about that historic commission meeting."

I couldn't imagine what he had found fault with within my story; after all, it had essentially been a straight reporting of the meeting, just the facts.

"Okay," I responded. "Is there something new to report?"

He cleared his throat. "She just wants to be sure we're all on the same page, that her new plan is a positive for the town. We're concerned that too much of this meddling and rehashing could become a stain on an otherwise promising project."

God, there we went again. I was finding small-town news to be a balancing act between reporting the news and gently, sometimes firmly, reminding those we wrote about that while my colleagues and I also lived in town, the news did need to be reported—even when it wasn't favorable. But son of a monkey, what was he thinking? In this case, we were covering a building plan *on a lot where someone had been murdered.* It had to be mentioned.

"You know, we both have a job to do here," I said. "And everything that happened the other night was on the public record."

He replied, "Yes, I know how this works, but I find myself

in a tricky spot." He stopped for a minute as if deciding what to reveal. "Our family firm has represented the Carmichaels for decades—going back to the fire, actually—and that means something in Exeter, even if you chose not to join the firm."

Again, with the digs. Piper the lone Greene not to become a lawyer.

"I hear you," I said. "But this murder and that lot are big news, probably the biggest news in years."

Well, aside from the murder of my former editor, Charlotte, over the summer, which had shocked everyone in town. But this story had deep roots in Exeter, and people were committed to it.

Chester went on. "There are things—some things I can't tell you because of confidentiality—that would make you look at this entirely differently."

That sounded like he knew something juicy. "Like about Roy's hot showgirl lady?" I prodded.

His voice was terse when he answered. "She won't be an issue for long," he said. "But I can't say anything more than that. I would remind you that you're a Greene and despite how you've behaved since you moved back, that is important."

I held back from telling him what I really thought out loud. Instead, I gave him a noncommittal response and created an excuse to hang up. I made a mental note to check the probate court filings where I might find more clues about Roy's beneficiary, especially given Chester's cryptic comment about how she wouldn't be an issue for long.

As I returned to viewing the coloring contest entries, I had to take a deep breath and remind myself that Chester was always like this. I knew how he behaved, how he poked me to get a reaction, and I needed to let my annoyance float off like the steam on a cup of cocoa.

Perhaps emboldened by Chester's reminder of my own decision to stand apart from the Greene pack and not become a lawyer, I chose the pumpkin that was colored purple and red, the only entry not orange, to celebrate the independent streak in the young artist. Then I opened my email, responded to a few invitations to cover new business openings, and got the "nothing new to report" from the state police major crimes people.

I said goodbye to Clara and headed toward the setup for the Beer and Chili fest, just a short walk over to Swasey Parkway. The riverfront parkway was considered by many the jewel of the downtown, and it was a popular place for people to walk along the Squamscott River. The road was blocked off with heavy orange barriers put in place by the Public Works Department to stop vehicles from entering. Volunteers who wanted a free ticket for tomorrow's event were doing their share of manual labor for their entry, pounding in wooden stakes and stringing up a plastic snow fence—also bright orange—to set a perimeter for the festival. At first glance this seemed like overkill, but I knew the fence made it easier for the organizers to ensure that everyone who entered had a ticket and an ID. Back when Richie was actually still speaking with me, he had mentioned that the police had also recommended the fence to keep any of the overzealous teenagers from getting in for a sip of the beers.

I waved to Tom Stone from the chamber of commerce, who was holding a mallet in one hand and tapping the top of a wooden stake with gusto. He had on jeans, a red plaid shirt, and Timberland hiking boots, a popular local footwear choice given the proximity of their headquarters one town over from Exeter.

Becky Bean was standing to the side of the crowd, her phone pressed up against her ear, and I wondered if she was relieved to finally be at the finish line for the event she had been promoting for months. As I approached, she slid her phone into the front pocket of her skinny jeans. She looked tired, with circles under her eyes, and her long hair, which was normally perfectly coiffed, was scrunched up in a messy ponytail. Either something was bothering her, or her regular Pilates classes hadn't been enough to maintain her stamina for this last-minute push.

"Hey, Becky," I said. "Big day tomorrow. I can't believe it's finally here."

"Yeah," she said, but her voice lacked enthusiasm.

"You okay?" I asked.

Her face crumpled briefly, but she quickly regained her composure. "Yes, fine, just a lot on my mind lately."

I saw an opening and plowed in, one of those moments where I blurted a question without thinking. "Because of Roy, right?"

She looked startled and, I daresay, a little fearful. "What do you mean?"

I lowered my voice. "Between us, I heard you were pretty friendly, if you know what I mean."

Her eyes widened in fright, like an animal in headlights, so I softened my voice and added, "I'm sorry. I know it must be hard."

She shook her head and started to back away from me. "I don't know how you learned about that. But, seriously, I can't do this right now."

Before I could respond, she turned and stomped off, leaving

me there with my mouth open. Even though she hadn't said much, I came away feeling like she'd confirmed her connection to Roy. But if that was the case, then why weren't the police talking to her? Or were they?

CHAPTER 29

The next morning, I briefly stepped outside but immediately returned to my closet to grab a fleece jacket. Though the sun was out, it was clearly going to be one of those typical mid-fall days that started with me wearing gloves and a jacket and ended up mild enough by afternoon for me to ditch the layers. My plan was to get to the Beer and Chili Fest early enough to take in all the excitement and to cheer on Jenny and Emily with their entry. I also was hoping for some clues about how their date had gone.

Before I hopped into Walter, I popped through the back-door of the Victorian to say good morning to Gladys. I knew that with her love of craft cocktails, she would not be heading downtown.

"Gladys," I called out.

Her muffled response sounded exasperated. "In here. Save me!"

Not sure if I should panic or not, I quickly followed the sound of music usually reserved for spas and dentist offices until I found her in the sunroom. She had on a pair of purple leggings with fluffy black socks that might have doubled as vintage 1980s leg warmers, and she appeared to be doing a tai chi exercise tape on her TV.

"Oh, Piper, thank God you stopped by. I know this is supposed to be good for you, but it's dreadfully boring. I don't know how I could do the whole class," she said. She held up a remote and paused the DVD she'd been watching. "They've got Stanley doing it at the rehab and I thought I'd give it a try—moral support and all."

I was relieved to know she was not only okay but also thinking of him. I asked, "Is he still coming home next week?"

Clearly done with the tai chi experiment, she sat down at the round table and poured herself a cup of tea from the teapot. She held the pot up to me with a questioning expression, and I shook my head no.

She replied, "That's the plan. Poor thing. He's got to be able to manage basic tasks before he can move back to his spot at the senior housing, and he's just barely there."

I decided to steer away from following up with any question about where Duncan was that day. I was still hoping it was time for him to move on so things could return to the way they had been before he had turned up.

"Well," I said, "I'm off to the big festival. I'll have a beer for you."

Gladys winced. "Oh, Piper," she said, "I know it's all the rage with the craft beers and all, but really, beer is just so ordinary, if you ask me—and don't get me started on those men who belch when they drink it. Dreadful, isn't it?"

Clearly, she also would not be attending the Beer and History event the next week at the museum downtown. Martinis and mussels were more her speed. I gave her a little hug and headed back out the way I'd come in, pausing to step over

Oscar, who had found a patch in the sun on the front walkway and was soaking up some vitamin D.

At times like this I was glad I could walk downtown and not have to deal with parking. While Exeter's downtown was quaint and charming, it was also not designed to hold the number of cars that would flow into town for the festival. I knew that overflow parking had been set up at an old car dealership on the outskirts of town, with a trolley to shuttle people to the event. Ahead of me, people were pulling little red wagons filled with camp chairs, blankets, and extra jackets. The closer I got to the entrance to Swasey Parkway, the more the crowd gained momentum. Jeans, hiking shoes, fleece vests, and sunglasses were the uniform of the day.

A group of volunteers for a local children's fund were set up at the entrance to the parkway, where they were promoting yet another charity duck race—Exeter's favorite fundraiser— for later in the day. I was not surprised to see that after the disastrous race at the last festival, where Pansy Bolton went tumbling into the river, today's competition was going to be a dry land race.

One of the women in the group flagged me down, and I called out to her, "What's with the switch? You don't want to take a refreshing dip in the old Squamscott River?"

She let out a cackle. "Ha, not after the last episode." She gestured to three people in full yellow duck mascot suits, and one of them waved at us.

"We'll have the running of the ducks later, about the time the people at the festival have had enough beer to think it's entertaining and open their wallets for a good cause."

Smart call, I thought. It's why silent auctions always did better when there was food and drink involved. She explained that the three mascots would race around a short course, and the winning duck would pull a name from the box of raffle tickets to be the winner. I could hardly stand the suspense. Just for fun, I bought a ticket and wrote Gladys's name on it.

With my ticket deposited into the box, I waved goodbye and headed toward the festival. Even though I knew the gate-keepers, I still showed my press pass to them, and then I entered the main area, jumping to the side when I heard a loud beeping sound behind me.

"Look out! Coming through! Beep beep!"

I jumped again and Todd barreled past me on a golf cart. I should have known; only Todd would actually yell, "Beep beep!"

"How on earth did you score that?" I asked, when he quickly came to a stop a few feet in front of me.

He shrugged. "Just my boyish good looks," he said. Then he added, more seriously, "I'm helping the TV crew shuttle gear into the festival. Want a lift?"

Never one to miss a spontaneous golf cart adventure, I hopped onto the seat next to him and held onto the railing. I grabbed the "o bleep" handle on the side as he careened down the middle of the road, dodging people like obstacles in a pin-ball machine.

As we whizzed by, I could see that the camera people were set up by the pavilion at the center of the park. The on-air talent guy, Jason, was standing by a mirror adjusting his sleek black hair. Tom Stone was just beaming next to the crew, clearly thrilled our town was in the spotlight. People had already gotten in line for the beer and chili samples. The regulars knew which restaurants they wanted to try and got to those booths before they ran out.

"Hey," I said to Todd, "where's Becky?"

He shrugged. "I don't know; I've been having too much fun driving this around. I mean, I love Scarlett and all, but this is a whole other type of fun." He stopped, then readdressed my initial question. "She's around somewhere. This is her baby, after all."

He was right; I was sure she was there. The crowd was huge, and she was no doubt in the middle of it somewhere basking in the satisfaction of reaching the actual event. Todd stopped the mad golf cart just long enough for me to jump off, and though logically I sensed I could run faster than the cart, I still felt lucky to have survived.

I scanned the booths, eager to see how Jenny and Emily were progressing. I spotted them on the corner in one of a line of E-Z Up tents. Theirs had a Tuck Tavern logo on the top, and I headed their way.

"Hey, ladies," I said, sidling up to the booth from the rear to cut the line. "How hot is your chili?"

Jenny tilted her head and made a face. "How hot do you like it?" She laughed and added, "So far, so good."

Emily placed a hand on Jenny's arm and added, "The addition of the hot honey to Jenny's magical corn bread really bumped us up a notch. I think this will become a regular menu special for the fall at the tavern."

Given Emily's gesture and their good moods, I assumed their date had gone well, but I was dying to hear the details when Jenny and I were alone. Though I loved them both, I'd never seen their relationship coming.

Jenny smiled at us and said, "I think we have a shot in the People's Choice award, but who knows with the judges they have this year."

The judges' tent was off to the side of the food tents, and I knew calling them *judges* was a bit of a loose interpretation of the word. The panel usually consisted of volunteers from various roles in town who got roped in for the duty. The fire chief usually sat in, supporting that stereotype about the five-alarm chili at the firehouse, along with the town manager and one of the local business owners.

Emily handed me a small sample of their chipotle chili with sweet potatoes, and I took a small taste, letting the flavors show themselves. Just the right mix of spicy and sweet, with a pleasing texture from Jenny's topper.

"Oh, my goodness, you two! This is amazing!" I said. "Wow, that honey has a kick."

Jenny winked at me. "Oh, does it ever."

An airhorn pierced the air, and people quickly looked around in shock, as if confusing it with the nuclear power plant alarm. Instead, it was one of the festival's organizers trying to get the attention of the crowd. A crackling sound came over the PA system from the pavilion, where Tom Stone stood before a microphone.

"I'd like to welcome you to the annual Beer and Chili Festival and welcome our guests from the *America's Festivals* show. It's such a great way to showcase all our little town has to offer, and now I'm going to turn it over to Becky Bean, the promoter of this year's festival, to say a few words."

Tom stepped back and looked around the crowd, as did the others with him on the stage, but Becky did not appear. After a few minutes, people returned to eating and drinking, and Tom picked up the microphone again.

"She must have gotten tied up. Enjoy the beer and chili, and we'll get back to you soon."

Becky's absence seemed off. I did another scan of the park. There was no sign of Becky, her shiny black boots, or her trademark good hair. I had a growing feeling of anxiety I couldn't shake. First, she'd admitted to having some type of contact with Roy, and now she wasn't at the big event she had been organizing for the past three months. You didn't have to be a detective to know that something was amiss.

CHAPTER 30

After months of buildup, it seemed like the town didn't know what to do once the Beer and Chili Fest was over. Jenny and Emily had taken home the People's Choice award, while the Terrace had garnered the judges' top marks. Todd, who had been savoring his role as official chili cook-off correspondent, began working on a follow-up feature story on the event. Halloween was still two weeks away, and without much breaking news in town, I was really looking forward to his zombie performance in *Thriller*. He'd taken an old pair of jeans, which were ripped, and rubbed them into the dirt in the backyard to give them an authentic zombie-from-the-underworld feel. It was rather inventive. I half expected to find him sleeping in the garden out back to really get the sense of being a corpse.

With nothing new in the murder investigation, I was relegated to much more mundane reporting: a roving troubadour who was creating quite a stir in the downtown area not only because he'd been busking without a permit, a requirement, but even more so because he only played one song, "Hurt" by Johnny Cash, which most people found extremely depressing. "I know, I know, it's not sexy," Hap told me, as I set out to find the busker. "But people are curious about him, and our job as a community paper is to report what happens in town, big or small."

He was right, of course, and honestly, I was curious about why one person could possibly play such a sad song so many times, so I set out to find him. He'd been spotted recently outside the other coffee shop downtown and near the boathouse for the prep school, so I started on that block. Guess he stuck to a routine, because there he was by a bench at the entrance to Swasey Parkway, strumming away. He was playing and singing at full volume—and getting looks of both annoyance and pity from passersby. I strode up to him.

"Hey," I said, "I'm Piper. I work at the paper here. How's it going?"

He had on a faded pair of Levi's, dusty brown cowboy boots, and a blue plaid shirt. There was a certain Hank Williams quality about him, and his brown beard really needed a trim. He looked at me and replied, "I can't complain. I'm spreading the word, you know."

Too bad no one else thought his word was that good.

"So," I said, one of those times where I had to really focus on my delivery. "People are super curious about you and your music. Would you be willing to be interviewed for a short story?"

I knew a lot of people found it exciting to be in the local paper, but I wasn't so sure how this guy would react. He stopped playing for a minute, and I felt it could go either way.

"What the heck, sure," he finally said. He stuck out his hand. "I'm Clancy."

He then proceeded to tell me his tale. He had arrived in Exeter via a roundabout walkabout of sorts. "My girlfriend left me for the drummer in our band when we were on tour in Texas. So, I went on to Tennessee and all the way to Maine, and you know, these lyrics, they just spoke to me," he said.

That was one way to put it. He went on. "When I got here to this town, it was just so nice, I decided the universe was telling me to put down roots."

"What about a permit?" I asked.

He said, "I didn't know I needed one. I was just out expressing myself. However, I'm working on getting one. The police chief's a pretty decent dude. Have you met him?"

I nodded. Had I ever.

"Want to hear my song?" he said. When I nodded again, he began strumming what I could only describe as the type of song lyrics that made people jump off the nearest bridge. He crooned about hurting himself, to see if he could still feel, and how the pain was the only thing that was real. God, it was awful. I tried not to cringe, but I knew I needed to get some more details to show compassion for the poor guy.

"Sounds like it was a rough breakup," I said.

He stopped and nodded somberly. "The worst thing is, she took my lucky belt buckle when she left," he said. I worried he might shed a tear. "I wore it at all of my shows, and without it, I just don't know how to find my groove, you know."

I nodded a third time, while trying to think of something sympathetic to say in response. All I could think of was how hard it was going to be to get those lyrics out of my head. But considering how much I missed Richie, I had to feel for the guy.

"I'm glad you have an outlet," I told him. Then I couldn't stop myself from adding, "Maybe mix up the songs a little, you know?"

The suggestion looked like a surprise to him, and I decided it was time to make an exit.

"Well, thanks, Clancy," I said. "It's been real. You'll be in the Friday paper if you want to get a copy."

He waved to me and began walking down the parkway, strumming as he went. He'd moved on to lyrics about a crown of thorns, broken thoughts, and how life was beyond repair. The poor guy. I hoped he was okay. Honestly, the song itself would make anyone depressed. Maybe he should just search for a duplicate belt buckle on eBay and move on.

I couldn't get back the office fast enough, and I immediately turned on the radio station that started playing Christmas music before Halloween and took five. "Holly Jolly Christmas" was the only antidote at that point.

Later on, with Clancy's voice finally out of my head, I put in a call to the town offices to get a quote about the rules for busking. Then I wrote up a quick story, which I finished just as Todd came walking in. He looked frustrated, which was saying a lot for him.

"What's wrong?" I asked him.

He grumbled and said, "Man, I can't finish my story because I can't get Becky to call me back."

Huh. She wasn't at the Beer and Chili Fest and now wasn't returning Todd's calls. My internal radar was squealing like a police siren on the way to an emergency.

Todd continued, "So, I went over to her place, and she's not there either." He stopped to push his shaggy blonde hair back from his forehead. "It kind of feels like she skipped town or something."

I had to admit, it did sound that way, but it really didn't make sense. Maybe the shock of Roy's death had finally hit her and she needed to take a break for a few days—but during the event she'd spent months promoting? That really didn't add up.

I still hadn't heard from Richie, who was holding firm on his break, but in light of the situation I decided to give him a ring. Becky's disappearance seemed like something we needed to follow up on, and I dialed his direct line at the station.

"Detective Collins, can I help you?"

I hadn't heard his voice in a while and felt more nervous than I had expected.

"Hey," I said. "I heard something you should know about."

There was a long pause. Then he said, in his most professional tone, "Go ahead." It was almost sterile, not the teasing or fun voice I was used to hearing on the other end of the line. Ouch.

"Well," I went on, "Becky Bean has ghosted. She wasn't at the chili fest and now she's not at her house." At that point, I decided to lay it all out for him. "And she basically confirmed to me that she'd had a fling with Roy before he died, and something just doesn't feel right."

He cleared his throat. "Okay, well, thanks for the call. I'll pass it along. I've got another call coming in."

And with that, he signed off without any term of endearment or promise to let me know how it panned out. Not even a thank-you for giving him what I thought was a big tip. I sat for a minute taking in the reality of the split.

As Todd wheeled his chair to my desk, I quashed down the feeling of irritation I felt toward him for his role in the mess.

"Anything?" he asked.

I shook my head. "No, he's still shutting me out."

We sat for a minute in silence before he wheeled back to his desk, and I pondered what I knew about Becky. Aside from the promotional materials she had shared at the start of the project, I didn't really know much about her past career. Todd had been the one following the Beer and Chili Fest, and honestly, it seemed he'd taken everything at face—or chest—level.

I opened the search browser on my work computer and started looking for anything I could find about Becky. I revisited her slick, expensive-looking website, which I'd already glanced at when she first came to town. This time, I slowed down and read through it carefully. I scrolled through the section that featured past jobs and wrote a list on a pad of paper. Then I returned to the search engine and started looking up the other events with her name, one by one. Most were big charity events, the kind that popped up with a link to the same-old, same-old, society page-type of black-tie photo spread.

Then I tried a general search using only her name and the word *event*. One result brought me to page 6 of the *New York Post*, which contained a story that suggested she had abruptly quit her work on a major celebrity chef event. When contacted by the reporter, Becky had refused to comment. It was just about six months before she had arrived in Exeter. Now, I knew I could find a conspiracy in the dairy aisle at the supermarket, and it was true that the *New York Post* also featured stories about Bigfoot, but I still had a funny feeling about this. I decided to put in a call to the organizers to see what I could learn. Sure, maybe Becky had simply found that the job had not been a good fit, but I had a niggling thought that was getting louder by the second. Was it possible that she had come to Exeter to get away from something—or someone?

CHAPTER 31

I settled into the Morning Musket the next day with Jenny's latest pastry creation before me: canelés cake, which she'd decided to try out in advance of the holiday season. Now, I knew this was technically a dessert and not breakfast, but, hey, what are best friends who serve as taste testers for if not to break rules? The rum-and-vanilla-flavored delicacy had a perfectly caramelized crust.

"Oh, Jenny," I called over to her, "I think I'm in love."

I was so caught up in the little cake that I momentarily forgot that day's *Exeter Independent*, laid out in front of me with Todd's story about the Beer and Chili Fest front and center. We'd gone to press without a comment from Becky, the only option we'd had as deadline loomed. I scanned the other stories, which were all things I knew about because Todd and I had written them, but there was still something about seeing them in print, laid out with photos, that was both satisfying and thrilling. Unlike authors of books, who often waited years to see their names in print, being a newspaper reporter gave me and my colleagues a certain level of instant gratification that could be addictive in terms of seeing our work published.

"I'm glad you're here," a voice called out. Winnie was slowly walking toward me, carefully holding her cup of tea in one hand and a colossal caramel-drizzled croissant in the other.

"That looks tasty," I commented.

"It's caramel and apple," she responded. "Of course, I knew Jenny just visited the orchard over off Pickpocket Road, so it's as fresh and local as it gets."

I gestured to the empty chair at my table. "Join me," I said.

She settled in, arranging her treat in front of her. "I'd love to, because I have some news for you." She winked and continued, "I was at the women's walking club today."

Ooh, I did love those ladies. I could only hope some variation of the group would be going when I got to be that age.

"Yeees," I said, in such a way I hoped conveyed my curiosity.

She took a bite of the croissant and nodded approvingly.

"Well," she said, then lowered her voice. "Apparently, they have an all-points bulletin out for Becky Bean. Seems she's skipped town, and they've learned she had more than just a friendship with poor dearly departed Roy, if you can believe it! He seemed a bit old for her, but maybe she was looking for—what do you call it—a sugar daddy?"

Eeew. With his dyed black hair and Vegas-style clothes, Roy was more like a sugar overdose. But I kept those thoughts to myself for now. Instead, I asked, "So, what do they think—scorned lover or something?"

Winnie shook her head. "No idea yet, but Cindy said it sounded serious."

Hmm. I filled Winnie in on what I'd inferred after I had talked with Becky, and I told her about Todd's efforts to find the publicity expert for his story.

"So, I just have a gut feeling that something is off," I told her.

She nodded eagerly. "I hope you're right, because I've been itching to update the old murder file. It's getting lonely."

Winnie had really been watching too much Jessica Fletcher, but she was one of the best researchers I knew, other than me. And not to beep my own bugle, but that was saying something.

"Meanwhile," I went on, "Tripp is still at the bed-and-breakfast downtown, and Pansy's on the war path. She actually ordered another rare rose hybrid from England just to get even. According to the garden club ladies I just interviewed for their fall feature story, it cost as much as my monthly salary."

Winnie's eyes opened wide, and she added, "I hadn't heard that, but I have to admit I feel badly for Tripp. Still, I am glad he paid the piper for his poker losses before this, or my England trip might have been only a virtual vacation."

I wondered if she'd found another gullible person to join her cutthroat secret poker games. Clearly, people never saw her coming when she fleeced them with a full house. Honestly, I was kind of in awe of her abilities.

My phone dinged with an alarm I'd set for myself—my latest attempt to stay on schedule whenever I got too caught up in all the local comings and goings.

"Sorry, Winnie, I've got to be on my way. Gladys has an appointment, and I'm her driver."

I didn't mention that the appointment was for her rainbow therapy, which she'd scheduled just before her upcoming outing with Duncan to ballroom dance class. I stood up and added, "But you know I will keep you posted if I hear anything."

She gave me a thumbs-up as she took another bite of the immense croissant, and I headed back toward the kitchen to say goodbye to Jenny, whom I hadn't seen much since the Beer and Chili Fest.

Jenny looked up from frosting some pumpkin cookies when I came in. She had been humming a love song, and I couldn't help but notice she was unusually bubbly that morning.

"Well, don't you look like the cat with the canary," I said. "Things must be going well with Emily."

She blushed. "Honestly, Piper, I still can't believe it. It's like we've been dating for years. She's just so great."

I gave her arm a little squeeze. "You totally deserve this after that nightmare with Armand, but I have to be honest: I'm still getting used to the idea of you and Emily being an item."

She blushed even more, if that was possible. "Me, too, and I promise I'll give you all the details when we find time to get together." She paused and held her arms out and gestured at her kitchen. "Between this bakery and Emily, my calendar has been full lately."

She leaned over and gave me a quick hug. I was glad she didn't ask about Richie. I didn't need to rehash the radio silence I was getting from him again. It was hard enough to try to push my feelings aside when I didn't need to share them out loud.

I made a quick stop at the newspaper office on the way to get Gladys. Hap wanted me to go by the elementary school that afternoon to get photos of their annual autumn display, a rite of passage for incoming third graders, who made all manner of creative scarecrows and set them up on the front lawn. I knew I would need the good camera for the photos, so I grabbed the camera bag that held it, waved to Clara, and headed out.

Gladys was waiting for me when I pulled up in front of

her purple Victorian, decked out in a claret-colored cashmere sweater and huge sunglasses.

"The fall chill is really here, my dear," she said, as she lowered herself into the Volvo. "And nothing keeps me warm like cashmere when I don't want to wear my furs."

I wanted to tell her she should put a little meat on her bones, because she seemed to get more rail-thin by the year, but whenever I tried this, she insisted that she needed to keep her lithe dancer's body and brushed off any suggestions about her weight.

"So, what color are you getting today?" I asked. Her light therapy involved different colored lights for different effects being shined into her veins.

She took this seriously and said, "Well, as you know, Duncan is taking me ballroom dancing quite soon, so I really need a dose of red to limber up my joints for that excursion. That color does free up the blockages, they say."

She went on to tell me that her color therapist had shared that red had high-penetrating properties that could stimulate her aura to such an extent that circulatory blockages could be cleared. I kept my skeptical thoughts to myself, knowing the treatments made her happy, and eased the car onto High Street.

"So, how long is Duncan staying in town?" I asked, as we drove toward the town line and passed Exeter's recreation facility and tennis courts.

She turned and replied, "He hasn't really said, but it seems like he's perhaps considering staying permanently. He says being around me makes him feel fifty years younger."

I couldn't argue with that—Gladys had a huge impact on everyone around her because of her infectious zest for life—but Duncan was wearing on me. From his ear-splitting CD, which he was now trying to sell at the music shop downtown, to his frequent habit of forgetting his credit card when it came time to pay the restaurant bill, my list of grievances against him was growing. This seemed like a great time to remind Gladys of an actual gentleman.

"So," I began, "I saw one of the ladies from the senior housing downtown, and she heard Stanley is getting set free by the weekend. We should have a little welcome home party for him."

Gladys nodded. "Oh, yes, the poor dear was just thrilled when I brought him a decent meal and a real martini. Honestly, I don't know how he's survived on that mush they call food at that place. Just the other day, Tootie and I brought him a dinner from the new bistro downtown: roasted-coffee-rubbed duck breast with a root vegetable mash. We also ordered some for ourselves, of course. It was remarkable!"

I was jealous about the missed meal but glad she'd found time to visit Stanley between the outings Duncan kept planning for her. I eased to a stop in front of the rainbow therapy office, which was next to an acupuncturist's office on the town line. After helping her inside, I returned to the car and scrolled on my phone to check work emails while she went in to get lit.

My phone buzzed with an incoming call, a number I recognized as the newspaper, and I quickly picked up.

"Greene, something just came across the scanner," Todd said, an edge of excitement in his voice. "It sounds like the police have found Becky's car. It's outside a hotel in Salisbury Beach."

Ooh, that was interesting.

He then said, "So, I don't have a car," a fact I knew since I had used Walter the Wagon to drive Gladys, "and it would take too long to drive Scarlett down there, so might you by any chance pick me up so we could go out there?"

I glanced at my watch. I knew Gladys would be in the treatment room for another twenty minutes. If I left now, I could pick up Todd and be back to get her before she was done. Then we could all drive to the beach to find out if Becky was still there. I wondered what color Gladys would need to get into peak form to chaperone our snooping.

CHAPTER 32

Gladys emerged from her rainbow therapy appointment in her large pair of sunglasses à la Jackie O. She resembled a vintage movie star getting ready to greet her public. She stopped abruptly when she saw Todd and me standing by the Volvo.

"Oh my, I've got both of you now! What? Are you waiting to whisk me off to the funny farm?"

Todd opened the front passenger door for her with a flourish. He said, "Oh, not today. You're going on an uncover mission with us. Just imagine I'm Bond, James Bond."

To be honest, she was elegant enough to have starred as any of the leading ladies who played across from Sean Connery during his tenure as the famous 007 secret agent. She lifted her glasses and peered at both of us with curiosity.

"Oh, do tell! Are we on the hunt for a killer?"

I got behind the wheel and allowed a bit of excitement to creep into my voice. "Well, actually, we just might be."

She clasped her hands together and let out a dignified shriek of delight. "I knew it! Adding that red to my session today was guaranteed to make life even more spectacular. And I even have my sunglasses to go undercover, like a real disguise."

Oh boy. I didn't have a poker face, but Gladys most definitely would get caught up in the thrill of a sting and blow our cover. We'd have to keep her contained.

We filled Gladys in on the news about Becky as I guided Walter toward Salisbury Beach, a beach town just over the border into Massachusetts. Salisbury Beach had really been rejuvenated since the days when I was growing up, compete with an upscale restaurant and music venue and a string of new oceanfront condos. Becky's car was at none of those spots, but we tracked it down at the Merry Go Round Motel, an older place off the main strip. An old red sign with the word *office* and an arrow was attached to the side of the building, but only half of the letters still lit up. A Salisbury marked police cruiser and an unmarked cruiser with New Hampshire plates were staged on the side of the road, and I braked to a stop behind them. I cringed when I saw Richie walk around the corner of the building. He paused when he saw the Volvo then headed toward us.

Gladys rolled down her window, delighting in her role on our escapade. "Oh, Richard, isn't this exciting! Do tell us if there is a murderer on the loose? Should we lock our doors? Do we need to take cover?"

Apparently, despite his issues with me, he couldn't resist Gladys's exuberance. "No, no, just following up on a lead. There's no call for public alarm," he told her.

He leaned over as he responded to her, looked at Todd and me, and frowned. "Really? Both of you felt it necessary to be here?"

I jumped in before Todd could respond, hoping to keep things level. "Well, to be fair, I had the car, and, yeah, it's a long story." I stopped for a minute to decide how to proceed.

Then I said, "So, since we're here, what can you tell us? Is Becky here? Is she okay?"

Richie looked at Gladys, clearly feeling those good Catholic boy roots that made it essential for him to respect his elders, and despite the uncomfortable dynamic between us, he responded. "I can't say anything official, but off the record, she's not here. You'll have to get that from either Salisbury or major crimes."

He excused himself and turned to leave. Every time he walked away from an encounter without giving me a playful wink or smile left a pit in my chest. I really did like him, but I still hadn't figured out how to convince him Todd was just a pesky roommate and not a romantic rival.

In the meantime, I was stuck with Todd. I looked in the rearview mirror and made eye contact with him. "Maybe you should get a few photos while we're here."

He nodded and hopped out of the car, pulled his ancient iPhone from his shirt pocket, and started snapping. Though he did push the boundaries, I noticed he made a point to stay behind the police line. The police might be cranky, but so long as they were out in the open like this, taking photos was fair game.

"Oh, Piper, dear," Gladys said, as we watched. "I do hope you patch things up with Richard. He's such a darling young man."

I didn't want to get into a big discussion with her about my love life, especially since Richie and Todd were both still in possible earshot of the car, so I just patted her arm and said, "Me too."

Todd lumbered around outside, then stopped and talked with a slight older man in a blue uniform shirt, who I suspected worked at the motel. The two of them leaned together as they talked, and a few times I saw Todd laugh a little, as if they were sharing a joke. Hard to imagine that a missing woman was funny, but everyone had their own techniques to get information during interviews. He finally slipped back into the car about ten minutes later.

"Oh, Todd, did you learn anything scandalous?" Gladys asked. "I do love a good scandal."

I was curious as well. I pulled back onto the road, headed north, and waited for him to respond.

Todd said, "Well, that guy's the manager, and he told me that Becky checked in a few days ago, but then she checked out and left her car. He wondered if she took a taxi somewhere, but he agreed that this seems odd. He also said she was upset when she paid her final bill, and it seemed like she was, quote, *dealing with something.* Those were the words he used."

Interesting, but where was she? Could she have waded in the chilly Atlantic and gotten swept out to sea? Left her car at the hotel and called an Uber to make a secret getaway? Had some sort of medical emergency that left her lying unconscious somewhere with no one but seagulls to find her? None of this made sense.

Todd didn't seem as convinced as I was that something nefarious was going on, but I couldn't help but wonder if Becky had a bigger role in Roy's death than we even suspected. Honestly, she had seemed off the last few times I'd seen her, she had missed the chili fest, and people didn't just leave their car and go missing like this for no reason.

I said, "I know you two spent some good times together. Are you sure she never said anything about Roy? If she didn't have something to hide, you'd think she might have mentioned it, especially if they were close, right?"

Todd shook his head and shrugged. "Now, I'm not saying she wasn't a bit of fun, but she wasn't exactly a warm-and-fuzzy type. With her big-city attitude, she was a bit cold, you know?"

I guess that could be one explanation—she wasn't the type of person to show or talk about her feelings—but that didn't match up at all with the hotel manager's conclusion that she appeared to be distressed.

Gladys piped up from her seat. "Well, if you ask me, I'd rather learn that Becky killed Roy than discover that someone from our dear town of Exeter did it. I'd hate for the town to have the stain of turning out a real-life murderer. At least your colleague Sheila wasn't originally from here."

Then she dug Duncan's CD out of her purse and popped it into the CD player, so I bit my tongue and tried to close my ears as she and Todd merrily sang along to Duncan's wretched *Cats* medley all the way home. His voice was burned in my mind, and not in a good way. Still, I couldn't help but fixate on the lyrics—"Memory, all alone in the moonlight, I can dream of the old days; Life was beautiful then"—and I wondered how it might sum up Roy's final moments in his chair at the edge of the river. Were the old days at the Exeter Playhouse *really* as magical as people recalled, or was the dark side of the theater finally coming to surface?By the time we got back to Exeter, I slowed only long enough to drop Gladys and Todd off on High Street, because I needed to beat feet to get to the elementary school to take pictures of the scarecrow characters display. When I arrived, my first task was to meet up with the young woman who had replaced my own childhood principal, Mr. Locke, who had retired recently after about forty years. We had prearranged for her to pair me with some of the more talkative kids who were still on site in the after-school program. The first one, a little girl with auburn braids, earnestly told me about her scarecrow creation.

"This is Miss Kitty, because I really love cats. I have five at home, but my dad doesn't like cats. But I do." She showed me how she had taped laundry baskets together to make the body before draping black velvet over them for the finished project.

I snapped some photos, confirmed the spelling of her name, and moved to the next student, a boy with a lightning bolt shaved in the size of his head, who led me to an impressive array of pigs made from pumpkins that had been painted pink.

Okay, right, I thought, *like this kid made this independently.* But I kept that thought to myself, wondering if his mother had found inspiration from a professional Pinterest board, and snapped some photos of him.

By the time I returned to the newsroom and uploaded my photos to the computer system, it was getting late and I was hungry. Gladys had texted to ask me to come by for dinner, so I quickly headed home. I was also feeling slightly anxious because she'd mentioned inviting Duncan and had told me they'd be sharing some news.

I found them in the sunroom, seltzers in hand. She never drank martinis on rainbow therapy treatment days in case the alcohol canceled out all the benefits of the treatment.

"Oh, Piper, I was just telling Duncan about our exhilarating outing today. A real-life stakeout! Anything new?"

I shook my head. "Not yet. The state police told me they could only confirm they had located a car belonging to Becky but nothing about the case or where she might be."

Gladys tsk-tsked and turned to smile at Duncan. "Well, I hate to change the subject from the big murder, but Duncan and I have thrilling news."

Oh, God. My stomach lurched, and I thought, *Please tell me the rousing news didn't involve him getting down on one knee.* I forced my face to stay neutral. "Oh really?"

Duncan jumped up, pulled a white captain's hat from behind his back, and placed it on his head. "Well, it's not the *SS Constitution,* but I do think it will be an affair to remember," he said, before breaking out in a deep baritone. "Our love affair is a wondrous thing; that we'll rejoice in remembering."

Ouch. His references to classic movies were always cringeworthy to me, but this time even Gladys made a face. She swatted her hand toward him and said, "He thinks he's Cary Grant or something, but would you believe he's surprised me with a passage on a Viking River cruise? You know I've always wanted to go. Those ads during *PBS Masterpiece* are to die for, and now I'm going! We leave next month!"

I almost spit out my drink.

"Isn't that fabulous?" she added.

I worked at keeping my face neutral while I decided how to proceed, but I didn't have to struggle too long because my phone dinged, and I looked down to see a text message from Todd. He'd received a tip he thought I should know about. It seemed the bird man of Exeter wasn't done trying to halt the construction project on the Carmichael lot just yet.

CHAPTER 33

The next morning I woke up before the alarm, so I mulled over the intel Todd had shared with me about the bird man. Apparently, Harry Trott had filed an official report about the rare Ross's gull. This meant Fiona's new plan for the property also required approval from the state's bird preservation group, whose expert was due in Exeter in a few hours to survey the bird activity around the area. This seemed like a great chance for me to snoop around the site for more leads. I hadn't figured out a way yet to determine why Harry had the old theater relics in his garage, but maybe that luck would turn next. I decided that later, when I got to the office, I would do some snooping on eBay to find out if there were any theater items currently up for sale.

After I'd laid under my warm down comforter for as long as I could get away with, I found myself silently cursing birds for getting me up way earlier than I would have preferred. I slugged down a quick cup of high-test coffee and stepped outside, where Oscar was sitting on my back step. The black-and-white cat rubbed up against my leg, arching his back up slightly, but then he scooted off like a shot when I bent to give him a pat. If nothing else, he was teaching me patience.

I pondered the rest of what Todd had shared with me. His intel was that the bird expert was coming in as part of a consulting job, but from what we'd heard, this guru was way over the top. According to Todd's tipster, this man had once halted an entire project because he had found a piece of an eggshell, even though there had been no other confirmation of any endangered bird being on the property. "This apparently cost a pretty penny to the developer," Todd had said. It gave a whole new meaning to "the price of eggs."

As I walked over the Great Bridge, the gateway to the downtown area, an almost ethereal mist rose from the water. Just offshore, a heron stood on one leg while it hunted fish in the shallow section of the river. The only people out at this hour were the serious runners, the occasional dog walkers, and I realized as I spotted a stooped and slight walker coming my way, Tootie, on her morning constitutional.

"What brings you out at this hour?" she asked, as she reached the middle of the bridge, where I'd been looking down the river.

I zipped my fleece up a bit more on my neck before I answered. Then I said, "Well, apparently, the bird specialist from the state is coming down, and I wanted to hear what he has to say."

She pulled her red tartan scarf a little snugger around her neck before she spoke again. I didn't blame her.

She said, "Makes sense. Harry's been home a few days now, but he's not really doing much. I see the visiting nurse people come in and out, but that's it." She shook her head slowly. "Poor guy. He really is all alone aside from those birds he loves so much."

Which reminded me that I still didn't have any clue about who fed his birds when he was in Maine or in the hospital. The list of reasons I needed to pay him a visit was growing. In the meantime, I decided to make the most of Tootie's keen observational superpower. "Anything interesting happening around town this morning?"

She looked over the water and tapped a finger against her temple as if conjuring up her memories. "Well, I did see the recycling outside Pansy's house. Seems she's been on a real bender. Filled with empty cans of diet cola and what looked like a few bottles of champagne, if you can believe it."

Geez, was she having parties in Tripp's absence? Knowing Pansy, I wouldn't be surprised, but that was still a bit harsh. Also, given that Roy had died by drinking champagne, this sent a red flag up for me, but I didn't have time to follow up before Tootie went on to tell me what she saw in the other recycling bins about town that she'd peeked in on her walk. She also mentioned the new tiki hut someone had constructed behind their house off Court Street. Apparently, it had a giant wooden parrot at the entrance, like something out of a Disney-themed display.

"Well, I'm signing off," she eventually said. She waved back at me as she headed up the street. She was using an old cross-country ski pole as she walked up the small hill from the bridge to the base of High Street. Not only did it help her balance in the winter, she had once told me, but it could fend off wild animals if she found herself face to face with a rabid racoon or worse, a coyote.

"You think it won't happen," she had said, "but there was that woman who had to choke a rabid fox to death on a local trail to save her dog. It was a real scene."

I walked the short distance to the vacant lot, where a navy-blue Audi with a vanity plate BIRDEE1 was parked. I slipped in through the fence, the same route I'd taken the morning I found Roy's body. A tall, rail-thin man with a nose more avian than human was bent over a hole in the ground. He had a pair of binoculars around his neck and a clipboard. Fiona stood next to him, arms crossed, with her short hair tucked under a sapphire-blue wool hat. She didn't look happy to see me.

"Really? Is this really necessary?" she asked.

I smiled and carried on. "Oh, I know, but Hap wanted to be sure we kept up on the process. There is just so much interest in town, you know."

She scowled. "This is private property, as I'm sure you're aware. But I don't want that to be in the paper—that I asked you to leave—so just don't make a scene."

I looked around and tried not to laugh. What kind of scene could I make here? She was starting to sound like Pansy. But I nodded anyway.

The tall bird man looked at me as if only realizing I was there. I stuck out my hand.

"Piper Greene, *Exeter Independent*. We've been covering this proposal, and I'd really love to learn more about the Ross's gull."

He was clearly in his element, and I could tell by his quick grin that he would like nothing more than to banter about birds.

"Well, see this," he said, as he leaned down and pointed to a mark on the ground. "We know that this type of marking is made by the bird. Our volunteer, Harry, has been out of commission, as I'm sure you know, but he was keeping tabs on these."

He went on to tell me that the preservation society had been very, very eager to learn more about this bird. They wanted to determine if it had been tagged or tracked anywhere else and where it had flown in from.

Fiona interjected. "We're glad to put up a little birdhouse if that's what it will take to make sure everyone is on board with this project."

Oh, yes, a birdhouse, I thought, *in the historic district.* I could just imagine the meeting where they would discuss the shingles and siding and whether it was historically accurate or not.

The bird man kept up his walk about the lot, alternating between his binoculars and a camera, which he used to take photos. I needed to do the same, but I waited until Fiona turned the other way before I snapped a few shots on my phone. No need to poke the beast and aggravate her even more. I was surprised that my brother, in his role as her attorney, wasn't there, but perhaps she wanted to handle this on her own.

The bird man stopped and beckoned to both of us, then raised his binoculars to gaze further down the river. "Would you look at that," he whispered. "A pair of bald eagles. That's a good sign for the local habitat. The fish population must be on the upswing."

I knew from some of the locals on the Conservation Commission that they'd hoped the fish population would rebound to its precolonial state after the recent removal of the dam, which had existed in some form or other between 1638 and 2016. I didn't want to burst his bubble, so I tried to look impressed, but in fact the women's walking club had been seeing the eagles all summer in a tree along Swasey Parkway.

Winnie had been quite excited the first time she saw the big male swoop over the river and fly toward Newfields. She'd insisted his wings must have been ten feet across when she'd told me the story.

"Such majestic creatures," Fiona said.

I glanced around the lot and tried to imagine what it must have looked like when the playhouse was there. It was hard to do. On one side there was a cavernous hole, with large granite foundation blocks in a mishmash heap, the way they'd been since the place burned. No doubt the rocks were almost as old as the town. Fiona would certainly have her work cut out for her when she was able to get the construction crews on site if her proposal was approved. In the meantime, I knew she planned to bring in an excavator this week to clear up the area, which seemed optimistic for her proposal but also might give the lot a less ramshackle appearance.

Several years ago, when I was home visiting Gladys for an extended Fourth of July weekend, the museum downtown had done foundation work at its own location and found a treasure trove of artifacts on a spot where a privy had once been situated, including an old pistol that had likely been used to shoot rats at the former dump site along the river. According to Winnie, people had disposed of more than one kind of waste in their toilets in those days. She had seemed quite disappointed to discover that it most likely had not been a murder weapon.

The sun was just starting to sneak through the clouds again when something caught my eye. It was glistening on the edge of the pile of rocks, down at the bottom. I leaned forward and did a doubletake. A gold chain of some sort was poking out from the edge of a large boulder. There was no way for me to reach it, but the light of the sun was hitting it just right for me to get a solid glimpse. It looked like a necklace with a locket, maybe just something that had been washed up during an earlier period of high water on the river, which had flooded in this spot on and off for years prior to the dam removal.

Before I could edge forward to determine if there was any way to grab it, my phone pinged with an incoming text. Hap wanted me to file the story as soon as I could, which meant I had to head out immediately. I waved goodbye to Fiona, who reluctantly gave me a nod, but the bird man was still peering at the ground and didn't see me. I shivered as the sun was blocked by another large cloud. If I hustled, I would have just enough time to go home for a hot shower.

CHAPTER 34

Finally warm again, I decided to quickly say good morning to Gladys before I left for the office. As I walked toward her door, I glanced at Todd's Jolly Dodger, which was still out back, and I wondered how long he would be able to park there before the code enforcement officer decided he was violating an ordinance or a rule in the town's zoning. Technically, Todd wasn't sleeping there because he was using a room in the main house, but I knew that it would only take one neighbor to insist that it was an eyesore, and then Gladys could be on the hot seat.

I found her sitting in her kitchen, poring over thick brochures for her upcoming Viking River Cruise. A large picture of a canal and the Eiffel Tower was spread across her white marble island, and she looked up only briefly when I called her name.

"Oh, Piper, this is just so exhilarating. I'm leaning toward the Danube Waltz itinerary, which goes from Passau to Budapest through what they term Europe's most enchanting countries along the Danube River," she said. "But the other one that goes from the heart of Paris to the heart of Normandy has some vineyards I'm interested in touring."

She flipped through the brochure, which featured glossy photos of the Wall of China, tulips in Holland, and dramatic castles in England.

"Oh, my dear," she said, "I know it must seem a bit sudden, but when you're my age, you've got to embrace the carpe diem approach."

I wanted to slow her down and remind her that Duncan had essentially ditched her decades ago on a whim, but I decided to hold my tongue for now.

"Well, it does sound like the trip of a lifetime," I said. I also didn't mention that he'd stuck her with the bill the last few times they'd gone to dinner. How was it he could afford a cruise? He surely wasn't funding it with his CD sales.

Gladys was sipping a cup of tea, no kombucha today. Lately it had been Yerba Matte, a chocolate caffeinated tea made popular as an alternative to coffee in South America. She said, "But enough of that. What's the latest with the big case? Did the bird expert have anything newsworthy to tell you?"

I shook my head. "Not really, just more of the same about the rare gull." I paused, then added, "But he about lost his marbles when he saw the Swasey Parkway eagles."

Like me, she'd already heard about the eagles, and she looked disappointed. I can't say I blamed her. This case was starting to feel stalled. Becky had just up and left, and there was no further news on her. Meanwhile, Richie still wasn't sharing any of the inside details owing to our split, and the state cops were about as helpful as talking to a wall in terms of the information they released. I decided that later in the day I would call and inquire about the necklace I'd spotted that morning. Even though I couldn't believe the police had overlooked evidence when they had the crime scene people onsite, there was something about it that niggled at my subconscious.

"Well, I've got to head into the newsroom to write up my story," I told Gladys. I stood up and walked toward the back door that led to my carriage house. "Good luck with the planning."

Todd had Scarlett, his scooter, that day, so I was able to take the Volvo. I was glad for the ability to get places on a faster—and warmer—schedule if need be.

Clara was laughing to herself and shaking her head when I walked into the office. "Okay, what's so funny?" I asked.

For a long moment she looked like she was trying to collect herself. She finally took a deep breath and answered, "Well, it's this 'Your Call Line.' It's just too much. The people calling in need to get a life." The "Your Call Line" was a new idea hatched by Hap's brother, Dick, as a way for residents to share tips and news around town without the worry of being called out as a tipster. But so far, it had only been used by people complaining about their neighbors, grumbling about the roving troubadour I'd interviewed recently, and keeping tabs on how long of a lunch break Chief Sinclair took. Talk about small-town grievances. Initially, I had wondered what they'd do if there was a real issue of concern, like, say, a murder? But so far, Roy's death hadn't resulted in any anonymous calls to the line, much to my dismay.

"Do I dare ask what people are griping about today?" I asked her.

Clara looked around the newsroom, even though we were the only ones there, and put her phone on speaker mode. She punched in her access code for the voicemail, and we waited.

"Yes," a muffled voice that sounded like the caller was in a closet began. "I saw the town's animal control officer walking his dog this week, and you'll never believe this! His dog did its business, and he didn't pick it up. Just left it on the ground! Can you believe it? Do you know how much he tickets people for doing this?"

Clara paused the voicemail, cackled hysterically, and said, "Like they're the poop police now? Can you believe it?"

She hit the play button and the recordings continued.

"Yes, um, hello? I just wanted to say that, like, my neighbor Joe, oh, wait, can I say his name? Anyway, my neighbor, um, Joe, put his recycling out on Monday? And our garbage day isn't until Tuesday? That's, like, illegal right? And a skunk came! It really stinks over here! Call me back!"

Needless to say, she had not left her number. Clara hit the play button again.

"Yes, this is Bob. I was in a support group with Sheila, who worked in your office. Anyway, I went to the town's recreation office last week to sign up for the Incident at Exeter workshop, and I'm certain that on my way out I encountered a ghost. There was definitely a steamy vapor rising up near the coffee pot. Kind of a hissing sound, too. I'd like to request that the town bring in a ghost whisperer. There might be a message from beyond."

Clara snorted as she laughed. "And don't get me started on the one who is upset about her neighbor's choice of music. Apparently, she would prefer light jazz, but he only plays honky-tonk."

Really. I loved my little town, but at times, I could see why others preferred the city, where people didn't even pay attention to their neighbors.

Clara was still laughing as I headed to my desk. I wanted to write up the bird expert story quickly so I could move on to my daily check-ins with the police and follow up on that necklace I'd spotted. Maybe they could finally release something new on the investigation into Roy's murder. I settled into my desk, flipped open my reporter's notebook, did a quick read-through of my notes to refresh my memory of specifics, and started to type.

BIRD EXPERT CONSULTS ON PLAYHOUSE PROJECT

By Piper Greene

EXETER__*A renowned bird expert visited the site of a proposed redevelopment of the Exeter Playhouse this week and said the plan can work if certain accommodations are made for an endangered gull.*

Clifford Singleton said the top priority is maintaining a familiar habitat for the Ross's gull at the vacant lot on Water Street. "This can be done by constructing a feeding station on the edge of the lot adjacent to the river," he said. "But care must be taken to keep it as realistic as possible; these birds are not easily fooled."

Fiona Carmichael, owner of the lot, said she would work with the organization to incorporate their recommendations within the proposal she has before the town. The lot, vacant since a fire destroyed the former Exeter Playhouse, is the site where Carmichael's brother, Roy, was found murdered recently. That investigation is still ongoing, and police said there is no new information to release as this time. However, Becky Bean, who sources say was having a romantic relationship with Roy prior to this death, has not been heard from in several days. Police in neighboring Salisbury, Mass., recently found her car at a hotel in that town. Exeter police declined to comment on Bean's connection to the case or where she might be holed up.

Ms. Carmichael says rebuilding the former theater is a way for the town to focus on something positive after a terrible time. "We are all mourning Roy. He was my little brother, and I loved him," she said. "But I hope this can be a rebirth of sorts, like a phoenix rising from the ashes, during a dark time in our town."

I read through the story a few times, tweaked a few words, and sent it over to Hap for his review. Then I turned to my work email and scrolled through to see if anything needed to be followed up on that afternoon. A local photographer who helped organize the town's annual Christmas Festival of Trees had sent me a press release about this year's event. Next up, the small town next to Exeter was having a town-wide debate about whether to get their own zip code or simply keep using Exeter's. "It's a real identity crisis," the woman who had emailed me insisted, and she had pled her case for the paper to write about it.

I was hoping to cut out early but wanted to put in a call to Chief Sinclair about that necklace. It was still on my mind, and I couldn't stop wondering why it had not been noticed when the crime scene people were there. As I was reaching for the phone, a commotion at the front door caught my attention. Todd came barreling in as fast as I'd ever seen him move.

"You've got the car, right?" he said, no preamble. When I nodded, he said, "Well, let's go. I just heard that Becky is at the PD and so is her lawyer—Darby Jones."

Ooh, our local top defense attorney representing the suspected lover of the deceased. I was up and out the door before Todd could say another word. Of course, it could be nothing. Maybe Becky was just upset about Roy's death and needed some time off. Then again, maybe the intrigue I'd been waiting for was about to unfold.

CHAPTER 35

Todd and I sat in the front seat of the Volvo and stared at the police station's door, as if we were in a stakeout in a movie. We'd both gone into the lobby upon our arrival, but the receptionist had let us know that it would be a while before someone came out to offer a statement. Back in the car, I wished we had some snacks with us. I was starving. I usually kept some of Jenny's homemade granola on hand for times like this, but I hadn't stocked up lately. She'd been so busy with Emily that she'd fallen off her schedule of making the crunchy treat.

Todd produced a dried beef stick in plastic, the type you'd see in a gas station—or maybe a pet aisle, for that matter—and held it over to me. "Want some?"

I held my face as neutral as possible as I shook my head no. Despite my growling stomach, I couldn't bring myself to take a piece. Who knew what was really in the smoked meat-like food? Sure, there were enough preservatives in there to keep it edible for a century, but was that really a good fact? And it smelled horrible.

I cracked my window to release the odor but kept the car

running for the heat, and Todd and I bounced around a few theories as we waited. *Becky killed Roy in a fit of passion because he led her on and broke things off. Becky broke things off and Roy poisoned himself, but a seagull flew off with his suicide note. ("Bonus points if it was that Ross's gull," Todd joked.) Becky accidentally poisoned Roy because she dropped his glass before filling it and there was rat poison on the lot. Someone else killed Roy and pinned it on Becky. Tripp Bolton poisoned Roy (mainly because he was the only person we knew with a fancy wine cellar that might stock the type of champagne found by Roy's chair).* We lost motivation the longer we sat there, because on some level, I just couldn't embrace the idea that Becky had murdered Roy. Our theories were just that—theories—and they sounded more like Hollywood fiction the more we brainstormed.

Two hours later, the front door to the station finally cracked open, and I knew the police were about to come out to make a statement to us, even though we were still the only two members of the media there. As the door was held open, we saw a parade of people exit, including police officers I knew and some other official-looking people in dark suits. I glanced toward the back parking lot of the police station and spotted Darby Jones walking across the darkened area where cruisers were kept. Todd and I looked at each other, and I knew we were both thinking the same thing.

I spoke first. "You take the cops, I'll take Darby."

He nodded and loped over to the sidewalk in front of the station. Given the tension with Richie, I felt it was better for me to chase Darby, one of the preeminent defense attorneys in the state. Recently, he'd also represented our former photographer, Andy, who had been fingered as a suspect in our editor's murder. I made a beeline for Darby across the grass behind the station, hustled past the picnic table set out for officers to eat lunch, and walked up behind him just as he got to his fancy black car with the vanity plate DEFNDM.

"Darby, hold up!" I called out.

He turned and briefly grimaced before clicking into his polished and practiced defense attorney mode. "I should have known you'd be here," he said.

I ignored the remark and jumped right in, knowing I had a limited window to get a comment since defense attorneys were notoriously closemouthed, always blaming it on their bar association ethics rules.

"Are you able to offer a comment on behalf of Becky Bean?" I began, going out on a limb to assume he planned to continue representing her. "Our sources say she was here to turn herself in."

He had already opened his driver side door and stood beside it, an escape hatch, clearly ready to jump ship the moment he felt my questioning went too far. But he kept up the façade and answered my question.

"What I can say is that Ms. Bean has come forward to the police with information about an accident. And given the situation, she wanted to be forthcoming about something that happened, an accident." He paused briefly then said, "There's a lot more to the story, but at this time, I will say I am prepared to vigorously defend her in court."

I scribbled as fast as I could, underlining direct quotes as I went, a system I'd developed over the years. Then I looked back up at him.

"And that will be when? Court, I mean?" I asked.

He placed his briefcase on the front seat of the car, and I

feared he was ready to make a getaway, but he continued. "It's not been confirmed. At this time, she is cooperating with the authorities, and that's all I can say."

With that, he lowered himself into the car, stopping to slide the briefcase to the passenger seat, and turned to give a little wave before he closed the door.

"Interview's over," he said with a smile, and I got the feeling that despite his annoyance, he appreciated my pluckiness.

I wished I'd gotten more, but I was still glad to be the only press on the scene, which meant we had the initial scoop. No television people had caught wind of the story yet, so no van, lights, or pancake makeup to compete with. Despite being in a small town, I didn't like being beaten by anyone else when news broke.

I walked around the side of the parking lot, past Chief Sinclair's unmarked Crown Victoria, toward the front of the police station. Todd had his head down and was furiously scribbling in his notebook. Chief Sinclair was standing behind a beefy man I recognized from the state police and a thin woman in a suit, who was probably one of the prosecutors from the state. They all turned to go inside after the state police guy announced that was all they would comment on.

"Anything good?" I asked Todd.

He nodded enthusiastically. "Oh yeah," he said. "She basically confessed but said it was an accident. We definitely need to get back to the newsroom and write this up ASAP."

We jumped into the Volvo and headed for the *Exeter Independent*, where, despite liking to do my own thing, I agreed to partner up to write the story.

Lara Bricker

POLICE HOLD PUBLIC RELATIONS
EXECUTIVE IN MURDER CASE

BY PIPER GREENE AND TODD TISDEN

EXETER__*A New York City public relations executive is being
held in the murder of a local man.*

*Becky Bean, who arrived in Exeter to do publicity for the
town's Beer and Chili Fest, turned herself in to police this afternoon in connection to the death of Roy Carmichael. Police said
that Bean admitted to serving Carmichael the champagne that
was found to be tainted with arsenic, originally in the form of
rat poison, but Chief Frank Sinclair declined to say more, only
that she is cooperating with the investigation.*

*"Ms. Bean, after some soul-searching, knew it was the right
thing to do to speak with us and voluntarily came in for questioning," the chief said. "Because this is an active investigation,
I am not at liberty to say anything else."*

*Prominent defense attorney Darby Jones, who confirmed
he is representing Ms. Bean, said that there was no intent on
Bean's part to poison or kill Carmichael and that he is confident she will be cleared when his own investigators delve into
the case.*

*Carmichael was found poisoned on the lot he hoped to turn
into an arcade. His sister, Fiona, just got approval from the
town to excavate on the lot now that it's been cleared as a crime
scene, part of her efforts to restore the property to a playhouse.*

Todd and I emailed the story to Hap and headed into his
office, where we sat down with him to brainstorm our plan

241

for coverage. We agreed that Todd would call the jail and the courthouse first thing in the morning to find out if Becky was an inmate at the local county lockup. He would also try to determine if the court had an arraignment scheduled, which would mean she was being charged with a crime. I would continue with the deep dive into Becky's background that I'd started and see if there was anyone else that I hadn't reached out to about that page-six story about the job she abruptly resigned from before taking the post in Exeter.

We broke our huddle, and I headed back to my desk. The adrenaline of a breaking news story kicked in as I dialed the phone and left a message for the charity that Becky had worked for before her arrival in Exeter.

I didn't understand why Becky would poison Roy. Surely their short dalliance was just that: a brief encounter. But Darby had said, more than once, that it was an accident. Could our crazy theory be right? Had she unintentionally dropped his glass in a pile of poison before filling it with champagne? That just seemed insane. But if they both drank the poison somehow, then why didn't she also get sick or die? None of this made any sense. I did suspect that if the police were holding Becky, then there was something else she'd shared or that they knew that had made charging her possible. Maybe her fingerprints were on the glass—but it seemed like they should have known that before now. God, my head was going to explode trying to figure it out. And I had forgotten to tell the chief about the necklace. Drat.

At times like these, as hard as it was, I knew I needed to slow down and be patient. I headed home and went to bed early that night, hoping to catch up on my sleep. But the sun had barely started to shine through my skylight when my cell phone rang. I rolled over and answered, still half asleep.

"This is Piper," I said, used to answering that way at work. The caller was Winnie, and she sounded excited.

"You might want to get up to the Carmichael lot right now," she said. "They just started digging with the excavator to clean up the site for the project, and you are not going to believe what they pulled up."

CHAPTER 36

By the time I got to the lot a crowd had formed, and I had to elbow my way through to get to the front, where Winnie was holding her ground. I was glad I'd grabbed a cup of coffee before I raced to the scene because this morning was already shaping up to be a big one. The old fence had come down, and we had a solid claim to the show. I noticed a gleam in Winnie's eye as she leaned toward me and pointed.

"It's a skeleton," she said. "I wonder if it's been there since the fire."

A skeleton! Now *this* was news. Finally! However, her question raised a good point. Was the body really that old? Surely if someone had been reported missing in the fire, the town's officials would have searched and found the body. But unless the skeleton dated back to Exeter's colonial or Native American times, I couldn't fathom any other scenario. It's not like someone could just drop a dead body on a vacant lot in the middle of downtown without being spotted—although the faithful followers of the infamous UFO sightings might suggest it had been beamed down by aliens. The newspaper's "Your Call Line" voicemail box would probably fill up again with conspiracy theories in no time.

The engine of a yellow excavator sputtered to a stop, and I caught a whiff of the burning diesel. The bucket was poised over the freshly dug up earth, its metal teeth resting just above what I surmised was a piece of bone. Police gathered around the hole, but there was no sign of Richie, and I suspected they'd have to wait for a specialized crime scene team to photograph the scene and extricate the skeleton. I had visions of archeologists using tiny brushes to sweep the soil away from the bones, and honestly, I didn't know if I had the patience to wait for that sort of a pedantic process to play out. My brain was already racing with the possibilities. First, could that locket I'd spotted be connected to the bones? And if so, why was the skeleton only coming to the surface now?

I leaned over toward Winnie and whispered, "Curious they never found the skeleton before now."

She tilted her head toward me and said, "Well, it was way underneath the rocks from the old foundation." She pointed toward the pile of gray granite boulders on the other side. "Didn't come up until they moved those to the side. Sounds like there was some sort of storage space by the old foundation that fell in when the building collapsed after the fire."

Hmm. I looked back at the gaggle of police who stood by the hole. Most of them were shaking their heads in a way that made it clear that another body in Exeter was the last thing they wanted to deal with. Fiona was standing by the foundation boulders, wringing her hands and looking like she could use a little dose of purple light for peace from Gladys's rainbow therapist. But let's be real: anyone would need a moment of serenity if they spent that much time with Chester, who was standing behind her. He was wearing a leather-trimmed field coat and a black scarf, and I could see a thick manilla file in his hands.

"Excuse us! Coming through!" a snappy man's voice announced behind me. I turned to see the lead state police investigator walking toward us with Richie. As they made their way through the crowd of the curious, Richie glanced at me only briefly before looking away.

Winnie and I stepped to the side so they could pass through in front of us. Richie eyed the large group, and I heard him mutter, "They should have left up that old fence."

They quickly lasered in on Fiona and my brother, bending their heads close together as they spoke. Unfortunately, I was too far away to hear the conversation.

"Do you think there's anything else under the bones?" I asked Winnie.

She pursed her lips and raised her eyebrows at me. "The lost treasures of Exeter?"

We laughed at that one, mostly from the absurdity of it. I'd never heard of any lost treasures in town, but boy, what a story that would be if they were unearthed. Of course, it would generate more interest if it was an alien. Our little town did have a special place in UFO history, as documented in the *Incident at Exeter* book, which explained how two police officers were among those who saw what they suspected was a spacecraft.

I said, "This could be the proof we need to cement our title as the East Coast Roswell. Let's just hope it's an authentic alien skeleton."

Winnie raised her eyebrows. "Think of the stories you could write!"

I forced myself to return my attention to Fiona, Chester,

Richie, and the lead investigator. I pulled out my phone to snap some photos of the scene, where a tarp had now been placed over the skeleton. Chester opened the manilla folder in his hand and handed a piece of paper to the state police investigator, who then made his way to one of the other officers. The officers then looked at something in a clear evidence bag—I could barely make out that the object was shiny and gold—then at the piece of paper. That object had to be the locket, and I suspected the paper had a photo or description of the locket.

The state police investigator nodded, then walked back toward Fiona. He leaned in toward her right ear and whispered something. Even with the distance, I heard her shriek, which could have peeled paint. Then she shouted, "Oh, my God, it can't be!"

My heart was pounding. This was clearly something big, and I could scarcely stand by just yards away and not know more.

"Who do you think it is?" I asked Winnie.

She replied, "No idea, but given the way Fiona screeched, I'd say she knows."

Richie walked toward us, and I reached out to grab his arm. In a low voice, I said, "Off the record? *Please?*"

He looked behind him, where the state police guy and the others had their backs to us now as they stared at the tarp.

"Skeleton," he whispered. "That's all I can say."

Gah, Richie, I knew that already. Even so, I smiled and thanked him, and he moved on. My mental Rolodex started flipping at warp speed as I wondered who it might be. I honestly had no idea.

Winnie and I stood in silence for a moment. I suspected

she was going through the same internal archives that I was: unsolved cases, missing people, anything that might indicate who was in that hole.

Richie came back through with a role of yellow crime scene tape, which he promptly strung across the front of the lot. He gave Winnie and me a warning look and said, "Please, you two, behave." It was as if he knew us or something.

"Who could it be?" I asked Winnie again.

She squinted, still deep in thought, and then said, "Well, who was around the Playhouse at the time of that last show, the fire?"

I went through the list of people I knew. The Carmichaels: Roy, Fiona, and Virginia. The actors and crew: Stanley, Tootie, Duncan. I got a twinge as I recalled another one.

"You know that leading lady who left town after the last show? What was her name?"

Winnie didn't miss a beat. "Vivian Hall."

Yes, that was the one. Gladys had heard speculation Vivian ran off with Duncan, but he had told us he assumed she went to Hollywood to pursue a career in film. Interesting. I wondered now if I could confirm what became of her career after Exeter. If I remembered the story correctly, Roy's mother had told me she had seemed on her own and hadn't mentioned any relatives locally. And given that Vivian was the only person from that time unaccounted for, it wasn't a leap to wonder if the skeleton was her. I quickly shared this with Winnie, who agreed that it sounded suspicious. I could feel my pulse pumping now with the adrenaline of a hot scoop. Thank goodness I'd inherited my mother's low blood pressure, because this kind of break had the potential to catapult a person into hypertension.

Officers were gently directing Chester and Fiona our way now that the lot was once again being treated as a crime scene. It had been just three weeks since the investigators had last removed the yellow tape, and I briefly wondered how—or even *if*—this tied in with Roy's murder.

They stopped in front of us, and Chester looked anything but pleased to see me at that moment. I, on the other hand, could not contain myself any longer without going full Piper Greene on them.

"Fiona," I said. I reminded myself to slow down and not look too eager, but that was a lost cause at this point. "Do you know who it is?"

She gave me a dirty look. "Really, I thought you were a little more community-minded—being an Exeter native and all. Where is your empathy? You couldn't wait to pounce, could you?"

Chester put his hand on her back in what appeared to be a subtle attempt to calm her down.

"I'm sorry," I told her. "It's just that I overheard them say it was a skeleton, and I got a bit ahead of myself. Hazard of the job, you know? Of course, it's a terrible thing."

She nodded, mollified slightly. "It's just too much. I'm starting to think this lot is cursed. First Roy, and now—I don't even want to think who that might be."

So, she was going to act like she hadn't just identified the body? I looked at Winnie and knew she was thinking the exact same thing: Had Fiona meant Vivian when she yelled, "It can't be?"

CHAPTER 37

By early afternoon, I was drinking a cup of cocoa in Winnie's office, and, thanks to Chief Sinclair's secretary, Cindy, we'd confirmed off the record whose skeleton was on the lot. A quick online search for Vivian's name had also confirmed that she had never made it to Hollywood. As we munched on snickerdoodles from Jenny's bakery, we patted ourselves on the back for our powers of deduction.

Winnie said, "If this was another time and place, we would be joining the Bletchley Circle!"

"Look into it when you visit England," I joked. "Maybe there's a modern-day version."

According to Cindy, whom we had bumped into at the Morning Musket, the skeleton was indeed presumed to be Vivian, the leading lady from the final play. The preliminary identification had been made by the locket, which had Vivian's initials, and an inscription inside that said "Forever my leading lady, RC." She wouldn't confirm it, but those initials certainly sounded like Roy Carmichael to me. The official confirmation would be made using dental records, but how she had gotten there and why no one had ever reported her missing for decades was still a mystery.

Todd had joined me at the lot shortly after I spoke with Chester, and when the investigators had declared that no formal announcement would be made until at least the morning, we had decided to split up the reporting duties to get prepared. He had stayed at the scene, and now that I'd finished my cocoa, I was going to track down Duncan and find out what he really knew. Winnie wished me luck and promised to gather more details from her files as quickly as she could. Then I headed home. I was surprised by how much the crowd had dwindled as I passed the lot.

I went straight to Gladys's kitchen to enlist her help in getting Duncan to answer some questions. After I explained what had transpired, her eyes welled with tears. I reached out and gave her a hug, and she said, "Oh, Piper, what a sad, sad end for dear Vivian—all these years in a windowless tomb, without even a proper burial."

Despite the emotional turmoil, she agreed that we needed to get to the bottom of this immediately. She quickly straightened her hair and dusted her cheeks with rouge. Then she called Duncan and asked him to meet us on the enclosed patio of the bed-and-breakfast downtown. I was glad she would at least have a bit of a treat if things really fell apart. I knew she loved their new high tea service, which they offered twice a week, and she was very fond of the charming innkeeper, who always remembered what Gladys liked.

When we drove past the lot on our way into town, she quickly averted her gaze, and I was glad to find an empty spot directly in front of the B&B. The innkeeper led us back to the stone patio, which was enclosed by a decorative fence and included a water feature and fireplace, like a European utopia within our very New Hampshire downtown. It did seem like an odd spot to talk about murder, but I needed to find out all I could about Vivian, and as the leading man, Duncan might have been one of the last people to see her alive.

A few minutes later, Duncan strolled over and joined us. His red ascot tie was neat but the jacket that he'd been wearing since we'd met was a bit rumpled, and I noticed a stain on the right sleeve. He furrowed his eyebrows and shook his head solemnly as he sat down across from me. Then he got right to the point and said, "What's this Glady tells me? They think a skeleton they found is poor Vivian? I hope this isn't true."

I nodded and filled him in on the day's events, Vivian's initials on the locket, the ongoing investigation, and the next steps the police would be taking to confirm her identity.

Then I said, "So really, what I'm hoping you can help me with is who she was as a person. Who were her friends? Any love interests?"

By this point, Duncan and Gladys had ordered the full afternoon tea service for all of us, and a petite woman, who looked barely strong enough to carry the heavy tray with a teapot, cups, and pastries, arrived.

Because nothing says murder talk like a good cup of tea and a cranberry dark-chocolate scone, I thought.

We paused our discussion while Duncan poured us each a cup of tea, and I reached for a scone, even though I was still pretty full of the cocoa and cookies I'd shared earlier with Winnie. Since we were at the precipice of a big break in the case, extra pastries were definitely called for.

Duncan added a spoonful of sugar to his tea and turned his attention back to me.

"Well, everyone wanted to be around Vivian," he said. "She just had something that was contagious. Her smile could light up a room."

I didn't want to be disrespectful to Vivian, but I rolled my eyes because he sounded just like Keith Morrison on *Dateline,* who described each crime victim featured on the show as having a smile that lit up the room. ("I guess we're safe," Jenny had told me once, "since our smiles aren't that bright.")

Duncan's dramatic voice pulled me back to the present. "But if Vivian was dating anyone, she kept that private, though you could say she had plenty of suitors."

I wanted to ask if that included him, but I didn't want to make him defensive, so I decided to hold back for now.

"Such as," I prompted.

He took a sip of his tea, added a whisper more sugar, and continued. "Well, he's not here to speak up, but I guess it's okay to tell you now. Roy was infatuated with her; he was really just over the moon. It was a little embarrassing, really, to watch the way he fawned over her."

Interesting. Virginia Carmichael had said the same thing and based on this, I decided it was almost certain that those initials with the inscription on the locket were Roy's. He was not long out of high school, maybe in his early twenties at that time.

"Was that reciprocated?" I asked.

Duncan shook his head. "I think she was flattered, but he was just a kid, really. Even Fiona, as young as she was, tried to talk sense into him about the way he fawned over Viv."

Gladys's eyes widened, as if she was surprised by that morsel. I knew I had to ask more.

I paused briefly to spoon a dollop of clotted cream onto my

scone and then launched into my next question.

"So, I hate to put you on the spot," I began, "but I know there are always rumors about the leading man and lady having off-stage romances. Was that the case here by any chance?"

His face darkened. Gladys looked intrigued but hid behind her teacup. After all, for years she had wondered if they had run off together.

"Not in this case," Duncan said firmly. "She was like a younger sister to me, a sweet girl with no family in the area. She came directly to Exeter from a small mill town in Maine. Her dream was to move on to Broadway. I tried to be a mentor to her, look out for her."

Gladys breathed a visible sigh of relief, but I wasn't done, so I forged ahead again. "So, what about Fiona and Virginia? How did they get along with Vivian?"

Duncan helped himself to a petits fours with an artful swirl of red glaze drizzled across the white icing. He ate half of it, shrugged, and said, "They all got along fine. Virginia was supportive of all of the actresses, but you could see she liked Vivian more; she even looked out for her. There was something sweet about Vivian that made people want to protect her."

I pushed a bit more. "And Fiona?"

Duncan popped the second half of the tiny cake into his mouth and finished chewing before he spoke. "Well, Fiona was still in high school, so she was not around the Playhouse as much as Roy was. In her spare time, she had a job at the Ioka Theater as a concession girl."

"Interesting," I said. "I wonder if she worked there when Harry Trott was running the projector?"

Gladys and Duncan looked at each other, both pondering

that question, but it was my aunt who spoke first.

"Could be. He was there for years until his retirement," she said. I made a mental note to check with him about his memories of the young Fiona. I knew from Tootie's latest report that he was home from the hospital, but I hadn't gone to check in with him yet, owing to everything else that had been going on. Still, the need to learn about the cache of theater memorabilia in his garage was strong, and it was only a matter of time before I cracked and showed up on his doorstep with some of Jenny's homemade soup, hoping to get the full story. I turned my attention back to Gladys and Duncan, who were both peering myopically at the assortment of treats on the silver tiered tray.

"Well, I hate to tea and run," I said, "but I've got to get to the historical society and see what Winnie's found in her files for me."

Like a caricature of an old-fashioned gentleman, Duncan rose briefly as I stood up, and Gladys said, "Well, please keep me posted. Duncan got a last-minute deal on two rooms at a lovely bed-and-breakfast down in Ipswich, and we might leave all this dreadfulness behind for a few days, though I hate to miss the news."

First the river cruise, now another romantic outing. Geez, Duncan was something else. But I didn't have time to stew over my grievances about his moves, because I needed to find out if Todd had any intel from the scene. Hap had already published a short breaking story about the discovery, with scant details and the promise of a full story when details became available. Our plan was to have our main story ready to print as soon as we could plug in the confirmation about the identity of the skeleton.

As usual, I was nervous about being scooped. I knew the television station in Manchester had interns charged with monitoring local newspaper websites for breaking news, and they would probably see our story posted online. Hap had insisted we wait for the official word to reveal anything more, and professionally I knew he was right, but that didn't help the overly competitive side of me that was pulling at the bit to run with the story.

I tried to push my worries aside, switching my focus to Winnie and the gems she always managed to mine from the records at the society. As I opened the back gate of the bed-and-breakfast, I nearly bumped into Tripp, who was heading inside. He didn't seem to notice and rushed past without even acknowledging me. His face was scrunched up in an angry grimace, and I wondered what Pansy had done now. Then I pushed thoughts of Tripp and any potential tidbit about him aside. I needed to see Winnie and learn what she'd found out.

CHAPTER 38

Given how amped up I was about the story, I didn't stay at Winnie's office long. I made copies of the old photos and articles about Vivian she'd found in the archives and promised I'd stop by again when I had more time to chat.

"You know where to find me," she joked. Then she turned back to her online research about Exeter, England.

With the nuggets she'd shared, as well as what I'd extracted from Duncan, I had my story written up by dinnertime, but because the police were not budging on an official confirmation, both my story and Todd's were just sitting in our newsroom computer system pending publication the following afternoon. Todd had scored a major coup and found one of Vivian's relatives in Maine who gave him an interview.

"Yeah, they said she wasn't super close with them, and when her last letter home talked about her dream to make it to Hollywood, they just assumed that's where she was," he said. "That she made it big and forgot her roots or something."

Huh, now if that were me, I might have sent a letter when I never heard from her in fifty years, but I knew there were all types of families. It's not exactly like I was close to Chester.

Out of habit, I checked in with Chief Sinclair, who still insisted it would be at least a few days before anything would be released about the identity of the skeleton or how it got there.

"Now, I know you're impatient," he told me, "but we just don't have the skill set here in Exeter to analyze old bones like that. We've got an expert headed up from Boston to help us, but it could be a bit of time."

This left me in a holding pattern and in search of other leads. Given the excitement I still felt about the discovery, the last thing I could do was sit still and wait for information to be released. But I needed to step back from all the hubbub about the bones and cross some of the loose ends off my list. Harry Trott and his theater relics, the mysterious person who had fed his birds, and most importantly, the status of Becky Bean. I put out some calls to the players in the case. Becky had been sent home from the county jail, per attorney Darby Jones, because they couldn't continue to keep her there without pressing charges. But police were still tight-lipped about whether she was going to be arrested in connection with Roy's death.

Darby still insisted she was innocent and that whatever had transpired with the poison and the champagne had been an accident. "Listen, Piper, I can tell you that Becky was just wracked with guilt because she feared she had inadvertently poisoned him when she poured champagne into the crystal flute," he said. "Once she heard the champagne was how he was poisoned, she spent weeks agonizing about what she should tell the police. She made the right decision to come forward, but she was in no way planning to poison him that night."

After Darby, I decided to try Richie, given how he'd slipped me one little tip about the discovery of the skeleton. There was a piece of me that hoped it meant he might be starting to come back around. My call went to his voice mail, and I left a message.

"Hey," I began. "I know you're still upset, and I get it, but it's really, really not what you think with Todd. Do you think we could talk later? I'll be home tonight if you want to come by."

So that was a total long shot, but I was nothing if not determined. I didn't have a lot of optimism about my prospects, but stranger things had happened.

Before I could follow up on the other loose ends, Todd and I were called into yet another big sit-down with Hap about whether to publish now, given that it seemed all but confirmed. Ultimately, he decided that he still wanted us to wait. "The paper has a good reputation for being responsible and careful about stories like this," he told us, "and we don't need that to change now."

As I returned to my desk, going stir crazy with the anticipation of the scoop, I couldn't help but speculate further about Vivian's death, unreported and undiscovered all these years, on the same property where Roy had died. It wasn't a leap to surmise there was a connection between the two. Virginia and Duncan had both mentioned that Roy had been infatuated with her. The locket was most likely a token of affection he gave her. Duncan had also stated that he had served as an older brother figure and mentor to her. According to Duncan, he had believed Vivian had left town for Hollywood after the last show, at the same time as his own move because his acting career had taken off. All of this had transpired at the same time as the fire. Fiona had been in high school, working up the street at the Ioka, where she hadn't had as much to do with Vivian but had worked with Harry Trott.

Honestly, Harry just kept turning up in the middle of the

case. Everything had started when he had invited me to the lot that morning to see the rare bird but I had found Roy instead. Harry had offered a plausible explanation for why he wasn't in town that morning—the potential Steller's sea eagle sighting in Maine—but when the police had found all of those relics from the Exeter Playhouse and the Ioka in his garage when he had been taken to the hospital, my radar had gone off again. Sure, this was New England and we'd all heard stories of old Yankees hiding valuables in their mattress or not knowing they had antiques worth millions in their old barn, but there was something about Harry's collection that left me uneasy. I couldn't help but think there was something else that connected these people and the old Playhouse. Surely, in a town with this much history, there must be *someone* who might hold the key to how they were linked.

I groaned inwardly as I realized who that person might be: my brother, Chester. Still, although it pained me, I knew it was worth following up on. Our family firm had been the lawyer of record for the Playhouse at the time of the fire. Now Chester was publicly representing Fiona, even as he was privately seeing her. That was something the state legal ethics board would certainly reprimand him for if it ever got out, but despite that fact, I knew he considered himself too professional to spill confidential client information. And yet, perhaps I could give him one more try? Though he was the type of person who never let his guard down, perhaps it would be my lucky day.

I packed up my bag in the newsroom and started the short walk over to his law office on Water Street. If there was one thing I'd learned as a reporter, it was that you had to be persistent, going back to the same source more than once before they opened up to you. I'd heard stories when I worked at the big metro paper of reporters developing sources over years before they finally got a story.

As I strode up the sidewalk, trying to slow myself before I burst into the office and blurted something I couldn't take back, I forced myself to take a breath and look at the Halloween decorations dotting the entrances to the shops: cornstalks, pumpkins, and the occasional plastic skeleton. Next week, the shops would all open for the traditional downtown trick-or-treat event after the town's annual Halloween parade, in which children, parents, and sometimes even their dogs marched from Swasey Parkway in a short loop before the best costumes were announced.

I steadied myself as I approached the law office, just past the Morning Musket, with a little inner pep talk: *This is my brother, and he is used to my constant questions. I can do this.*

I pulled open the door, but the secretary wasn't out front. Perhaps she'd stepped out for a coffee, which gave me an opening to be nosy. I moseyed down the hallway toward Chester's office, and within seconds, Teddy poked his head out of his own office.

"Oh, hey," he said. He smiled as usual, such a contrast to Chester. "Looking for Chester?"

I nodded. "Yes, I need to talk with him about something."

Teddy crossed his arms and responded, "He just stepped out to get a coffee." Then he turned his head toward his office, where the phone was ringing. "I've got to take that call. Make yourself comfortable until he gets here."

I mean, that was basically an invitation to snoop in Chester's office, right? I pushed open the door to my brother's office and went in. His desk light and computer were on, and it felt like he could return at any moment. I did a quick scan, and my eyes came to rest on a thick manilla folder on his desk. Holy gua-camole Batman, it couldn't be. I looked over my shoulder and crept forward, looked at the name on the tab: Carmichael. Oh goodie, Christmas had come early this year for Piper Greene.

I knew I should sit down and wait patiently, but I couldn't contain myself, so I flipped it open. I skimmed the papers as quickly as I could, grateful that speed reading had always been a superpower of mine. My heart was thumping against my breastbone at the reality of what I was doing. Spying in a lawyer's office was not part of the journalistic code of ethics, but I couldn't stop now. I glanced at the door again, held my breath, and listened. When I heard nothing but my own heartbeat, I returned to my totally unscrupulous and illegal read through. The file was several inches thick, and I knew I only had moments before Chester returned, so I went back to the front of the file and skimmed the latest paperwork on top: what appeared to be a new lawsuit that was ready to be filed against Anastasia Rose. I read the details as fast as I could, gasping audibly when I read that she would have to report to New Hampshire for the case. Now, that was going to be something I would never miss witnessing.

I flipped to later pages and filed away all of the tidbits in my mind. It was a gold mine. I picked up a typed memo, dated the day after Roy's murder.

"NOTE TO FILE
RE: EXETER PLAYHOUSE MEMENTOS."

Client Fiona Carmichael came to my house late at night on the abovementioned date and asked me to make a record of the following:

While working as a concession girl at the Ioka Theater, Ms. Carmichael came to know one Harry Trott. Mr. Trott ran the projector at the theater and often stopped to speak with Ms. Carmichael when he got sodas from the concession. Ms. Carmichael stated that Mr. Trott was a kind, but lonely, man and they became friends. Ms. Carmichael further stated that she observed Mr. Trott leave the Ioka Theater one evening with a framed photo from the lobby under his jacket. When Mr. Trott realized that she'd seen this, he told her that he was preserving the theater's history and asked her not to say anything. She confirmed that she did not say anything.

On another occasion, Ms. Carmichael saw Mr. Trott at the Exeter Playhouse for a performance of Oklahoma! *As she'd seen at the Ioka Theater, she observed Mr. Trott slip an autographed photo from the theater into his jacket and leave the theater. Ms. Carmichael again did not say anything but suspected after the fire at the Playhouse that Mr. Trott had some of the prized items from the theater that were presumed destroyed in the blaze.*

She maintained a friendship with Mr. Trott over the years and recently went to his residence to speak with him about the photographs she believed he'd stolen to find out if he still had them. He agreed to give her some of the items from the Exeter Playhouse, which he said he occasionally sold to collectors to fund his work in bird preservation. Mr. Trott asked Ms. Carmichael for a favor in return for the pieces he gave her. He told Ms. Carmichael that he occasionally needed help feeding his birds and gave her a key to his garage and house for those times. Ms. Carmichael stated that she only fed the birds a few times, accessing his garage to get the birdseed, and twice taking bread to the Exeter Playhouse lot for the seagulls. She also felt

Mr. Trott's experience with the birds might be able to help her find a way to halt her brother's proposed construction of an arcade on the lot, but they did not directly discuss it. Ms. Carmichael asked my opinion on the legality of not reporting Mr. Trott's thefts all those years back, and later taking possession of some of those items herself. I advised her that at this time, the statute of limitations had expired, and that she could not be prosecuted.

I heard the automated ding-dong indicating the front door had opened, so I slammed the folder shut and sat down in the visitor chair just as Chester walked in. I slid my hands under my legs to hide the fact that they were shaky.

"Teddy told me to wait here for you," I offered, working hard not to sound out of breath from my adrenaline rush.

He grimaced as usual. "I don't have time for your antics today."

Now normally I would have put up a fight, but after what I'd just read, it wasn't worth it. "Okay," I said. "You know I had to try. If you change your mind, you know where to find me."

He waved me off, already holding his phone up to his ear as I left. But it didn't matter, I'd already turned to race out the door, going so fast that I tripped on a rug in the lobby, and barely avoided landing flat on my face. I caught myself, stopped, took a deep breath, and tried to steady my hands as the adrenaline rush of preparing to face Fiona hit me. Chief Sinclair was going to be really angry when he found out I once again faced a murderess on my own, but it was a lost cause. I could no longer hold back as I pushed open the front door, and bolted toward her house on High Street.

CHAPTER 39

I channeled my best inner power walker as I headed up High Street toward Fiona's house, which was further up High Street than Gladys's house. I remembered the theory of Occam's Razor, which my favorite cynical podcaster often referenced: the most obvious solution is usually the answer. Who had the most to gain from Roy's death? Fiona. Who had felt cheated out of her majority stake in the lot? Fiona. Who had never wanted to see the tacky arcade in town? Fiona. Who had wanted to embrace Exeter's history by bringing the Playhouse back? Fiona. Who had access to the poison at Harry Trott's house? Fiona.

The documents I'd seen in the file on my brother's desk had brought it all together for me. Initially, Fiona hadn't known about Roy's plan to leave Anastasia Rose the majority ownership of the Playhouse lot—none of us had—so in her mind, killing him would have allowed her to proceed with her plans. Now she was filing a lawsuit against Roy's Las Vegas showgirl, who had definitely inherited the majority share of the lot in his will. There were also affidavits attached to the filing from staff at the assisted living home, who had heard Roy pushing his mother to sign the paperwork while she was disabled with dementia. And then there was Fiona's alibi on the night of the murder: Chester. Based on his memo, it seemed more likely that he'd been working with her that evening as he'd claimed, instead of doing the horizontal mamba as I'd suspected. That was kind of a relief because I'd never really been able to believe that he would compromise his law practice by getting involved with a client. Of course, none of this explained how the leading lady, Vivian, fit into the picture, but I'd deal with that later. Time was of the essence. What if Fiona hunted down Anastasia and killed her next?

I picked up my pace even more as I approached the other side of the Great Bridge, where the historical wooden "Welcome to Exeter" sign included the alewife fish on the town seal. I powered up the hill and loped past the old corner market, which had once sold a winning one-million-dollar lottery ticket.

I didn't have exact plans for what I would do when I got to Fiona's house, and I paused for a minute to catch my breath and consider my options. If I stopped at my carriage house, I could get the pepper spray Gladys had given me for my birthday. I always left it at home, afraid I'd accidentally spray and blind myself, but since I was about to face a killer, it probably would be best not to go in completely empty-handed.

I made a detour over the path around the side of Glady's house and stopped dead in my tracks when I heard a male voice filter out the sunroom window.

"Oh, Glady, who even balances their checkbook these days? You're far too precise. That was always your downfall. I only wrote myself a few hundred-dollar checks!"

I didn't catch her reply, but it didn't take long for him to continue.

"You've ruined everything. I really didn't want to have to do this. We could have been in Ipswich by now and you'd be none the wiser."

Though he didn't say what *this* was, I got an icy shiver up my back. Gladys was in danger.

I was relieved to finally hear her speak. "Now, Duncan, this is not befitting of you. Let's just sit down and be civilized. I don't care that you can't pay for the cruise or the weekend, but why did you lie about your finances and steal from me? Really, I would have just lent you money if you needed it that badly."

I crouched down and crept toward the window, making sure to say behind the shrubs as I got closer.

Duncan responded, "My finances would have been fine if that leach Roy hadn't bled me dry all these years!"

I got right up to the wall and slowly pulled myself up so that I could see in the window. Gladys was facing me, her back up against the far side of the room. Duncan was in front of her, not moving but emitting a menacing energy. I popped up a bit higher and tried to make eye contact with Gladys. She moved her head ever so slightly and locked eyes with me. I pointed to the other direction, indicating I was going to come around the back. She blinked twice.

Now I know I should have called the police, but all I could think about was getting to Gladys. Duncan sounded like a madman. I lowered myself down and crawled around the side of the sunroom, only standing up when I'd gotten out of sight of the windows. I very slowly opened the back door so as not to make noise, and then I tiptoed around the other side of the house so that I could come into the rear of the sunroom.

I paused in the hallway outside the sunroom door, and it

occurred to me that I still didn't have anything on me to protect myself or Gladys. I looked around and spotted the marble bust of Marlene Dietrich, which Gladys kept on a pedestal because she admired the actress's feisty attitude, including her confidence to wear trousers in Hollywood when it was taboo in the 1930s. Gladys was also prone to quote the actress, who famously said, "I dress for the image. Not for myself, not for the public, not for fashion, not for men."

Sorry, Ms. Dietrich, I thought. I picked it up and tucked her under my arm like a football.

Gladys's voice rose again. "But, Duncan, why? Why would you do this?"

Duncan said, "It wasn't supposed to happen like that. Roy was blackmailing me for years. He saw me with Vivian's body the night of the fire."

He paused for a second and then carried on. "It wasn't supposed to end that way. Viv was supposed to leave town with me. I know you and I had a thing, but Vivian? That was a once in a lifetime chance."

Poor Gladys, I thought. *What a lousy thing to say.*

His voice sounded bitter now. He said, "We were going to take Broadway by storm. Roy ruined it when he gave Vivian that locket. She came into my dressing room and showed it to me and tried to break off our plans. I couldn't believe she'd chosen a little lovesick boy barely out of high school over a leading man. Of course, he'd promised they'd run the theater together one day, and she believed him. I tried to rip off her necklace, but she lost her balance, and ..."

He paused again for a moment, and then his voice rose as if he was giving his last great theatrical performance, which needed to reach the back row.

"Vivian fell backward and hit her head very sharply on the edge of the makeup counter. She was gone, I knew that, and what was I to do? She wouldn't have wanted me to lose my career over an accident. Setting the fire was my only hope."

Duncan's voice was getting more agitated now, and I could hear him pacing back and forth as he spoke.

"What's done is done, Glady. There's no going back. It all happened so fast."

By now my mind was really racing, but Gladys kept her cool. She said, "If Roy saw you with Vivian's body, why didn't he just go to the police?" Duncan replied, "Greedy little menace! How do you think he got the money to start his first arcade over on Hampton Beach? Over the years he just kept asking for more and more, until I had nothing. For the past few years, I've been reduced to living in a prop room at the theater, and before I came back to Exeter, I even lost that. I had nowhere to go and was trying to live off the royalties from that awful CD."

Well, that was something we agreed on. That CD was truly dreadful.

Duncan seemed to become more and more emboldened with each word.

"Honestly, Glady, you have to believe me. I was only going to the vacant lot that night to talk with Roy, tell him the money was gone, plead for mercy. He'd promised to meet me there, but he must have forgotten our plans, because when I showed up, he was having a tete-a-tete with Becky Bean. I stayed by the gate, but I could see them on folding chairs next to a picnic blanket; there was just enough light from the restaurant next door.

"He was opening champagne, if you can believe it." Duncan

was muttering now. "A Cretan like him, with his tasteless dye job and suits, as if he even drank Veuve Clicquot. Why a woman like Becky would want to be around him was beyond me, and I wasn't surprised when they quarreled."

"What really happened, Roy?" Gladys asked gently.

"They had champagne. She poured him a glass. Then they argued. I couldn't hear the exact words, but Roy reached for her waist, and she pushed him. He fell and she stormed off, but he didn't get back up. I was grateful she didn't see me. Then he crawled to the fence on the side of the lot and just lay there."

"Was he dead?" Gladys asked.

"Of course not!" Duncan said, "Although I guess she must have thought so. He must have started drinking long before she turned up, because he was three sheets to the wind. As soon as Becky was gone, I marched right in to tell him the blackmail was over. I'd already paid for my sins multiple times. Really what did he expect? I had brought some arsenic just as a backup—you can buy most anything on the internet these days—and when Roy demanded one last payday, well, that was his fatal mistake."

Gladys gasped, but Duncan plowed ahead with his confessions, as if he was truly savoring the spotlight.

"Good thing I'm an actor," he said. "I played along and said we'd just let the past stay behind us. Then I helped Roy into one of the chairs. He babbled some drivel about still loving Vivian, and when he dozed off, I slipped some of the powder in the champagne. Then I woke him back up, agreed to make one more payment, and suggested a toast to seal the deal. It seemed quite poetic—the final curtain call. It was almost too easy, if you think about it."

Gladys gasped again. "My God, you were just carrying poison around like that and then you decided to use it? Duncan, really, how could you?"

I was tempted to gasp myself. She'd been cozied up to a murderer for weeks. What would Stanley think when he found all this out?

However, there was no time to dwell on that, because Duncan suddenly said, "Now we're also going to have some champagne. I really hate that I have to do this, but you've given me no choice. You know the truth and I can't have that."

She let out a delicate shriek and I lost it. I burst into the room and smashed Marlene Dietrich's marble bust right over Duncan's head. He went down like a ton of Exeter alewives, all floppy and flippy as he hit the ground. Marlene lost an ear but was otherwise intact.

Gladys let out a shaky breath. "Oh my, Piper, that was quite a move. Do you think we killed him?"

She leaned down, peered at him closely, and shook her head. "A trickle of blood but still breathing."

I gave her a huge hug and then turned my attention back to Duncan, who was still out cold. But for how long? I quickly looked around. What could I use to keep him there? Gladys's scarf from her belly dancing class was on the back of a chair. I picked it up, wound it up, and used it to bind his wrists together. He groaned, but at least now he wasn't going anywhere.

Just as I was making the last loop, I heard the door open.

Gladys called out, "Back here! Quick!"

I thought it was probably Todd, home from work and looking to score a free dinner. But it was Richie who burst into the sunroom. He'd never returned my call, and in the midst of all the chaos, I'd forgotten that I'd invited him over. He looked around the room, instantly snapped into police mode, and said, "Are you both okay?"

Gladys nodded, though I noticed she was making quick work of downing her martini. We'd need to save the champagne for forensics.

I turned to Richie. I couldn't resist.

"Well, I managed to apprehend the murderer!" I announced. Then I winked at him and added, "But if you want to take it from here, have at it. I'll accept compensation later."

He blushed and looked away. Perhaps the murderer wasn't the only person I'd caught that day.

Made in USA - North Chelmsford, MA
1332177_9781737631927
09.13.2022 1652